THE CAT KING OF HAVANA

THE
CAT KING
OF
HAVANA

Tom Crosshill

KATHERINE TEGEN BOOKS
An Imprint of HarperCollins Publishers

Katherine Tegen Books is an imprint of HarperCollins Publishers.

The Cat King of Havana

Library of Congress Control Number: 2016931710
ISBN 978-0-06-242283-5

Typography by Carla Weise
16 17 18 19 20 PC/RRDH 10 9 8 7 6 5 4 3 2 1
❖
First Edition

To those who have left and those who remain

PART ONE

This Cat Can Dance

chapter one

I MEET ANA CABRERA

In a few pages, I meet Ana Cabrera.

That's called fulfilling your promise to the audience. Say I upload this video called "OMG cutest kitty evah can haz backflipz meow." A title like that will get me clicks—it's a hook. I don't just want to catch a fish, though. I want it to go tell its friends how awesome it is, getting a fishhook through your lip. If I want retweets and shares, my clip had better feature Fluffsters getting his circus on.

I can go a step further. You open my clip expecting catrobatics. You see a kitten on a trampoline. Fluffsters jumps, Fluffsters bounces, here comes the backflip—look at him go! So far, so good.

Then "Eye of the Tiger" plays, the vid goes into slow motion, and you realize there's something on the kitten's back. Yes . . . yes, it's a water cannon!

Kitten paws pull levers. Water bursts from the cannon. Fluffsters shoots into the sky atop a pillar of glory.

The vid cuts to black. Samuel L. Jackson growls, "I can haz backflipz meow." And then, quickly: "No kittens were hurt in the making of this film."

That's what I call a cat video. A million clicks guaranteed.

Take this book. I call it *The Cat King of Havana*. Between felines and Cuba, that's two different tags to maximize eyeballs.

I'll deliver what I'm promising—an edge-of-your-seat tale of the mean streets of Havana, full of adventurous salsa dancing, dangerous romance, and cats. Lolcats, specifically. But that's an appetizer. That's Fluffsters doing backflips. You want a jet-pack kitten blazing across the sky? Read the book.

But hey, what do I know about it? I'm only Rick Gutiérrez, the Last Catbender. That's the name I go by on my website, CatoTrope.com. We get 30 percent of all non-YouTube cat video traffic. Among my fellow students at Manhattan Secondary, I'm known as That Cat Guy.

Which brings us back to Ana Cabrera.

ᥱᦓ

Two people contributed to my meeting Ana.

The first was Rachel Snow, this punk rocker girl, my first and only girlfriend.

"There's something profoundly existential about waiting for the L train at three in the morning," were the first words Rachel spoke to me.

"Uhh . . . umm . . . yeah," were the first words I spoke to Rachel.

She didn't let that stop her. We never took that L train. A few hours later we kissed on the Williamsburg Bridge.

Rachel was a redheaded, Pabst-chugging, Ginsberg-quoting whirlwind. With her, nerdy me became the kind of guy who sang along to the Black Keys and walked barefoot down Broadway at 3:00 a.m. and licked clean the lid of a bucket of plain yogurt. Kissing was about as hot as our romance got over the next few months—but I didn't try to rush things. I could imagine spending a lifetime with her.

Rachel dumped me on the twentieth of January, my sixteenth birthday.

She had come over to my place with a surprise present—two tickets to the Amazeballs Groove, playing at Birdland that night. "They're the new wave in punk jazz," she explained, perched on the edge of my desk, long legs swinging, small bare feet poking from torn jeans. "They're amazing and they've got balls and they know how to groove. Show starts in an hour. Let's go."

"That sounds awesome," I said, though I would have preferred to stay in and snuggle. I clicked away at my website. "I just need to upload a CATastrophe of the month."

"Look," Rachel said fifteen minutes later while practicing a handstand against the wall, "I know this website is like a tribute to your mother and everything. But can we—"

"The video's processing," I said.

Maybe I shouldn't have cut Rachel off, but I didn't want to discuss Mom with her. Sure, the inspiration for my site had come from the folder full of cat videos I'd discovered on Mom's desktop after she died. She'd spent hours looking at the things, and it turned out she'd saved the best ones. I posted one on Facebook and got like a thousand shares—and so a business idea was born. But CatoTrope was a site full of cats pushing little carts across the floor. It didn't feel right to call it a tribute to my mother.

Even if she would have loved it.

"I'll go get us seats," Rachel said after another while.

"Would you?" I pecked her on the cheek. "I'm almost done here."

Five minutes after Rachel left the apartment, I received a Facebook message from her. I reproduce her missive here, because without it I may never have met Ana Cabrera:

Dearest Rick,

  I'm dumping you.

  I wanted to see what it felt like, dating a geek. It's not for me. I mean, Ewoks, Dr. Manhattan, Arya Stark, those guys are fun. I like a good lolcat as much as the next girl. But that's, like, all your life. Every time I tried to drag you to do something fun, that's what it felt like—dragging you, kicking and yelling.

Fix your own life. Read less! Turn off your
computer! Get off your ass! I haven't got the energy to
be your gung-ho manic girlfriend.
  Wishing you the very best in all your future
endeavors,
  Rachel

And that was that for Rick Gutiérrez and Rachel Snow.

You might figure her final message sent me on a voyage of self-discovery, culminating in the realization that Geeks Are Good and Everyone's a Special Flower and You Shouldn't Let Other People Tell You How to Live Your Life. If so, you've been watching too many indie films with quirky teenage protagonists.

I read Rachel's message and decided she had a point.

It took me a few days to accept it. A few days holed up in my room, binging on *Battlestar Galactica* and stuffing myself with schnitzel, my dad's special recipe.

"Schnitzel makes everything better," was all that Dad said to me, which was about as much paternal advice as he ever gave me, now that Mom was gone.

(Dad's from Leipzig, where they take their schnitzel seriously. Perhaps I should mention that my full name is Richard Hahn Gutiérrez. Technically I should introduce myself as Rick Hahn, but I have stayed away from that name since this kid in middle school pointed out Hahn means cock—as in rooster. So I stick with the name Mom brought with her from Havana—my grandfather's name—and leave Dad's for special occasions.)

But things fall apart, the center cannot hold, and nothing lasts, not even *Battlestar Galactica*. Soon enough I had to confront reality. Rachel had dumped me on my birthday. She hadn't been nice about it. No, really, she'd been a little mean. But she wasn't wrong.

I was a geeky loner. And I didn't like it. I didn't even know why I'd resisted Rachel's outings. They'd been some of the best fun I'd ever had.

It was time for a change.

Why should I be that quiet guy in the corner, always last to be picked for the game? I'd rather be the guy who started the game. The guy who had adventures instead of reading about them. And yeah, the guy who dumped instead of getting dumped.

This is what I resolved:

I would become that guy.

Funny thing about resolutions. You make one, and it feels great and decisive and liberating. Then you look in the mirror and see the same old you staring back. And you realize you need a plan.

Which brings us to the second person who contributed to my meeting Ana. The man with the plan. My pal Lettuceleaf Igorov.

His real name is Vladislav, but our resident bully Rob

Kenna can't pronounce that, and Lettuceleaf is so much funnier—because he's fat, you see, haha, hilarious. Lettuce is into anime and video games. And he plays classical guitar.

I'm not talking elevator classical. I'm talking Joaquín Rodrigo and Francisco Tárrega and Isaac Albéniz (look them up on YouTube). This intricate, beautiful, haunting stuff. He played a school concert once, did Rodrigo's "Invocación y Danza." I shivered listening to him. But in the back row, Kenna's catcall brigade worked overtime.

"Oh, man," I told Lettuce afterward. "That was awesome."

"I know," he said. "If only those imbeciles appreciated quality."

That's the other thing about Lettuce. He's modest.

We'd been buddies for years. Both of us nerdy, both of us outcasts, and hey, getting picked on isn't as bad when you've got company. Then, a few weeks before Rachel dumped me, Lettuce discovered rock.

It took one show. One gig with the BlueNuts, our school band, where he went wild on a metal-ish version of the *Pink Panther* theme, fingers ripping through violent chord progressions and complex riffs, his massive frame shaking, eyes rolled up in ecstasy. The rest of the band looked like kindergartners by comparison.

From that day on, Lettuce could do no wrong in the eyes of the school. His size gave him a rock star's gravity. His arrogance became a stage persona to be admired. Kenna quipped that the school band should be called Lettuce's RainbowNuts

(Lettuce is gay), but no one laughed.

After my dumpage, I turned to Lettuce for advice. I told him my tale of woe during a break at school. "I need a plan," I told him. "How do I turn my life around?"

Lettuce considered the issue, then nodded decisively. "You have to find your own thing."

"What do you mean, my own thing?"

"I mean, something social. Something that lets you meet people. Like, maybe start a cat video appreciation society that actually meets in real life."

"Umm." Running my website was fun, but I didn't really want to find out what kind of people hid behind usernames like FurryMasterXY and BroomstickRiderTexas. "Maybe something a bit cooler?"

"What else are you good at?" Lettuce asked. "Like, in my case, I'm good at guitar. Except you know, playing Bach and stuff is great, but that was me in a room, alone all day, practicing. Playing rock—a whole 'nother game."

"I can play the conga drums a bit," I said dubiously.

"That's not what I meant," he said. Then he got thoughtful. "Can you join a salsa band or something?"

"I'm not very good," I said.

Mom had made me take lessons. "When Fidel is dead we'll go back to Havana," she'd told me. "My old friends will hear you play and they'll say—*Agua!* That's María's son, all right."

That had been Mom's dream, not mine. She might have

claimed that she had given up on Cuba—"We're Americans now, and don't you forget it." But a photo of Havana's Malecón always sat on her desk, and a volume of poetry by José Martí on her bedside table, and she never tired of making plans for a future after Fidel.

A future she hadn't lived to see.

To me, Cuba was a distant dream, almost mythical. A fascinating fantasy, not quite real. I enjoyed listening to salsa music because the clave beat spurred my imagination. It let me picture what it might have been like to grow up on the streets my mother once walked. But I didn't love it enough to practice the congas every day.

After Mom died, I stopped playing altogether. I had tried not to even think about anything Cuban these past two years. Whenever someone mentioned Fidel or Buena Vista Social Club or the *bloqueo* or what have you, visions of Mom flashed before my eyes and I heard her voice ranting against "those communist pigs" again. And, well, that was not how I wanted to remember her.

Maybe it was time I got over it.

"You don't need to play the congas well," Lettuce said now. "You just need to find others as bad as you."

I stared at Lettuce for a long while. Then cried out in sudden epiphany. "Craigslist!"

Lettuce grinned. "That wonderful flea market of the internet."

❧

A few days later, I found what I needed.

We play salsa covers, nothing too complicated, wrote Patrick, the bandleader. *We've got our own congas, but our guy broke his hand. Come by on Wednesday, we'll try you out.*

"I'll be home late," I told Dad early Wednesday evening. "I'm trying out for a salsa band."

"Good job," Dad told me as he clicked morosely at his remote—cooking show to reality TV to soap opera and back.

I'd hoped the mention of salsa, Mom's favorite music, might stir his attention. But perhaps that had been wishful thinking. If I'd been avoiding thoughts of Cuba these past two years since Mom's death, Dad had been avoiding thoughts of *anything.* Or so it seemed to me sometimes.

The address Patrick had given me was for a community center in Gramercy. We were in a meeting room on the third floor. Low-ceilinged, carpeted in severe gray, lit by cold fluorescents. There were a couple of older, white-bearded drummers on bongos and timbales. Two women who looked like sisters handled maracas and trumpet. A lanky black kid my age had a bass guitar. Patrick himself, a tall pasty twenty-something with blond dreadlocks, waved about clave sticks as he talked.

"This is Rick," he introduced me. "Our new conga player."

People nodded, said hi. No one seemed eager to make friends and improve my social life.

"Get ready," Patrick told me. "They'll be here soon."

"Wait, what?" I floundered. "Who?"

"We're accompanying a dance class," Patrick said. "It's

their last practice together so they decided to pay for a band."

Blood rushed to my face, with all those eyes on me. "I haven't played in a while—"

"It's a beginners' class," Patrick said. "We'll play basic salsa. Do the tumbao, nothing more."

That's the problem with leaving your apartment. You end up having to do things.

The dancers trickled in. Fifty-something women in black slacks and pale blouses. Gray-haired men with silver belt buckles and summery polo shirts. They looked around uneasily, as if they didn't know what they were doing here any more than I did.

Then Ana walked in.

⤳

She was poised and slim, with inky black hair down to her shoulders. It framed a heart-shaped brown face, smooth and soft, naive, almost childlike—except for her eyes, set unusually deep in her face. Those eyes seemed amused, like this girl knew things you didn't and found it funny.

Don't get me wrong—it wasn't love at first sight. You see lots of cute girls in Manhattan, and you know they won't ever feature in your life except as passersby. Besides, I was too nervous to pay her much attention.

The girl had entered together with a stringy thirtysomething white guy who looked like he spent too much time at a tanning salon.

"Hey, Gregoire," Patrick greeted him, but he was looking at the girl. "How's it going, Ana?"

"Hey," she said easily.

The tanned guy, Gregoire, turned to the class. "All right, everyone. Let's warm up."

"One, two, one two three four," Patrick counted. He started on the claves—clack clack clack, clack-clack. On the next bar, the maracas came in, and the bongos.

I realized I was still staring at Ana. Hurriedly, I attacked the congas. My first strokes went wobbly, off time, but then—face burning—I fell into the beat.

Not that anyone noticed. We played a basic percussive pattern, steady and even. The trumpet came in with a simple, cheerful melody.

The class rolled their shoulders and circled their hips, stepped forward and back and sideways, and turned around in place. Ana and Gregoire moved with a light, casual elegance at the front of the room. Everyone else plodded like a bunch of rusty Transformers in bad weather conditions. Jerky steps, now slower, now faster, and tripping over their own feet.

Not that I had a right to judge anyone's dancing. A few years ago at a school party, Flavia Martinez took one look at my dance interpretation of "Poker Face" and laughed. "You really Cuban, dude?" she had asked me, in front of everyone. I hadn't danced a step since.

The dancers paired up and shuffled back and forth, left and right in unison, like a roomful of badly made mario-nettes. It was painful to watch. So I watched Ana instead. The languid way she rolled her shoulders, a mesmerizing figure eight. The elegant shift of her torso from side to side in time to the beat. The way her hips rocked—

My fingers tripped, and I missed a beat.

"Focus," Patrick hissed.

In my defense, Ana's hips.

By the end of the class, I arrived at two conclusions. One, salsa was a shuffling dance for old people. Two, my plan was a failure. I wasn't good enough to play with this band. I wasn't good enough to play with any band.

We'd finished the last piece and I was already getting up when one of the students spoke to Ana and Gregoire. "Would you dance for us?"

They looked at each other. Ana shrugged. Gregoire turned to Patrick. "Can you give us something interesting?"

Patrick considered for a moment. "'Mi Cama Huele a Ti'?"

We played. It was a relaxed piece with a sweet melody on the trumpet, a salsa cover of a Tito "El Bambino" reggaeton piece that I had heard on Spotify. A dozen bars in, the guitar kid started singing in flawless Spanish, his voice smooth, adult.

I barely noticed. I barely had the presence of mind to keep time.

In the beginning, Ana and Gregoire hardly moved, shifting from side to side, their torsos swaying in graceful small undulations. They fell into the basic step, forward and back, just like the class had done except there was a charge to their every moment, a supple tension, so that theirs was not a dull lack of motion—it was fire held in check.

Gregoire raised Ana's arm in the air, and she spun once elegantly. He guided her around him in a graceful walk. He hooked his elbows over hers and drew her close, and they circled each other in an intimate embrace.

How I wished to be him.

The bongo player switched to cowbell, ringing loud and clear. The singer launched into the refrain, a sonorous complaint of how his bed smelled of the girl who'd left him. The music surged.

So did Ana and Gregoire.

They swung apart, arms outstretched, not touching. They spun in place, once, twice, thrice, perfectly poised. They circled each other in taut, stalking steps, watching each other. They rushed forward, except they never collided, but came together and spun, spun, spun around the floor, Beauty and the Beast in their ballroom.

It was not a thing for words, their dance. I won't give you the blow-by-blow. The best I can do is tell you how I felt, watching it. My heart raced ahead of the salsa beat, and my breath came fast, and shivers shot up and down my body. I no longer saw Ana, only the dance itself. Lost in it, drunk on it, at once ecstatic to behold it—and frustrated that I couldn't be part of it.

When they finished, it took me a while to realize that my fingers no longer moved. That the class had been applauding.

In a daze, I rose from the congas. If I had let myself think,

I would have stopped. Quickly, I walked to where Ana drank from her water bottle.

"You were awesome," I said to her.

She looked me over nonchalantly. "You weren't."

"Er . . . ," I said. "I'm not really a drummer."

"You're that cat guy," she said then.

I blinked. "You've heard of me?"

She pointed at my chest, the corner of her lip twitching.

I looked down and saw my T-shirt. It featured a fat gray tomcat squished upside down into a glass preserve jar. Except the cat's got my face Photoshopped on. Above the picture, red letters spell out THAT CAT GUY in Comic Sans.

Rob Kenna gave me that shirt on my birthday, in front of the whole class. I put it on right there, out of principle. To show that bastard he couldn't get to me. I told everyone I liked the thing—and managed to convince even myself.

Now, with Ana's eyes on me, I was acutely aware how I must look in it. Skinny brown arms sticking out of baggy sleeves.

No choice but to go all in.

"That's right," I told her. "I'm New York's first cat video tycoon. My site, CatoTrope.com, is the go-to destination for feline footage connoisseurs."

"Cato-trope?"

"Like zoetrope," I said. "Or like catastrophe."

"So you're like a cat lady except younger?"

"I don't even have a cat," I said. "I just make money off

them. It's sort of a family business."

Which was almost true, if you considered Mom's folder of cat videos my start-up capital.

"Fascinating," Ana said. "I need to set up a website. Could you help me?"

I flinched.

A website. So that's why she was still talking to me.

I wanted to tell her to build her own damn website.

What I said instead was, "Sure! Just tell me what you need. Let me give you my email. Oh, and here's my cell. Call me anytime!"

Yeah. I'm smooth.

"The thing is," Ana said, "I don't have much of a budget."

"Well . . . ," I began. "Maybe you could . . ."

I stopped. Remembering all the times I'd been called a klutz. Remembering what Flavia Martinez said about my "Poker Face" dance. Knowing I had no chance in hell at getting as good as Ana.

But I remembered also what it had felt like to watch her dance.

"Maybe you could teach me salsa," I forced out.

The world kept right on spinning.

"What kind of salsa do you want to learn?" Ana asked.

"I don't know," I said. "The stuff you were dancing."

"Cuban, then. Salsa casino."

"My mom was Cuban," I said. "I don't think she was much of a dancer, though." For all the salsa we listened to at home, I'd never seen her dance.

"Just because you're Spanish doesn't mean you can do the paso doble. I'm Puerto Rican. *Boricua, ya tú sabes.* But I learned to dance from this French guy." Ana tossed her head at Gregoire. "You've danced before?"

"No," I said.

"I don't teach," Ana said. "But come dance with us. At our school. I'll get you a discount."

So maybe I should have bargained, should have said a discount wasn't enough to pay for a new website. But I didn't care about that in the least.

Ana hadn't laughed at my request. She hadn't called me crazy. She'd said, "Come dance with us."

Funny thing about failed plans. They get you places all the same.

chapter two

I CONNECT WITH
MY ROOTS

An observation:

You upload a video where Mr. Porcelain leaps from sink to kitchen island, lands elegantly, and proceeds to drink the milk from your bowl of cornflakes.

It gets a thousand views.

You put up the same video, except with more footage. First, Mr. Porcelain leaps and falls to the ground short of the island. He leaps again and hits the edge of the island, and tumbles to the ground. Finally, he takes a running start and leaps and makes it. To a background of trumpets, he laps up your milk.

This version gets fifteen thousand views.

Interpretation:

Up to you, really. Perhaps we enjoy watching the suffering of others. Perhaps we enjoy feeling superior. Plausible explanations, both of them. I'm sure there's some truth to both.

I have another theory. I figure watching someone struggle gets us into their skin. When Mr. Porcelain plummets to the floor, we identify with his problem because we too learn by trial and error. Seeing him fail, we consider what we'd do in his place. We get invested in his struggle as a kind of mental role-play. When Mr. Porcelain succeeds we cheer not only him, but also ourselves.

That's why the second video gets fifteen times more viewers. Not because Mr. Porcelain bonking his head against the kitchen island is hilarious. Because people empathize with his fight. That's what I choose to believe.

Why do I mention this? Oh, no reason.

No reason at all.

᥯

Some weeks later, on the first of March, Ana met me at the door of Chévere Dance Academy.

"There you are," she said. "I wondered if you'd show."

My lips tugged up into a smile. Ana wore skintight leggings and a sports tee, and let's just say I was distracted. "Did you?"

"Sure. Come to the office."

Chévere occupied a three-story brick building off the

Gowanus Canal in Brooklyn. The first-floor dance hall was long and narrow, hemmed in by mirror-covered walls. Soaring ceilings gave it a cavernous feel. An enormous fan turned in one corner, but the humid air smelled of Pine-Sol and sweat. Large colorful photos of Cuban street scenes covered the walls. I recognized the grand colonial houses of Trinidad, Mom's birthplace.

Ana led me to a glass office in the far corner. That tanned-looking French guy, Gregoire, looked up from a computer.

"This is Rick from Patrick's band," Ana said. "He's here for your new class. Give him a month free on my account." To me, she said, "We'll talk about my website later."

She left.

"I'll need you to fill out this form," Gregoire said.

"Okay," I said, trying not to sound too deflated. "Is she also in the class?"

"Who? Oh, Ana?" Gregoire shook his head. "She's in advanced study. That's our performance team. You're in beginners."

"Umm . . ." My face heated up. "How long does it take before you get to advanced study?"

Now Gregoire really looked at me, as if taking me in for the first time. "You're Hispanic, aren't you? Got Latin roots?"

I blinked. I get my looks from Mom's side, but people don't usually straight up blurt it out like that. Not white people. They tend to dance around it. ("Where are you from? I mean, originally. And your family, where are they from?")

"My mother was from Cuba," I said.

"Great," he said. "So you've been dancing since you were little."

I shifted uncomfortably. "Not exactly."

Gregoire looked disappointed, as if that was the wrong answer.

Maybe it was. I always told people I was Cuban—but in our home, you didn't mention Cuba unless you wanted to hear a diatribe. "That communist *comemierda* screwed up our country," Mom had said. "I don't want you to waste your life hating him. We're Americans now."

Mom had come to the United States on a boat during the Mariel exodus of 1980, when she was eighteen. The rest of her family had stayed in Cuba. Mom didn't talk to them and didn't talk about them, not even when I asked questions. I only knew that something had happened to her, back in Havana, something that made her want to forget. The only connection she'd maintained with the island had been her salsa collection and a few books—Del Monte, Villaverde, Martí. Pre-Revolution, all of them.

Naturally, Mom's refusal to talk about Cuba had made me a fanatic about it. For a while in ninth grade I'd watched every movie, read every book about it that I could get my hands on. Castro's Revolution, Hemingway's submarine hunts, the Bay of Pigs invasion, the Special Period, blogs like Generación Y and Here is Havana, anything. But it was intellectual knowledge, all of it, and it would help me little on the dance floor.

"So about that advanced team?" I asked.

Gregoire shrugged. "It takes most people a few years to get there."

"Okay," I said.

Protip: when you find yourself saying okay to years of hard work, that's life telling you something.

This wasn't even about Ana, not really. I wanted to dance with her, yes—but not simply because I was attracted to her. I wanted to experience what she had, that evening with Gregoire. I'd seen snatches of their dance in my dreams.

The beginners' class had twelve girls and seven guys. Most were teens, the oldest in her early twenties. All white kids, except for two black girls and me.

Everyone else seemed to have arrived with friends and chatted among themselves. I stood off to the side and circled my knees as in PE class—which was my sole prior exposure to any sort of organized exercise. I might have convinced myself I looked like I knew what I was doing, except the mirror told me I looked like a bony kid in sweatpants too big for him.

"Welcome to Chévere." Gregoire paced the front of the class with his hands behind his back. "We dance Cuban salsa—the dance called casino, after the *Casino Deportivo* social clubs in Cuba. Everyone else in this town dances New York style. What we can't make up in numbers, we make up in quality. We won't start you off with flashy moves and fancy patterns. You will stay in this beginners' class until you've learned the basics." Gregoire stopped to face us, hands on his hips. "A dancer without basics is a baboon."

It seemed to me that Gregoire had watched too many war movies—the sort featuring a grizzled old drill sergeant.

He put music on. I recognized the song, "Malditos Celos," a slow tune by Manolito Simonet. My hands tapped out the tumbao beat on my hips. My knees trembled on the verge of motion.

"First, we listen," Gregoire said.

Huh.

He drew the rhythmic structure of salsa on the mirror with a marker. He explained where the phrase began, where the drums came in and where the bell rang, and what the bass played. He had us close our eyes and tap our foot on the 1 beat, the beat on which we would begin to dance.

I took my first salsa steps twenty minutes into the class. It was the basic back-and-forth step I'd watched the other class practice with disdain.

We spent the next half hour on that step, plus a side-to-side variation.

"Transfer your weight!" Gregoire yelled over the music, and then he'd come up behind you to give you a nudge. "Listen to the beat!" he'd say, accompanied by a loud clap of his hands right in your ear. Or he'd cry "Don't bounce!" and do a little jerky pantomime of our dancing prowess.

Toward the end of class, we did ten minutes in couples. I ended up with a tall blond girl who moved in strange, tilting steps, like she was constantly about to stumble. I took her hand and put my other hand on her back, as Gregoire showed us, and tried to lead her in the basic step.

The experience felt about as graceful as one of those county fair three-legged races. A quick glance at the mirror assured me this was, in fact, an accurate description. The girl's scowl told me she agreed and that she wasn't to blame.

Suffice to say, I finished the class somewhat dispirited. I wasn't the only one. I heard some other kids talk about not coming back. "I signed up to have fun, not to get bored out of my skull," muttered the blond girl I'd danced with. I wasn't ready to give up myself—I could stand a little boredom if it meant I might get good at this. But I did wonder if Gregoire the drill sergeant was the right teacher for me.

I ran into Ana on the way out.

What? It's true. I ran into her because I lingered by the bulletin board for ten minutes—pretending to browse flyers until she came downstairs.

She was breathing hard, a sheen of sweat on her face, her dark hair in disarray. I decided to pass by as she drank from the wall fountain.

"Hey, Ana."

She straightened, wiped her mouth. "Hey, Rick. *Qué hay?* How was your first class?"

I shrugged. "Gregoire takes this basics thing seriously."

"I know, right? So awesome."

I schooled my face into the appropriate expression of agreement. "Yes. Awesome."

"That's what I love about this place," Ana said. "Gregoire doesn't really need the money, so he doesn't worry about losing students."

"I see." Specifically, I saw that it was a strange way to run a school.

"That's what they don't get, the people who leave," Ana said. "This is the fastest way to learn. Other schools, they turn out people who dance for years and do all this flashy stuff, and still they're bad. Like, *en candela*. But here—here you get good or you quit."

Had Gregoire said this stuff, I might have brushed it off. Ana spoke with an excitement that made my heart speed up.

I was going to learn my basics. I was going to get good faster than anybody Ana had ever met.

"Well, uh," I said instead. "So what kind of website do you want? A dance blog?"

If you're going to brag, best stick to things you've already accomplished.

"A portfolio," Ana said. "For my films."

"Films?"

"I'm a filmmaker," Ana said, with simple conviction—not I'm going to be a filmmaker, not I want to be a filmmaker, but I *am* a filmmaker.

"Huh," I said. "I didn't know that."

"You mean to say, why didn't you see that when you stalked me online?"

"Umm . . ."

Ana laughed. "Clearly I need that website."

"Clearly," I said.

On which graceful note I fled the conversation.

⌒

Dad finally noticed my new hobby—and he wasn't thrilled.

We live in Peter Cooper Village. Our building is a red-brick housing project-turned-overpriced apartment block near First Avenue and Twentieth Street in Manhattan. We can only afford it because of rent control—Dad has lived here for all thirty years of his career as a Metro-North ticket puncher.

The place has the sound isolation of a matchbox.

I blasted Charanga Habanera from my speakers and practiced torso isolations while doing math homework. I practiced my basic step at 1:00 a.m. when I couldn't sleep. I spun in place while watching *Breaking Bad* reruns—round and round and round again, until my world swayed like Jesse Pinkman's.

Dad's a tolerant kind of guy. His motto is live and let live (although he hadn't been so good at the first part since Mom's passing). But when I lost my balance and toppled over my bookcase one afternoon a couple of weeks in, he finally spoke up.

"Don't you think you're taking this dance thing too seriously?" he asked, after we'd picked up the collected volumes of *Ex Machina* and *Sandman*.

"You've got to practice the basics," I told him. "It's the fastest way to learn."

"When did you last watch a movie?" Dad asked. "Did you see that new one, what's it called, with the robots? You used to really like those."

"Dancing feels like nothing else," I said.

"Shouldn't you update your site?" Dad asked. "The last Catfestation was in January."

I winced. The word "Catfestation" should never pass a father's lips. Spoken with Dad's German accent, it sounded more like a venereal disease.

But at least he'd noticed. "I didn't know you kept up with my site."

"You kidding?" he asked. "That's all I do at work, in low-traffic hours."

"You actually like the videos?"

Dad snorted. "Who do you think sent Mom her first cat video? 'Cat riding a tricycle across the parking lot.' She loved it."

"That's a classic," I said.

I felt strangely happy to realize Dad had been following the website all these months. We'd never even talked about it. But then, we talked about little these days. Ours had been a quiet apartment since Mom had passed away.

"People might start to notice that you're not updating," Dad said.

"I run a content aggregator." A cat-tent aggregator, says my site, with an appropriate graphic of a camping feline. "People can upload their videos without my help."

He was right, though. If you don't keep updating—new features, new contests, new flame wars in the forums—you die.

"It's about that girl, isn't it," Dad said. "About Rachel."

At this, I experienced one of those mouth malfunctions that had been affecting me lately. Dad took my silence as agreement. He sank onto my bed. "A girl can really mess with your head."

I gathered this was meant to be a buddy moment. I didn't feel like having a buddy moment. But I couldn't remember the last time Dad had spoken to me like this, serious, adult to adult.

"I think my head's all right," I said. "Sure, Rachel got me thinking about a few things, but—"

"When I met your mother," Dad cut in, "I forgot who I was for a while. I stopped playing soccer. I started reading books. I went to poetry readings with her. Me, going to poetry readings! I thought I needed to do all that if I was going to date a literature teacher."

"I really get salsa," I said. "It's my thing."

"It took us years to figure out how to stay ourselves," Dad said, still gazing at the ceiling. "That I didn't have to care about her books, and she about my soccer matches, and it was fine."

"You're right about the website," I said. "I'll pick it back up."

"Sometimes I miss her so much," Dad said.

At that point, I realized this conversation wasn't really about me.

"I miss her too," I said.

Even now, two years later, I woke up some mornings expecting to hear her puttering about in the kitchen. Even now when I got sucked into some new book I thought, Mom's gonna love this. And when it hit me . . .

We had to live on, though. Except Dad, it seemed he could only think of the life we'd had before.

Before the blood on her lips. Before the doctor's appointment. Before the endless hacking cough in the night. Before the breakfasts, those horrible breakfasts where we smiled and joked and talked about school and the weather and everything and nothing. Before the silence in the apartment, that flat ticktock silence that came after.

I blinked hard, shutting down that thought.

Dad too started as if awakened. He gave me one of his trademark stern gazes that he uses on Metro-North fare dodgers. "So you should be careful with this salsa obsession."

His reasoning didn't seem very convincing to me, but I said, "The style I dance comes from Cuba. Maybe that's why I'm into it. You know, connecting with my roots and stuff."

It seemed a clever deflection as I said it. Dad appeared to chew it over for a few seconds, his brow furrowed. Then a light came on in his eyes. He shot up from my bed with new-found energy.

"You should absolutely connect with your roots," he said. "Hold on."

"Hold on for what?" I asked, too late.

Minutes later he reappeared, holding his phone and a little black book, its cover streaked with dust. He flipped through the book with one hand, still clutching the phone in the other. I hadn't seen him this excited since Germany won the World Cup.

"Is that . . . Mom's notebook?"

"She said to call once you were ready." He found the page he was looking for, held it open with his thumb, and started dialing.

"What are you talking about? Who are you calling?"

"Your aunt Juanita," Dad said. "In Havana."

"Uhh . . ." That escalated quickly. "I'm not sure I have anything to say to—"

"Hello? Hello?" Dad started into loud American-speak, something he did well despite his German accent. "Can you hear me? CAN-YOU-HEAR-ME? This is Rudolf Hahn from New York. NEW YORK, yes. Can I speak with Juanita? JUANITA?"

Dad held his cell away from his ear, stared at it reproachfully. He handed it to me. "They're not making any sense."

I accepted the phone as one accepts a specimen of tapeworm offered for your examination. You want nothing to do with the thing, but it would be rude to refuse.

"Hello?"

"Sí? Quién e'? Qué quiere?" Yes? Who's there? What do you want? A woman's voice, in rapid Spanish. "If you want Yosvany, he's in the street."

I struggled to keep up with the stream of words. My Spanish had been getting rusty since Mom died, and she'd made a point of speaking clear, proper *castellano*. The words coming across the crackly line blended together and tripped over each other like tourists in Times Square.

"Uh, I'm Rick," I said. "From New York. The son of María Gutiérrez Peña?"

The line went quiet—even the crackling seemed to subside, until I thought the connection had dropped.

"Rick?" the woman asked then. Her voice trembled. "It's you, *hijo*? Really?"

"Aunt Juanita? How are things?"

I hoped that question didn't sound too vague. I knew nothing about this Aunt Juanita.

"I never thought I'd hear your voice," Aunt Juanita said. "You sound exactly like María when she was younger."

"Oh." I sounded like a girl. Awesome.

"Wait until I tell Yosvany. He won't believe his cousin from New York called."

So I had a cousin. "It's nice talking to you too."

"You must come visit, meet your family. We have a room for you. Hot water, bathroom, elevator." She sounded particularly proud of the last.

"Great," I said. I doubted they had broadband.

"There's a color TV," she said.

Definitely no broadband.

"Fresh fruit for breakfast, *guayaba*, *plátano*, *fruta bomba*. Oh, and there's bread with cheese and ham."

This was starting to sound pretty dire. You can start a day perfectly fine without eggs, bacon, and blueberry pancakes— but when bread with cheese and ham becomes a selling point, it's time to run.

Seriously, though, here's the thing. In my family, Cuba had been the forbidden land—and so of course I'd always wanted to go. Whenever Mom raged up and down the living room decrying Fidel's latest atrocity—"We're never going back as long as that *hijo de puta* is alive"—I'd secretly thought to myself that I would, as soon as I got a chance. But since Mom's death I hadn't considered going even once. It was as if the island had lost its pull, now that there was no longer anyone around to forbid the trip.

Or perhaps I simply wasn't ready to face the trip and all the memories of Mom it would bring back.

In any case, I wasn't ready to commit. So I did what I always do in such situations.

"That sounds wonderful, *tía*," I said. "I really want to come."

"Really?" Aunt Juanita asked. "We would love to see you."

"I'll find a way to make it happen. Now, I've got to run. I'll talk to you soon, all right?"

"All right, *cariño*. I'm so happy you called!"

Most kids, adults ask them to do something annoying, they'll say no, make a big scene, and in the end get forced to do it anyway. But there's a smarter way. Just smile and nod, and do nothing.

I mean, face it, Uncle Otto's perfectly capable of mowing his own lawn—no need to make it a lesson on the value of honest work for his nephew (especially if said nephew is a cat video entrepreneur already).

After I'd hung up, I went to compile the best videos of the month for my site. The Spring Catfestation Extravaganza couldn't wait any longer.

chapter three

DANCE MACHINE

I spent five weeks in Chévere's beginners' class. I'd like to say my conga background, my daily exercises, my single-minded focus let me move up faster than anyone else, but four other guys graduated first. My dedication to salsa only compensated partway for years of a different dedication—to not moving my butt from the couch. Even so, it was a novelty not being last.

I could do the basic step without losing the beat, alone and with a girl. I could do an *enchufla* turn and an *exhibela* and a *setenta*—a pair move that initially seemed like a maze of arms, but soon became second nature, me and my partner circling each other in something approaching coordination.

It was time to go social dancing.

Gregoire harangued us on the subject every time. "You have to get out there and dance! You can't learn salsa from a class."

Which seemed a peculiar admission for a teacher to make, but Ana backed it up. "Class teaches you moves, but the girls know what's coming so they'll do the moves even if you screw up. At a club, the girls have no idea what you're thinking. Don't lead a move right? *Olvídalo ya.* It ain't gonna happen."

This sounded about as pleasant as sticking my arm down a garbage disposal. But when she texted me that everyone was going to the White Hamster a few days later, I wasn't about to stay home.

The Hamster was a smallish bar on Houston. Exposed brick walls, cheap furniture, cheaper beer. The guy at the door let me in after a raised eyebrow at my fake ID, something that suggested I shouldn't try my luck at the bar. Timba, a modern Cuban form of salsa, blasted loud over the speakers. The air was hot and humid. The packed crowd was half Chévere students practicing their school-learned steps and half Latinos, who danced steps that I didn't recognize.

"Only a few are Cuban," Ana explained, after waving me over to her table. "You've got Puerto Rican, Venezuelan, Colombian, Dominican salsa here."

Before we could swap more than a few sentences, a heavy-set black guy with a bright red sweatband strolled up to the table and offered Ana his arm. She smiled and went with him. "*Vamos, muchacho!*" she yelled over her shoulder.

I watched them dance for a minute. The guy was smooth and quick on his feet, despite his considerable size. At last I gathered all my courage, took a deep breath, and went in search of a partner.

As it turned out, my fears of how the night would go were inaccurate. The girls didn't scowl at me. They stared glassily instead and nodded thanks and beat a quick retreat as soon as we'd finished the song.

If not for Ana, I would have given up after a dance or two. But she hardly ever rested—every guy in the bar seemed to want to dance with her. My pride wouldn't let me sit in a corner, alone and quiet.

I didn't get up the courage to invite Ana herself until late in the night, when the floor was starting to empty. My feet ached. I'd changed my shirt already, and the new one was getting damp. I saw Ana sitting still for a moment, and asked her.

"To this song?" she asked. "I guess it fits."

I listened for a moment. Adalberto Álvarez was playing "Máquina Para Bailar," one of Mom's favorites. A playful piece about a dance machine, someone so hard and stiff no one could possibly dance with them. Blood rushed to my face.

"Just kidding, man." Ana grinned, gesturing me toward the floor. "Loosen up."

It occurred to me Ana's pedagogical technique left something to be desired. But she didn't need to know that.

We started into the basic step. Ana winked at me. The

warmth of her body under my hands, the rose scent of her perfume, the way she moved, it made me forget—

"How do you do that?" she asked, a curious tilt to her head.

"Do what?"

"This . . . thing?" She shook her shoulders in ragged, choppy motions, like C-3PO electrocuted. "Amazing."

"Your pedagogical technique leaves something to be desired," I said, deciding maybe she did need to know.

Ana snorted. "Starting out is hard, I know. *Pero vale la pena.*"

It's worth it.

That became the refrain I repeated to myself over the weeks that followed. I went to at least one party a week, more often two, and forced myself to ask all the experienced girls for a dance. I pretended not to notice the hesitations and little sighs—or rather took them as signals that I needed to adjust my technique.

"Thank you for the dance," I said to rolled eyes.

"I enjoyed that," I said to retreating backs.

"Very nice," I said to forced smiles.

And occasionally, when some girl actually thanked *me* for the dance and smiled encouragingly, I told myself I was imagining the pity in her eyes.

"I'm getting used to embarrassment," I explained to Lettuce one Sunday, while we played the latest *Gears of War* on his living room couch. "Soon I won't care what people think anymore."

At the time he only nodded, as if impressed. I felt satisfied with myself (I wonder when I'll finally learn to recognize life's little warning signs).

The next day at school, Lettuce invited me to sit with his band at lunch. "We need a website," he explained to me. "I could do it, but I figured maybe you'd want to build it for us. Get to meet everyone, you know."

"Everyone" in this case turned out to be three skinny white guys in ragged jeans and black T-shirts—short little Mitch the singer, blond Luke the drummer, and Joe the bass guy.

"Rick's a wizard with websites," Lettuce introduced me. "He'll get us set up."

"The cat guy," Mitch said.

"That's right," I said.

"Man's got a gift for pussies," Luke said, drumming chicken thighs on his lunch plate.

I forced a smile, wondering if this was a compliment.

"Rick's a chick magnet all right," Lettuce said. "He's a salsa dancer."

I gave him a look. It was a look to give you radiation poisoning. But he only nodded encouragingly, as if he'd handed me the opportunity of a lifetime.

His friends were all watching me. So, naturally, my mouth opened and words came out.

"That's right," I said. "I dance with hot girls every day, up close and personal."

"Yeah, right," Mitch said.

"It's true," Lettuce said. "He's known as the King of Salsa."

"Uhh," I said.

"Well, he is Mexican," Luke said.

"Cuban. And I'm no Salsa King."

"Thought so," Mitch said.

"I'm pretty good, though," I said. "They do call me the dance machine."

Not like they were going to show up at the White Hamster to check.

"Hey, here's an idea." Joe put down his burger and leaned forward intently. "Use him to fill the gap."

"That's right." A gleam came into Mitch's eyes. "That's brilliant."

"Umm," I said.

"We're programming the spring concert," Joe explained. "There's a five-minute gap while we change equipment between bands. Perfect for a dance show."

"Awesome," Lettuce said. "When else are you going to get a chance to show off to the entire school?"

Ah, yes. Me, dancing in front of the entire school.

"So we're set," Luke said.

At this point, the smart thing to do was obvious. Backtrack like hell and hope these guys let me live it down.

I looked at Lettuce for help, with my best plaintive expression.

"Rick doesn't even get stage fright," Lettuce said. "That's what he told me. He doesn't care what people think anymore."

"You should hire Lettuce to be your agent," Mitch said. "He's got me starting to believe."

"The show's in five weeks." Luke clapped me on the back. "Looking forward to it."

"Okay," I said.

I could have said no. I really could have. But even now—sitting at that lunch table and shivering with a cold no one else seemed to feel—I saw a vision in my mind's eye.

Of shining lights. Of a roaring crowd. Of Ana and me, turning, turning, turning in dance.

chapter four

ANA SAYS

Five weeks wasn't a lot of time to prepare. That's why I delayed for days before asking Ana if she'd do the show with me.

Bowel-emptying fear may also have had something to do with it.

Then she texted me over the weekend. *I've worked out the concept for my website. Come over to my place?*

As if I might actually say no.

Ana lived with her mother and stepfather in a two-bedroom railroad apartment in Williamsburg, just off the L train. It was a place of waxed wooden floors and stylishly uncomfortable vintage furniture. The air smelled of paint; Ana's mother was an artist.

"Nice place," I said.

"I suppose." Ana had a distracted look to her. In black jeans and a gray sweater, she hugged herself though it wasn't cold. "At our old apartment, I slept in the walk-in closet."

"Seriously?"

"My parents hadn't divorced yet, so it was the closet or sharing the room with the two of them." Ana stared off into the distance. "And, well, that would have been a disaster."

"That bad, huh," I said.

"You know how sometimes kids won't accept their stepfather?" Ana asked.

I nodded uncertainly.

"All my mother had to do was tell me she'd found someone who didn't drink," Ana said.

"Oh." After a moment, I added, "I'm sorry."

Ana shrugged. "My drunk of a dad is out of our lives now, and my mom has someone who loves her. That's all I care about."

Even to my ears, she didn't sound quite convincing. But I made no further comment.

Ana's eyes focused on me again. "We can work on my mom's machine."

That machine was a giant tower of a computer, with lots of blinking lights. It must have been a beast back when I was in diapers. Still, it ran Chrome all right, which was all we needed. Ana showed me a few indie filmmaker sites she liked; we discussed the pros and cons of WordPress versus a custom-made site.

"I want a gallery to show off my short films," she said. "Plus a page for my new project, a film about Cuban salsa in New York."

I asked to see one of her short films, to get a sense of her style.

"My stepdad gave me a camera his first Christmas with us," she said. "So I went out and made this with my friends."

Ana's first film starred a giant walking teddy bear with a top hat and a wide sewn-on grin. He woke up in Ana's apartment every morning, had breakfast, and took the L train into the city. He stood all day in Union Square—grinning that sewn-on grin, holding a sign that said *Free Hug!* Except no one ever came for the hugs. Day after day, month after month, year after year.

It wasn't a cheery film.

"Huh," I said.

"I wasn't very good back then," Ana said. "The lighting's crap, some of the composition makes me wince, and that shaky camera . . . ugh."

"Well, yeah," I said, "but I like it."

"You do?"

"I was expecting some reversal," I said. "Someone comes in and gets his spirits up, you know."

"Her spirits," Ana said. "The bear's Angelina."

"Oh." I scratched my neck. "Yes, of course."

"I was planning to do something like that. But I decided this version was more true to life in New York City."

There was an energy to Ana as she spoke, an enthusiasm

that she rarely showed off the dance floor. Something swelled in my chest as I listened to her. It was a strange, buoyant, exhilarating feeling. I wanted to tell her that she inspired me to . . . to . . .

To do what? Create a spinoff site for pony videos?

I'd built CatoTrope mostly as a distraction after Mom's death. Now that it brought in money I felt proud of it, but it was hardly *War and Peace*—not even the *War and Peace* of lolcats.

Listening to Ana, I could almost imagine what that must feel like—having something that consumed you, that drove you, that meant everything to you. I had never felt that way about anything.

Except maybe the first time I'd seen Ana dance . . .

I spoke before I could stop myself. "I've got a problem, Ana."

"Huh?"

"It's about this school concert."

Ana watched me blankly.

"I . . . umm . . . I kind of agreed to dance salsa in front of the whole school."

Ana nodded appreciatively. "*Estás jodido.*"

"Yeah. I don't even have a partner yet . . ."

There followed a silence. Patrick Rothfuss, my favorite author, might have called it a silence of three parts. The part where my self-respect curled up quietly to die. The part where desperation sank its stiletto blade into my gut. The part where

I implored Ana for help with mute, mournful eyes.

She started. "No," she said. "Go away."

I added a trembling lip. Not intentionally. It just happened.

"I'm too busy. School. Exams. My new film."

"You could use me for your salsa film," I said. "Clumsy beginner makes good."

Ana's face told me this plot summary didn't seem likely to her.

"If I don't do this, I'm finished at school," I said.

Ana's face told me how much this prospect upset her.

"I'll pay you," I said. "Like for a gig. A hundred bucks. Two hundred."

Ana threw her hands in the air. "Shut it. I'm not doing this for money."

"But—?"

"What makes you think there's a *but*?"

"Optimism? Desperation?"

"If I agree, you're going to make me the spiffiest website on the intertubes," Ana said.

"Of course!" I was nodding so hard my neck hurt.

"Just one more thing," Ana said.

"Anything," I said.

"I won't be your girlfriend."

I gaped. I choked. I sputtered. All the repertoire appropriate to such an announcement. "What do you . . . I don't . . . I mean . . . I didn't even . . ."

"Come on, Rick," she said. "I'm not blind. You follow me around, you make puppy eyes, you ask Gregoire about me."

My jaw constricted. Damn you, Gregoire.

"Look," Ana said. "It's fine. I'm not annoyed or anything. I just figured I'd save us both trouble. I'm not looking right now and you're probably not my type anyway. Sorry."

She sounded so reasonable about it. That was the thing—so damn reasonable.

"So what do you think?" Ana asked me. "Can we just be friends?"

I could give you some wise advice at this point. If a girl you really like says let's just be friends, you should nod and smile and get the heck away from her. Once you get over her, sure, be friends—if you liked her enough to want to date her, presumably you like her enough to be pals. Until then? Clear the blast radius.

"Sure," I told her. "We can just be friends."

By which I meant one day you'll see my brilliance! One day you'll realize how great I am! Me, Rick Gutiérrez, Cat Guy Extraordinaire!

You're probably not my type, she'd said. *Probably.*

&

Cue training sequence.

You know how those go. Rousing music plays. An awkward but likably scrappy kid trains hard at the dance studio. Practices his steps on the empty subway platform. Taps his feet under his desk at school. Runs through the Siberian snow with salsa shoes tied around his neck.

Montage of a wall clock in fast-forward. Then green leaves sprouting on trees, days crossed off a calendar, and, voilà, you're in late May.

It was almost like that, except for all of Ana's cursing. You would have needed an industrial grade bleep-machine to censor it.

We practiced for forty minutes after class every day, alone at Chévere—they trusted Ana with the keys. For our choreography we'd picked "Me Dicen Cuba," a gentle, sweet tune by Alexander Abreu y Havana D'Primera. It seemed to have little effect on Ana.

"Get a flashlight and dig your foot out of your ass," was about the sweetest suggestion on her spectrum. Her comments always came with a smile.

But as the weeks went on, something strange happened. Ana got quieter and quieter. Her attacks faded, but so did her smiles. Often she'd stare into the distance for minutes at a time, like that first time at her place.

I caught myself wishing she'd go back to the cursing.

"What's wrong?" I asked her often.

"Shut up and dance," was her usual answer, spoken quietly, as if she didn't really care if I did or not.

"You can tell me," I said to her after practice one night. "We're friends, remember?"

She kept quiet as she wiped sweat from her face with a towel. She put it aside and sighed. "It's family stuff, okay? My

47

stepdad's sick and my mom's in denial, and I'm caught in the middle. I don't want to talk about it."

"I'm sorry to hear that." Ana had always mentioned her stepdad with fondness in her voice, but I didn't know much about him. I only knew he was Dominican, and that he'd hooked up with Ana's mom shortly after they'd moved to Williamsburg—away from Ana's father. And that he'd been a good parent to her. "Look, I've been through some medical stuff in my family. If there's anything I can help with . . . I mean, I'll listen if you need to talk."

"I don't," she said.

I knew what that felt like, so I didn't push her.

Our evenings at Chévere became grim, quiet affairs. I wondered why Ana kept working with me. I almost told her not to bother, to take care of her family and forget about our show.

I might have, if not for the oh-so-encouraging support of my schoolmates.

"Give us a twirl now," Kenna demanded in PE, swinging his finger in the air.

"I'm going to record your show," Flavia told me. "Instant YouTube classic!"

Luke from the band put up a poster on the concert's Facebook event page. *Featuring Rick Gutiérrez, King of Salsa*, it said. The comments section sported a dancing cats compilation video—from my own website!—along with the quality humor I had come to expect of my peers (*My eyes, they bleed already*).

"I hear you're dancing at the school concert," Dad said over breakfast, the day before the show.

I nearly spilled my cereal. How did he find out?

"I'll be there," he said.

I did spill my cereal. "What? Why?" Dad never came to these things.

"I'm happy for you, son," he said. "You're exploring your mother's culture. She would have liked to be there for you."

"Um, uh . . ." I sighed. "Thanks for your support, Dad."

"I know I've been a bit . . . not there for you, these past couple of years," Dad said. "But recently, you know, watching you dance, I'm realizing some things." There was red in his cheeks, but he pressed on. "Mom would be so happy for you. So happy to see you having fun."

"She'd be happy to see you having fun too," I said.

Dad said nothing to this, only nodded, his eyes down on the table. After some time, he said, "You should call Aunt Juanita again sometime."

Calling Havana was the last thing on my mind. "It's crazy expensive."

"It's family," Dad said. "Don't worry about the money."

"Mom would say that's putting cash in Fidel's pocket." As if I really cared about the *bloqueo*.

"Yeah, and how well has that worked?" Dad asked. "Fifty years and he's still there."

I stared at him. He wouldn't have said such a thing when Mom was around.

"You forget I lived under communism too," Dad said. "You can squeeze the country all you want. The guys at the top will steal enough from their own people to sit happy. Take North Korea now—"

"I'd love to take North Korea," I cut in quickly, "but I gotta run to class."

"I'm looking forward to tomorrow!" Dad said.

I shuddered. If tomorrow never came, that would be all right with me.

Unless, of course, it was because of a plague of flesh-eating goo that swept across New York and ate us alive.

You've got to keep perspective.

chapter five

SALSA KING

Tomorrows tend to become todays without much help. Even if you spend the night half awake, twisted up in sweaty sheets, kicking your legs to Alexander Abreu's voice in your head. Even if you reset your alarm three times and skip breakfast. Even if you text Lettuce Igorov asking if the concert's been postponed.

Curtain at 6 he texted back.

On the plus side, no flesh-eating goo.

School provided the expected dose of spitballs, witticisms about my upcoming performance, and pantomime on the theme of "Gangnam Style" wherever I went. It seemed the whole school was ready to watch me bomb. The best that can be said of the day was that I managed to keep my lunch down.

Ana had agreed to meet me at five outside school. When I showed up, she was already there, sitting on a bench by the curb. Legs together, hands in her lap, still—so very still. That stillness seemed incongruous with her punchy outfit of bright red jeans and a white tee.

"Hey, Rick." She might have sounded happier to see a parking ticket.

What happened? I almost asked. But I'd learned not to push her. "Let's go. They want us for a sound check."

A few sophomores were setting up a bake sale inside the auditorium. Overhead, a maze of colored streamers spread wall to wall, the sort of decoration that should be grounds for decollation (look it up).

Lettuce and the band kids were setting up on stage. They turned when I said hi. A smirk crept onto Mitch's face. He started to say something—then he noticed Ana. His jaw clicked shut.

I won't lie—that felt pretty good.

"Hey, guys," Lettuce said, unbearably cheerful, like he'd forgotten this was his fault.

I introduced Ana to everyone. She seemed to hardly notice them.

"The jazz guys will finish and we'll drop the curtain for five minutes," Lettuce explained. "That's your cue. You get into position, and the DJ will play your song."

I double-checked the space in front of the curtain. There

was plenty of room. I glanced at the band kids, gathered my courage, and asked Ana, "Shall we run through it?"

Ana shook her head, staring past me. "Where's the bathroom?"

"I'll show you."

In the hallway outside, away from everyone, Ana stopped and leaned against the windowsill, as if supporting a great weight. "Let's stay here for a bit."

"I thought you needed . . ."

"I'm sorry."

Ana looked up at me, met my eyes for the first time that day. And I saw uncertainty in her.

"Sorry for what?"

"It's my stepdad," she said.

A chill shot through me.

"We buried him this morning," she said.

I froze.

You came here from a funeral?

I didn't ask that question, though. Not because I was too considerate or too intelligent. Because someone seemed to have dumped ice down my shirt.

This sensation, it was a memory. An afterimage of a pale morning when I'd picked up coarse damp soil in one hand and tossed it on my mother's coffin. That morning, I couldn't make myself speak. Couldn't even cry. The kids from school, Mom's students, they cried—but I stood there and I couldn't. Inert. Locked inside a cold, heavy body.

"I'm sorry," I said. "What are you even doing here? The show doesn't matter. We'll dance some other time."

Ana turned on me, sharp. "No!" Then, softer, "No. I need this. I can forget, when I'm dancing."

"Okay," I said.

"Let's go through the steps," Ana said. "Right here, okay?"

We did. Ana danced by rote, mechanically. I couldn't even remember the steps, watching her face.

In short, we sucked. In a few minutes, we'd suck in front of my whole school.

"Are you sure you want to do this?" I asked.

"Dance with me," she said. "Please."

She might as well have pointed a gun at my head.

"Play it cool when you present us," I told Lettuce before the show. "Whatever you do, don't oversell us, all right?"

Half an hour later, the jazz club walked off the stage to polite applause. The curtain descended. Mitch's voice boomed over the speakers: "And now, ladies and gentlemen! A spectacle never before seen in our school! Straight from the sunny beaches of Cuba! Presenting our very own Salsa King, Rick 'Cat Guy' Gutiérrez, and his partner, Ana Cabrera!"

"Salsa King, huh," Ana said. As huhs go, it was expressive.

Applause pitter-pattered. The lights cut out. We walked out into the darkness and took positions on stage a few feet apart, facing each other. Shadows in the gloom.

My knees shook. I felt cold as a penguin, and about as graceful.

From the dark auditorium came laughter and cries: "Rick!" "Ricky!" "Meow!"

Drums rolled. The piano sang out. Havana D'Primera played.

A spotlight blasted on, bright in my eyes.

Step, step, slide.

Step, step, slide.

I moved by reflex, my body a mirror to Ana's. Spin to one side. Spin to the other. Shoot my foot out, my hand in the air. Then—

Then I saw Ana, really saw her. Not her stylish outfit. Not the elegant, effortless way she moved. Those things were no surprise. No. I saw her smile.

She smiled like a Madison Square Garden spotlight. She smiled as if dancing with me were her life's dream. She smiled like she'd never felt hurt in her life.

It was a shock, that smile. I tripped, stumbled, shot out my foot to brace myself.

Ana matched me. She tripped too, except gracefully, with an elegance that said—I meant to do this. Together we fell into the next step, as if nothing had gone wrong.

The music changed. We approached, locked hands, locked frames, turned round each other—round and round, as Alexander Abreu crooned about the beauty of his home-land.

At first I plodded from step to step, terrified. But Ana was a solid presence against me, her hand on my shoulder steady and sure. My feet grew light and the beat of the music entered me. Fear left me and I danced.

Ana had composed a simple, languid choreography for us. It was the story of two lovers drawn together and repelled and drawn together once again, unable to resist though they knew there was no future for them.

We circled each other and approached warily, and spun apart, and made as if to leave, only to find ourselves locked body against body once again. One rhythm, one being, moving to the steady beat of the salsa bell.

I missed a few steps, forgot to roll my shoulders for an accent, but the music carried me through, as did Ana's reassuring hold. I got this urge to sing. To cry out together with Alexander Abreu. I didn't—I would have lost the beat for sure—but I felt the song pass through me all the same.

The song culminated. We broke into a complex turn pattern, arms interlaced—she turning under my arm, I ducking under hers. We made a maze of our bodies as if seeking to find a way to break free but unable to do so.

As the music faded, we gave up the fight. I hooked my elbows over Ana's and drew her close. We rocked side to side, in time to the last beats of the song.

I smiled at her.

She smiled at me.

Our bodies came to rest but inside me the dance surged,

surged, surged. And it felt *right*, me, being here on stage with Ana, dancing in front of the whole school.

The lights went out.

Applause.

I'd like to say it was thunderous, an ovation. In truth, it was merely decent, even ragged. But ragged applause was better than I'd expected from this audience.

I was thinking about this when Ana hugged me, there in the dark. Squeezed me tight, her body warm against mine. Put her forehead against mine, skin on sweaty skin. Her breath hot on my lips.

I froze.

She broke away from me.

The lights came back on.

Ana's smile was gone as if it had never been.

A renewed coldness passed through me when I saw that. But Ana turned to face the audience and I followed suit. We bowed.

The applause pulsed. There were a few whistles. Someone cried, "*Wepa!*" and I thought it was Flavia Martinez. Someone else yelled, "Nice moves, Rick!"

Rick. Not Cat Guy.

That made me stand straighter.

When we walked off the stage, in the greenroom, Lettuce gave me a high five. "Nice job, man." The band guys echoed him as they hurried onstage for their own gig.

That made me grin like a fool.

And then, as she wiped down her neck with a towel, Ana said, "That could have gone worse."

Now that . . . that was the sweet taste of victory.

"Thank you for doing this." I stood there drenched in sweat, clueless of the right thing to say. "Especially today."

"For a moment there, we were actually dancing," she said, as if she hadn't heard.

"Do you want to hang out?" I asked. "I don't need to stay until the end."

"Stay. I'm heading home."

I hesitated, then spoke all in a rush. "I'm here for you, if you need to talk."

"What I need is to go see if my mother is holding it together," she said. "What I need is to crawl into bed and not talk to anyone. Okay?"

I nodded.

Something shifted in Ana's face. "Thank you, Rick. You're trying to help. I know. I wish . . ." She hesitated. "I'll call you if I need anything."

With that she left.

I spent the rest of the show thinking about those words. I wish . . . what did she wish for?

The question retreated into the background once the concert ended. I had some viewer comments to field as I mingled through the bake sale crowd.

"Good job, kid," Dad said.

"No need to sound so surprised," I said.

Then Flavia Martinez approached. "You need to loosen up your shoulders. You're like a wood block."

"Oh."

"But, you know, that actually looked like dancing."

"I'll take that," I said.

I definitely would.

"I didn't know you could dance," said, well, a lot of people. A number of them girls.

Last to approach me was Rob Kenna. I preened inside as I saw him ambling over, a sheepish look on his face. Would he finally—

"Hey, cat guy," he said. "That girl you danced with. Does she have a boyfriend?"

I stared at him. I considered his question.

"Yes," I said. "Yes, she does."

I didn't lie because I was an asshole or possessive (Who? Me?). I lied because friends don't introduce friends to Rob Kenna.

"It really took me back, seeing you guys go," Dad said on the way home as we waited for the streetlight by the Flatiron. It was a warm Friday evening, and we were lost in a mass of people out for the night. "You never saw Mom dance, did you?"

I blinked. "Mom could dance?"

"Boy, could she. Like a movie star. She didn't much. She said it reminded her of home. But sometimes when she—" Dad glanced at me sideways. "When she got a bit tipsy, she'd start doing this thing with her hips. . . ."

"Don't use that tone when talking about my mother," I said. "It's creepy."

I tried not to show it, but it hurt, finding out Mom had been a dancer. I might be as good as Ana by now, if she'd taught me. But she'd kept it from me, as she had the many other secrets of her past.

"What's that girl's name?" Dad asked, as if he hadn't heard. "The one you danced with? I saw the way you looked at her."

"Ana." Then, quickly, "And that was just for show."

"Bring her over for dinner sometime," Dad said. "I'll make my special schnitzel."

I gave him a look to cast fear into the hearts of men.

"Something got in your eye?" Dad asked.

"An older German guy."

"All I'm saying is, you looked good together. Like you belonged there, dancing with her."

"Uh-huh."

"Maybe one day you guys will dance together in Havana," Dad said.

"Yeah," I said. "Sure."

⁓

I heard nothing from Ana for a week (dance class was on break). Then, late one evening, she sent me a Facebook message. *Call me. If you've got time.*

I rushed to my room, shut the door, grabbed my phone, and then sat down on my bed for a minute to calm my breathing. And dialed Ana's number.

"Hello." She sounded dull—not unfriendly exactly, but tired.

"Hey," I said.

There was a silence. It stretched for many seconds.

I didn't dare to break it.

She spoke at last. "So I came home today and my dad was there. Sitting at the kitchen table with my mother."

I blinked. Hadn't Ana just buried . . . oh, her biological father. "What did he want?"

"Said he'd come to help us out. In our time of need." Ana paused. "He didn't look drunk, but I could smell liquor on him."

"I'm sorry, Ana. Did you . . ." I searched for the right words. "Did you have any trouble with him?"

Ana laughed. It was a short, humorless sound. "No trouble. He's moving in."

"Huh?"

"My mom said we need the help. Told me she needs a shoulder to cry on. I guess mine isn't enough."

I closed my eyes. Breathed deep, trying to imagine what Ana was feeling. Recoiled from the result.

I'd known in the abstract that all families weren't like mine, nor all parents. But it was a different thing to be confronted with the reality.

"I'm so sorry," I said, though the words felt weak, inadequate.

"She could never say no to him," Ana said. "She only left him because he stepped over the line one night and he . . . and now it's been years, and he was always so convincing with his apologies. . . . I can't do this, Rick. I can't live in the same apartment with that guy. Not even for my mother's sake."

"Then don't," I said, more confident than I felt. "Move out. Stay at my place for a while. I'm sure I can convince my dad. We'll figure something out."

"Mom would never let me," Ana said. "I won't even turn seventeen until September. . . . She's not stupid, you know— my mom. She's just hurting, like, a lot. She'll remember what kind of man my father is soon enough." She paused. "I just don't want to be there while she does. I'm sorry, maybe that's selfish, but I don't."

"You shouldn't have to," I said.

In that moment, as I searched with all my heart for an exit from Ana's conundrum, inspiration struck.

Something Dad had said came back to me—words he'd spoken on our walk back from the school concert.

Maybe one day you guys will dance together in Havana . . .

My heart banged fast and hard in my chest and my mouth went dry, and I swallowed in a futile effort to clear my throat. But I said it.

"Let's go to Cuba for a while. Let's spend the summer studying salsa in Havana."

ஒ

Remember Mr. Porcelain, leaping for that bowl of corn-flakes?

We established this: you watch a video like that, you want

him to fail. That's what gets you excited. Instant success is boring.

Except when Mr. Porcelain *expects* to fail. When kitty goes for this big, hopeless leap to the kitchen island . . . and makes it, and scampers about in wide-eyed celebration. He's so startled at his own success, you don't have it in your heart to hold it against him.

Besides, you know he'll be butting his head against the wall again soon enough.

☙

Naturally, Ana responded to my proposal with an enthusiastic, "Let's do what now?"

I could take a few chapters to outline how I convinced her. To tell you how we sold our parents on the idea, how we made arrangements, how we prepared and budgeted. But—let me double-check—no, this book isn't called *Logistics of Foreign Travel, 3rd Ed., With Updated Chapter on Parental Psychology*.

I'll hit the highlights instead. Ana went through three stages.

(Stage 1: Denial, later that night in a Facebook chat window.) *Estás marea'o, man. One does not simply go to Cuba.* She included with the last a GIF of Sean Bean's Boromir.

Of course one does not simply go to Cuba, I replied. *One flies instead. Down to Cancún and across to Havana.* Being half Cuban, I could have flown directly from the US—but even with the recently relaxed regulations, Ana's situation was trickier.

Isn't that, like, illegal?

So is holding hands in school in Tennessee, I wrote, after a bit of googling for a handy comparison. *Doesn't make it wrong.*

I knew Mom would have been scandalized. But I also recalled what Dad had said about the *bloqueo*. More than fifty years and Castro's still there. Still feeding off his people, no matter how the rest of the world squeezed them.

The point is, we can sell your mom on this, I wrote. *Tell her you want to connect to your Latino roots—works great with my dad. And you'll buy yourself a couple of months away from home. Time enough for your parents to figure things out.*

This is crazy, Ana wrote.

Don't you want to do something crazy occasionally? It felt brash and daring to write that. *To get away and dance and forget everything and everyone for a while?*

Ana didn't respond for a long time. *To forget*, she wrote at last. *That would be nice.*

(Stage 2: Bargaining, the next day over lunch at Ess-a-Bagel.)

"No way I can afford two months in Havana." Ana bit into two slices of pumpernickel bagel separated by an ocean of cream cheese. "The flights, maybe. But hotels?"

"We can stay with my aunt Juanita," I said. "I'm dipping into my college fund for the rest."

Ana stared. "You what?"

"Just a little." I had eighteen grand saved from my site—I figured if I spent five, the remainder would still be more than most freshmen had. "Besides, I figure I can get into a good school. Full scholarship, you know. That's total socialism. They take all your savings and cover the rest. So it's a good idea to be poor when you apply."

"That," Ana said, "is so stupid I don't know where to begin. There's no guarantee you'll get into a great school, or that they'll pay for you."

"I want to reconnect with my family," I said. "Get to know the Cuba my mom grew up in. Isn't that worth a little money?"

Ana gave me a frank look. "Is that really why you want to go?"

"Sure." It wasn't a lie, not exactly. I also wanted to help Ana—and, hey, get close to her—but there was no need to spell all that out. "I also want to get better at dancing."

A smirk tugged at the corner of Ana's mouth. "I can hear them now. Rick Gutiérrez! The Salsa King of Havana!"

I winced. "That sounds unlikely, I admit. But—"

"I'm sorry," Ana said quickly. "I was being mean. I'm sure you'll get very good."

I shrugged. "Maybe we can shoot a film about salsa in Havana."

Ana's eyes lit up. "Or combine it with my New York film, make it a compare-and-contrast thing, salsa here and over there. We could shoot at clubs, do some street scenes, maybe interview some timba bands . . ." She smiled. "I would like to finish a film this year. For my stepdad."

(Stage 3: Acceptance, on a sunlit bench by the East River.)

"I suppose we could go." Ana pulled her feet up under her. "*Pero dime una cosa.*"

"Yes?"

"You're not doing this to get into my pants, are you?" She looked me in the eyes. "Because I'm not in a good place for that, not now. You understand?"

"Of course," I said.

I still recalled that hug, close and tight, up on stage after our dance. Not now, she'd said . . . that didn't mean *never.*

I wouldn't hit on Ana. We'd just go to Havana together. And sip piña coladas by the ocean. And dance in the surf. If she changed her mind . . . well, that wouldn't be my fault.

PART TWO

Rumba in Havana

chapter six

DUCT TAPE

Somewhere over the Gulf of Mexico, between Cancún and Havana, I gave in to terror.

Not that I'd been entirely calm all day. The flight to Mexico went fine, but the leg to Havana got delayed so we sat down to wait. And I made a strategic mistake.

I googled our airline for this final segment of our journey—Cubana de Aviación.

You know that happy excitement you feel when you google your airline and the related searches box suggests "air crash," "air disaster," and "air fatalities"? That burst of adventurous spirit, when you look up safety statistics and find your airline is last in the world—not among the bottom quartile, not worse than most, but *last*?

"I thought you knew." Ana spoke distractedly, fidgeting with her handheld camera. She turned the lens on me, red eye blinking. "Haven't you been doing your research?"

"I didn't have time. I had to prepare two months of content for my site." I looked straight into the camera. "CatoTrope .com, your one-stop catstination. Check it out today!"

Ana rolled her eyes, lowered the camera. "When something breaks, the Cubans can't replace it. They patch it up with duct tape."

"No way we're flying on a duct-taped plane," I said.

"A Tupolev 204," Ana said. "A classic Soviet bird."

"You sound like you're looking forward to it."

Ana gave me a weighing look. There were dark circles under her eyes—a constant presence this past month—but her lips twitched with amusement. "I thought you wanted to get to know the real Cuba."

"I also want to survive," I said.

"Did you know Havana used to be run by the American Mafia? Before the Revolution?"

"What's that got to do with it?"

"We screwed up their country," Ana said. "They got fed up and revolted, so we embargoed them. Now you complain they can't afford to fix their airplanes?"

Under normal circumstances, I would have sooner answered an email from a Nigerian prince than engage this question. But I needed the distraction from our looming trip aboard Uncle Lenin's Death Machine. So we passed a lovely couple of hours debating whether Cuba's problems were due to the *bloqueo* or theft by Castro's government, or simply the inevitable failure of communism.

"Communism has its problems," Ana said finally. "But there's something to be said for free rent and health care and education for everybody. If you'd grown up in Washington Heights, with a working mom and a drunk-ass deadbeat father, you might see it differently."

At which point she grew quiet and our conversation dropped off.

When we bussed out to our plane, the sight of it was a relief. A gleaming white two-engine jet, it looked modern.

"This isn't so bad," I said to Ana as we trudged up the stairs to board, buffeted by a warm breeze across the airfield.

She only nodded at the nearest wing.

There, wrapped around that finlike thing right under the wing, silvery gray, was that . . .

Duct tape?

Duct tape.

From my first minutes aboard, snatches of overheard conversation caught my attention.

". . . *sí, asere, pero sí que sí* . . ."

". . . *lo que yo metí fue candela* . . ."

". . . *tiene tremenda pinta, hermano* . . ."

Those half-swallowed vowels, that run-together cadence, they snapped me immediately to my aunt Juanita's voice.

71

Only half the passengers were Cuban, but each lumbered aboard with enough rollers and shopping bags to start a corner bodega in Havana, or to supply an extended family with shoes, clothes, and kitchen appliances, which seemed more likely. One guy had somehow gotten an electronic keyboard through security, still in its box. He struggled for five minutes to jam it into an overhead bin.

Soon I sat cramped in my seat, high over the Gulf of Mexico. Ana tried to distract me from the death roar of the Tupolev engines by telling me about her trip to her father's village in Puerto Rico—a story that involved country dancing, mountains of pork, and extensive hours spent hugging a toilet bowl. I tried to listen to her, but my eyes were locked on the window.

Maybe half an hour passed. It seemed like the trip had barely started. Then we banked and turned slightly, and I saw land.

A stretch of white sand, then green, so much green— empty fields and then forest, and then fields again. Here and there patches of bright red soil, like some kid had stuck Plasticine pancakes to a rolled-out map.

Cuba.

That's when I realized I was trembling. Not a mild tremor either. My hands shook visibly in my lap. My teeth chattered.

"You all right, Rick?" Ana asked. "We're safe, you know. It's more dangerous driving on the New Jersey Turnpike."

But that wasn't it. I wasn't worried about a crash.

In another twenty minutes, I'd be standing on Cuban soil.

I'd step on the ground Mom last touched thirty-five years ago. I'd walk the streets she'd grown up on. I'd come face-to-face with the family she'd abandoned, the regime that drove her to exile.

To exile and to silence. For fifteen years she'd kept her past from me. For fifteen years I'd had this vacuum in my life—not the simple absence of Cuba but an *active* lack of it, like an organ that should have been there but wasn't.

I didn't know which possibility scared me more. That I would feel like just another tourist, with my Americanized Spanish and my Dockers pants, a camera around my neck— or that Cuba would seem like home.

I watched the green fields and forests of the island pass by with a singular, undivided attention. Before I knew it, we began our descent. The fields gave way to concrete, a flattish grid of roads and buildings. The captain told the cabin crew to sit down. A few more minutes and the ground came rushing up at us.

The shadow of the plane raced across grass. The runway swept into view.

We clanged down. Bounced. Dropped. Decelerated violently. Rolled across the runway.

We were on the ground.

Somebody in the back of the plane applauded. Like they hadn't really believed the pilots were up to the task.

I noticed Ana was gripping my hand, hard.

I looked down at it. "It's okay, Ana. I think we're going to make it."

She let go of me as if scalded. "Look who's talking, hero."

The thing was, I wasn't trembling anymore. A calm had come over me, as abrupt as the terror of before.

A damp, sweltering heat enveloped us in the jetway, markedly more intense than in New York or Cancún. A few steps and I was covered in sweat. Then we entered an air-conditioned hallway, and my T-shirt hung clammy against my skin.

We followed a winding route to immigration and joined a line before a booth where an official in a light-blue uniform wielded the power invested in him by his little stamp.

"Just like home," I said.

The immigration agents sat in cubicles much like those at JFK, even if these looked older and uglier. The three uniformed soldiers by the wall with their holstered guns wouldn't have seemed out of place at an American airport. If anything, the posters on the walls—sandy beaches and colonial city squares, branded *Auténtica Cuba*—were more welcoming than the TSA's stern notices.

"Do you know how many people get detained at the US border for no good reason?" Ana asked.

We edged slowly toward the booth. Our officer was mustached and portly, and a philosopher. He paused between questions and spent long minutes studying his computer screen and demonstrated an admirable contempt for the frantic pace of modern living. Eventually we made it and *buenos días*-ed him.

He looked at our dark blue passports on the counter, back at us. "You speak Spanish?"

We nodded.

"You're Americans."

Ana shifted uneasily.

"Yes," I said.

He took the passports. Flipped through mine. Flipped through Ana's. Took out the tourist visas that we'd purchased in Cancún.

"What's the purpose of your visit?"

"To visit family," I said.

"Tourism." Ana's Spanish sounded self-conscious all of a sudden, almost as if it were a foreign language for her. "Exploring Cuba."

The official squinted at the two of us with the attitude of Sherlock Holmes on the snoop. "Which is it?"

"My mother was Cuban," I explained. "I want to meet her family and see her country. And this is my friend."

The officer grunted. "Where are you staying? Hotel?"

"A *casa particular*." That was the local term for bed-and-breakfasts run by private citizens. Juanita had instructed me to give this answer until we got to her place and sorted out some paperwork that would let us stay with her legally.

"You're under eighteen."

We handed him our parental consent forms, translated to

Spanish and notarized. He took them. Studied them. Turned to his computer, typed something. Clicked, scrolled. Typed something else.

Come on. Just stamp our visas already.

The officer turned back to us. Pursed his lips. Cleared his throat.

"We support the Revolution," Ana said.

I blinked.

The officer blinked.

We all blinked.

"You what?" the officer asked.

Ana hesitated. "The Revolution? We support it?"

The officer raised his radio to his lips. "Vasquez, come to ten. Vasquez, to ten."

"Officer, what's the—" I began.

He cut me off with a wave of his hand. He stared at us like he couldn't risk taking his eyes off us. Which might have made me feel like Rick Gutiérrez, dashing rogue of international crime—if I hadn't been in danger of crapping my pants.

I glanced at Ana. She glanced at me.

Pictures flashed through my head. They'd deport us. They'd lock us up. They'd find Ana's video camera and accuse us of spying.

Behind the officer, a door opened. Another man in uniform stepped in, lean, pale. Vasquez, I guessed.

"What's up?" he asked.

"Girl here says she supports the Revolution."

"She what?" Vasquez turned to Ana. "Why would you say such a thing?"

"Why?" Ana looked confused. "Batista was a dictator. I think Fidel and Che had many good ideas."

Vasquez looked at her. Looked at the other officer. Back at her.

"We're really just here to see the country," I said. "And to dance."

Vasquez leaned over the officer, whispered something. It sounded like, "I think she's serious."

The officer gave the slightest shake of his head, as if to say, what a thing. What he actually said was, "Welcome to Cuba."

We got our visas stamped. We got our photos taken. We got buzzed through the door.

Moments later, I stood at the baggage carousel, staring at the belt going round and round, amazed that I'd managed to keep my lunch inside myself.

"I don't understand," Ana muttered beside me. "What did I say?"

"I guess it's like someone showing up at the US border and announcing they love the Constitution," I said. "It makes you sound like a nutcase."

"Is that so," Ana said.

"I mean, you don't expect someone to go like—oh, man, Obama, he's so awesome. And how about those drone strikes!"

"Is that what I was doing," Ana said.

That didn't sound like a question. Which finally made me notice the look in her eyes.

"Not that you're a nutcase," I said.

"That's a relief."

"You just sounded like one—"

"Just . . . stop."

I grinned. After a moment, Ana did too.

We'd made it. We were in Cuba.

chapter seven

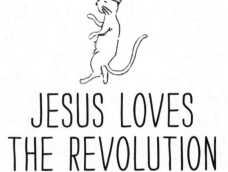

JESUS LOVES
THE REVOLUTION

A mass of people milled about a cavernous, dilapidated arrivals hall. Waiting, chatting, holding signs. Entire families pressed against a metal barrier, here to pick up their loved ones. Elsewhere a group of teenagers sat on a stack of luggage, each bag wrapped in clear plastic. They were eating sandwiches with the patient, indifferent look of people who had nowhere much to be.

As we pushed our way into this crowd, a gaunt man in ragged Nike shorts tugged at my shoulder. "Cigars? Cigars?" As if I might suddenly get the urge to smoke in the middle of the airport.

"We don't need anything. Thank you."

The man drifted off without a word, already searching past me.

"How are we going to find your aunt?" Ana asked.

I shrugged. So many faces here like Mom's. So many voices like Aunt Juanita's . . . she'd emailed me a photo, but—

"Rick!"

There she was. A rotund woman with silvery hair and a round face, and skin the same shade of brown as mine. She pushed her way toward me with happy disregard of the people in her way. She wore a faded denim jacket and blue jeans cut off below her knees, leaving her ample calves bare. I wouldn't have imagined it possible, but she totally pulled the look off.

I smiled. "*Tía!* I—"

She swallowed me in a hug. She smelled of perfume and, faintly, sweat.

"Rick, *mijo*," she said in her rapid-fire Spanish. "You look like your mother."

Great. I looked like a girl. "I'm surprised you recognized me."

"Of course I recognized you."

"On the second try," said a woman by her side, maybe twenty-five and solidly built, in a plain white dress. She wore a smile that seemed out of place on her face somehow, as if she wasn't used to the expression. "The first guy she hugged freaked out."

"Pssht." Juanita waved her hand. "Rick, meet my daughter Yolanda, your cousin. She's the brains of the family."

"Good to meet you, *primo*," Yolanda said. "And this is?"

I started, realizing I'd neglected Ana. She stood to the side, hands in her pockets, trying on her cool look.

"Guys, this is Ana Cabrera, my friend and dance partner. Ana, this is my family."

"Hi," Ana said. "Nice to meet you."

Juanita went in for a hug, engulfed her as enthusiastically as she'd engulfed me. "Lovely to meet you, *cariño*."

"How was your trip?" Yolanda asked.

"Good," I said. "Just a slight hiccup at immigration."

"Yes?" Juanita asked.

Ana shot me a warning look. I pretended not to notice.

"We expressed our support for the Revolution," I said. "They didn't like that."

"Is that so?" Yolanda's smile had faded. "What do you know about the Revolution?"

"Let's go get your money changed," Juanita said, all cheer, as if Yolanda hadn't spoken.

Cuba had two sets of currency: the convertible peso or CUC, worth about a dollar, and the national peso, worth twenty-five times less. Juanita instructed us to get some of both and to learn the difference between the two currencies so we wouldn't get scammed.

"People will do anything to get their hands on five CUC," she said.

"We Cubans get paid in national pesos," Yolanda added. "Which are worth crap."

"Don't be crude," Juanita said. "*Dale, vámonos.*"

She grabbed Ana's suitcase and sped toward the door, as if it were suddenly urgent we left. Ana raced after her to reclaim her bag, without success.

We left the building. It was early evening but you couldn't tell by the heat that rolled over us. The sidewalk was a free-for-all, tourists wrestling with luggage and fighting off locals offering their services, and trying to flag down a cab.

Wiping sweat from my face with one hand and dragging my suitcase with the other, I followed Juanita—across the road, down a path between some palms, to an open-air parking lot.

I'd seen many romanticized photos of old American cars rattling down bustling Havana streets, but I'd figured the photos were just that. Romanticized, exaggerated, a touristy shtick. Now I was confronted with a sea of hulking museum pieces. Massive automobiles with protruding hoods and shiny-chromed door handles and gleaming paint jobs, green and red and deep blue.

Not that all the cars were like that. There were a few modern ones scattered here and there, Kias and Hyundais and VWs. But the one Juanita led us to was different altogether. Painted a dull tan, it was small and spare and boxy, all right angles, like a thing made of Lego bricks.

"I've seen a car like this," I said. "In a museum in Germany."

"My Lada." Juanita popped the trunk, heaved in Ana's bag with one mighty motion. "Good old Soviet beast."

I wondered if Soviet cars were as safe as Soviet airplanes. My sense of self-preservation warned me against asking this.

I loaded my suitcase and took the backseat with Ana. It was painfully hot inside, the seat scalding to the touch.

Juanita slid behind the wheel. Beside her, Yolanda said, "Roll down the windows and buckle up."

I cast about for a seat belt. Couldn't find one.

Yolanda laughed. "That one always gets the tourists."

"Pay attention, *niños*." Juanita started up the Lada—it took three tries. The motor roared like a race car's. "You'll never get to see Havana for the first time again."

The Lada was sluggish to move but gathered speed. We pulled out of the parking lot and got onto a busy highway. Ana and I sat with our heads halfway out our respective windows, more for the breeze than for the view. I'd have stuck my tongue out like a dog if I'd thought it might help.

The airport sat on the outskirts of the city. We drove past grassy fields interspersed with the occasional shack or run-down hangar. If not for the stubby palms lining the road and the ancient cars—they rattled like tin cans and spewed black smoke—you could have mistaken this for rust belt America.

But no, I realized. This couldn't be America. There were no billboards.

Except there, I spotted one, plain white letters on blue. *Las Ideas Son el Arma Esencial en La Lucha de la Humanidad.*

Ideas are the essential weapon in humanity's battle. There was no indication what that battle might be.

As she drove, Juanita told us about the dinner she was cooking tonight, about Yolanda's boyfriend who was coming over, about the sights we had to see in Havana. "We'll take you to all the places your mother loved to go," she said at one point, and choked up a bit. "If only she could have come home with you."

Farther along the highway, warehouses and industrial buildings became more common, and occasionally even a low storefront. Everything had a worn-out air—long rust streaks on metal doors, peeling paint, sagging wooden fences, warped sidewalks, faded lawns.

Up ahead, a looming tower came into view. An angular spire in the shape of a five-pointed star, stabbing at the sky.

"That's the José Martí Memorial," Juanita said. "You know Martí?"

"Of course." Martí was a pre-Castro figure, a nineteenth-century Cuban revolutionary, writer, journalist, philosopher, and all-around national hero. "My mother loved Martí."

"I remember. She'd quote him at me when I wanted to pull her outdoors." Juanita's voice caught. "*Un grano de poesía es suficiente para perfumar un siglo.*"

I recognized the inflection, the cadence of those words. I'd heard Mom speak them once, near the end in her hospital bed, gaunt fingers clutched around a thin black volume of Martí's works.

A grain of poetry is enough to perfume a century.

My eye caught on something else. The Martí Memorial was in the middle of a large square. From the wall of one building beside the square, a monumental mural of Che Guevara looked down. But there was another giant face on a different building—bearded, smiling, with a wide hat.

"Is that . . ." I struggled to make sense of it. "Jesus?"

"What?" Juanita asked. "Where?"

Yolanda looked at me. Looked where I was pointing. Guffawed.

Ana rolled her eyes at me. "The Revolution doesn't support religion, don't you know?"

"No, no." Yolanda was still laughing. "I see the resemblance."

"That's Camilo Cienfuegos, hero of the Revolution." Juanita spoke in a serious tone, but in the end a snort escaped her. "Some people think he was better than Jesus."

"He died young," Yolanda said. "Right after the Revolution. Didn't have time to get his hands dirty."

Juanita started to say something, then bit it back. Yolanda looked at her for a moment, then out the window.

I let the silence stretch. Mistaking national heroes for religious figures saps your confidence.

"*Coño*," Ana said abruptly. She rummaged in her bag, pulled out her camera, nestled her arm on the door to shoot the passing scenery. "Can't believe I forgot."

We stopped at a red light. A boxy red convertible with the

roof down pulled up on Ana's side. The driver, a gray-haired grandfather type, grinned when he noticed her filming.

"I think it's amazing, the way you preserve the past here in Cuba," Ana said. "Fixing old cars instead of buying a new one every few years."

"Like we have a choice," Yolanda said.

There came another one of those uncomfortable silences. A bit like when someone lets rip a good one at a fancy dinner party and everyone stares at their plates pretending they didn't notice.

"This is Vedado," Juanita said after a while. "Pretty, no?"

We rolled down a broad avenue with a wide grassy promenade in the middle, complete with palm trees and voluminous green shrubs sheared into neat round shapes. The buildings that lined the road seemed relatively modern and clean—here a concrete apartment building, there a red-roofed house that could almost be called a mansion. Clusters of teenagers and twentysomethings sat on the benches of the promenade and at the tables of a corner café.

"Yes," I said. "Very pretty."

"The next part is even prettier," Yolanda said. "Our neighborhood. Centro Habana."

chapter eight

CENTRO HABANA

My eyes watered, and not from joy.

Black exhaust hung in the air. On this narrow street, hemmed in by three- and four-story buildings, that air sat hot and heavy, and still. Almost as still as us, barely edging along in the traffic. It was misery, and I barely noticed. The street held all my attention.

A collapsed balcony, concrete remnants protruding from the wall. A gaping hole in the sidewalk, covered over by a couple of planks. A cloudy, milky-looking puddle on the pavement, seasoned with a rotting banana peel. At one corner only the outer wall of a building remained, the rest a heap of rubble that two boys in bright red shorts scampered across.

You know how in *Fallout* you emerge from your underground vault to discover the world a bombed-out ruin? This place wasn't like that—most buildings were still standing—but looking around gave me that same uneasy feeling.

Except people lived here. They walked along the sidewalk and in the street, weaving among the cars. Here a muscled man lounged in a doorway, his arms crossed and the flat of his foot against the door, talking to a granny permanently hunched forward at the waist. A freckled teenage girl leaned out of a third-story window, carrying on a yelled conversation with a short black guy dressed all in white—completely comfortable shouting back and forth, and no one even giving them a second glance.

It was hard to miss the contrast between these people and their surroundings. A woman in fine white slacks and a purple blouse, her leather handbag gleaming new, could have been walking down Fifth Avenue in Manhattan—except that she had to veer around some concrete debris on the street corner. A guy in cutoff jeans and a black tee could have walked off the set of a rap video, complete with sunglasses and a gold chain around his neck.

Not that everyone looked like this. There was also an older guy in a once-white shirt with yellow pit stains, and plenty of people in clothes that showed their age. At one corner a long line had formed, men and women with ragged canvas shopping bags.

"Waiting for the new iPhone," I said to Ana in English, feeling witty.

"They're waiting for toilet paper," Yolanda answered in Spanish. "The shops have been out for weeks."

Yeah. I'm a real comedian.

We turned into a quieter side street. "Here we are," Juanita said.

We pulled up at the door of a seven-story apartment building. Its yellow paint job had faded, and the first floor was an abandoned shop. Strips of blue tape marked Xs on dusty storefront windows. Even so, the edifice had a reassuring solidity to it.

"We've lived here almost forty-five years," Juanita said. "Since my dad was reassigned to Havana, when your mother was ten years old."

I looked up and down the street. No shops here, only dusty buildings, a bicycle rickshaw parked in front of one.

I tried to picture Mom as a girl here, walking to school, playing jump rope on the sidewalk. All that came to me was an image of Mom in her last days—gaunt, with a scarf around her bald head. She leaned against the nearest building, an unlit cigarette dangling from her fingers. Defiant, like she knew what was coming and didn't care.

But Mom hadn't smoked at the end, not once she got her diagnosis. She had cared. She'd cared so damn much, and it hadn't made any difference.

Ana poked my shoulder. "You taking a nap?"

I started. This was why I'd felt reluctant to come to Cuba. I'd have to remember things.

We lugged our bags into a bare, dusty lobby. There was an

ornate, ancient-looking metal cage in the middle of a stairwell. With some knocking of knees, I recognized it as an elevator.

"Get in, get in." Juanita herded us into the narrow cage. Yolanda dragged the gate closed behind us. A fan turned slowly on the ceiling, wheezing as it went.

"Our elevator is seventy years old," Juanita said.

An elevator is not a fine wine. I don't need to know the vintage.

"Behind you, Rick," Yolanda said.

I turned. Stared. There were no buttons here—only a lever protruding from a metal plate, currently vertical.

This thing was manual.

"I'll tell you when to stop," Juanita said.

I took a deep breath and pulled the lever.

There came a rumbling from far above. The elevator groaned. The elevator shifted. We rose into the air—slow and steady.

Lurch.

Slow, anyway.

There were clangs as the ground fell away below us. There were mysterious squeaks as we passed the second floor. Between the fourth and fifth floors, the elevator shook from side to side.

"Your mom and I would go up and down, up and down, fifteen times in a row," Juanita said. "One day our father caught us and gave us a thrashing. After that, we made sure he wasn't around."

Which made me wonder how many places like this were there in the world, where you could return thirty-five years after your mother left and find things the same.

"What floor?" Ana asked in a small voice.

"Seven," Juanita said.

I had a feeling Ana and I were going to climb a lot of stairs.

"Now!" Juanita cried. "*Dale, ya!*"

I started, let go the lever. The elevator stopped a foot above floor level.

"Take it down a bit."

I edged the lever back, and we eased down gently.

Yolanda pulled open the gate. We poured out onto the landing. As my feet crossed the threshold, I felt like Odysseus emerging from Hades into the mortal world. (What? I read.)

Juanita's apartment had an outer grille made of iron bars and a steel door on the inside. Getting through wasn't easy— unlock the grille, reach inside the bars, lift a hidden latch, pull the grille open, unlock the deadbolt on the inner door, stick another key into the main lock, lift the inner door up by the handle, turn the key and pull at the same time. I doubted if anyone short of Houdini could have copied this ritual on first try.

Juanita's apartment was airy, bright, with minimal furniture and stone floors and tall ceilings. A worn, comfortable-looking sofa and three wooden rocking chairs faced an analog TV, complete with chromed knobs and a metal antenna. In the corner sat an antique dressing table with a tall mirror. The surface of the table was covered in enough porcelain figurines of pigs, cows, and donkeys to stage a production of *Animal Farm*.

A ceiling fan turned in the breeze from the open windows. And those windows . . . I stared all the way across the rooftops of Centro Habana, to a monumental domed building, gleaming white in the sun.

"Nice view of the *capitolio*, isn't it," Juanita said.

They must have taken inspiration from the one in Washington, back in the days when Cuba and the US were tight.

Juanita showed us the bathroom. It was clean and tiled in blue, though with no plastic seat on the toilet—you had to perch on the ceramic edge. "Seats are expensive," Juanita said. "Let me know in advance when you need hot water. It takes fifteen minutes to run the heater."

Next door, the kitchen seemed modern enough, with fridge and microwave and oven, and a bunch of bananas in a bowl on the table.

All in all, this wasn't so bad. So maybe there was no AC, and I saw no sign of a computer, let alone broadband, but the apartment looked comfortable enough.

"Here we are," Juanita said. "You're staying here."

We stood in the door of a small bedroom, with an ancient upright piano in the corner and a heavy carved dresser by the wall. The bed was wide and spacious, covered in a green quilt.

"Who's staying here?" I asked, to clarify.

"Why, you two."

There was a silence.

In that silence, some looks may have been exchanged. Some arms may have been crossed. Some faces may have flushed.

"Umm," I said.

"Yeah, Ricky," Ana said in English. "Umm."

"Ana's my friend," I said. "Not my girlfriend."

Juanita crossed her arms, stood side by side with Ana. "She's not your girlfriend."

"Hey, I told you on the phone, I'm coming with a friend." I was discovering it was possible to sweat more indoors than in the Cuban sun. *"Una amiga, te acuerdas?"*

"In this family, when a man says he's coming over with an *amiga*, they usually mean something else," Juanita said. "Yolanda?"

Yolanda poked her head around the corner. *"Sí?"*

"They're not *novios*."

Yolanda raised one eyebrow. "I did think she was quite a girl for him."

"Hey—"

"Not that you're ugly," Yolanda reassured me. "Just . . ."

"Flojo," Juanita said. "A bit of a wallflower."

"Great." I tried to look like I found this funny.

"Uh," Ana said. "I'm sorry about this. We didn't want to cause you guys trouble . . ."

"Oh, we're happy to have you." Juanita gave me a look.

"Your *amigo* Rick will sleep in my son Yosvany's room. There's a sofa. Yosvany!"

"He's in the street," Yolanda said.

"Come, Rick," Juanita said. "I'll show you your room. Let *your friend* get settled."

I could tell this was going to get old.

Juanita pushed open a door farther down the hallway. "This is it."

Apparently, Yosvany was not a great believer in the washing of socks. Maybe a dozen lay scattered across the windowsill, the (rumpled) bed and the (messy) desk. A faint scent in the air attested to their ripeness.

"You'll sleep there." Juanita waved at the sofa, barely visible under a finely curated selection of one T-shirt, one pair of jeans, an old acoustic guitar, four or five different drumsticks, one white sneaker, a cracked leather belt, a simple canvas backpack, and a large, rust-streaked barbell that I'd probably need two hands to lift. "You can dump all that stuff on his bed."

"Okay," I said.

"We eat in half an hour. Make yourself at home."

I found it difficult to implement this suggestion once Juanita left. I'd never shared a room with anyone, let alone with a cousin I'd never met. I knew how I'd feel if I came home one day to find a stranger in my room and all my stuff moved.

So I was still standing beside that sofa five minutes later, when Yosvany came home. He rattled his way through the locks on the door and greeted Juanita with a jaunty "*Buenas tardes, jefa!*"—and then he stood before me.

Yosvany was my height and not much older. The biceps bulging from his shirt made me feel small, though, as did the jeans riding low on his hips—swathes of checkered underpants on display. He was darker-skinned and had a bony, angular face, and didn't resemble his mother and sister much.

Yosvany's gaze latched onto me like a tractor beam on the *Millennium Falcon*. "Who are you?"

"Rick Gutiérrez? *Tu primo?*" I squeaked. Then, forcing my voice lower as I wrestled with a tongue that suddenly refused to speak Spanish, "Uhh . . . your mom said I'm supposed to stay on your sofa?"

I could sense him cataloging the ways he could dispose of me. Toss me out the window? Launch me down the stairs? Lock me in the elevator and wait for a heart attack?

"A *yuma*'s staying with me?" Yosvany grinned. "*Empingao.*" He stretched out his hand.

I almost tripped over myself hurrying to shake it. "Uh . . . what's a *yuma*?"

"You." Yosvany grabbed an armload of stuff off the sofa— the single sneaker flopping to the ground—and plopped it all down on his bed. "You-mai-friend, *entiendes?*"

I made a mental note to double-check that translation. "Sorry to intrude."

"No problem," he said. "We'll have fun together, yes? Go out?"

"Sure."

Cool kids didn't often ask if I'd hang out with them. But I'd read enough Cuba travel forums to figure this might simply mean—will you pay for us to go out? If so, that was all right. I wasn't above bribery if that meant getting along with my new roommate.

"So you're from New York? What's it like? Do you go to a lot of concerts? Do you see famous people on the street? Derek Jeter? Mark Teixeira?" Yosvany kept on this stream of questions without waiting for an answer. "I thought you were coming with your girlfriend."

"I—"

"She's not his girlfriend," Juanita called, passing by in the hallway with laundry in her arms.

Yosvany stopped. Looked at me with newfound interest. "She pretty?"

"Well . . . ," I said.

Yosvany must have seen something in my face. He went to the door and shut it. "I see," he said, all serious. "You want her."

"Well . . ."

"Don't worry," he said. "I won't touch her."

Were I a better man, I would have explained that wasn't how it worked. I would have explained that Ana made her own decisions and we had no business deciding who was going to touch her.

"Okay," I said.

I mean, I believed those things. I really did. I just couldn't bring myself to say them. Not if it might send Yosvany after Ana.

"I'll help you," Yosvany said. "You'll see. I'm an expert at this. Soon she'll be your girlfriend."

"Really?"

"Of course. I'm your cousin, you know? And I have only one rule in life."

"What's that?"

"*Hay que chingar*, my friend. *Hay que chingar.*"

chapter nine

JUST KISS HER

Sometimes when bored I play Match the Cat. The goal of this sophisticated mental game is to find the perfect celebrity cat to match the people around you.

Lettuce, for example, is the Great White Cloud. He's white, he's great, and, like his namesake, he drifts through the world with an unshakable knowledge of his own excellence.

Ana's Queen of Pillow Fights. Serene, elegant, and secure in her beauty, but rouse her anger and feathers will fly.

Yosvany, now . . . Yosvany is Al Capone Jr. He's the hippest guy in town, cool as ice, above it all. When he spots something interesting—a balloon or some yarn or an empty water bottle—he'll strut past like it's nothing to him. But give him a minute and he'll be back. Circling. Circling. Look away for an instant—and he'll pounce.

I didn't know this at first, though.

∽

Yosvany seemed to take our conversation about Ana as some kind of challenge. He waited until she left her room and introduced himself in the hallway, his Spanish slurred and careless. "*Qué vuelta*, I'm Yosvany."

"I'm Ana," she said. "*Mucho gusto.*"

He walked straight past her, then turned as if he'd just remembered. "Rick mentioned you're dancers. There's a salsa party at the Milocho tonight. Want to go?"

"The Milocho?"

"Club 1830," he said. "Best place to dance casino in Havana."

"Awesome," she said. "Can I take my camera? Shoot video there?"

"Of course," Yosvany said. "You want me to introduce you to the show dancers?"

"Sure," she said. "I mean, if it's not a bother."

Yosvany assured her that it wasn't.

"So here's the deal," he said once back in the room. "I've got her figured out."

"What?" I picked through my suitcase. "How? You just met her."

"Experience," he said. "I've had enough girls that I can tell."

99

"People are different," I said.

Yosvany shrugged. "Then call it a theory. I have a theory that can help you get with her."

On the one hand, Yosvany figuring out Ana at a glance felt vaguely offensive, as if he were lessening her by making the claim. On the other hand, getting with Ana.

"She's one of those hot girls who get hit on all the time," Yosvany said. "You can't do the same. You know, things like, you're pretty, you're nice, I like you, do you want to go out sometime, all that crap. You have to stand out. *Meterle el dedo completo.*"

I sat up from the suitcase, scandalized. "What do you mean, *meterle el dedo completo*?"

A word of caution. If you're the easily offended type, don't google Yosvany's Spanish.

I mean, I could censor it, but writing Yosvany without foul language would be like playing a guitar with three strings missing. It would be like leaving out the smile on the *Mona Lisa*. If I had to try, I'd be—to borrow Yosvany's own term—*embarca'o.*

"I don't mean it literally," Yosvany said. "Not yet." He snorted. "What I mean is, surprise her. Make her feel like she's in a movie. Say things to her that no one's ever said to her."

"Like what?"

"Take Cristina, this girl I met last week," Yosvany said. "I took her to this cool little club in Miramar. We're grooving to a bachata and I whisper in her ear: 'Forgive me if I'm too honest, but I've never felt like this dancing with anyone. You're the most beautiful girl here and the best dancer. I don't know what's happening to me.'"

I cringed just to imagine saying those things. But presumably Yosvany knew better.

"You're lucky to find a girl that makes you feel like that," I said.

"That's what I say to everyone."

"You lie to them?"

Yosvany shook his head, as if disappointed in me. "You've got to lie to women, cousin. The more lies, the better."

I felt dirty listening to him, like I'd googled "relationship advice" and ended up at a porn site. There seemed to be something uniquely icky about the idea of lying to someone so they would get with me.

Maybe I should have denounced Yosvany's philosophy loud and clear. But, thinking of the weeks ahead, I said, "I think we have different styles when it comes to girls."

"Really?" Yosvany asked, as if genuinely curious. "What's your style?"

My style was standing there with my hands in my pockets, staring at my shoes, until the girl lost interest. Thankfully, I didn't have to explain this because Juanita walked in (people didn't seem to bother knocking in this apartment).

"Dinner's ready. Benny's here, *asi que a comer!*"

Dinner was thick slices of ham with rice and beans, a

vegetable salad, and crunchy fried bananas. Hardly a feast for the senses, but tasty—and the papaya juice Juanita poured us was rich and sweet.

"You'll eat here every day," Juanita instructed us. "We wash everything with chlorine bleach. You have to be careful, because there's cholera in Havana."

Cholera. Things were getting better and better.

Benny was Yolanda's boyfriend, a wiry, spectacled black man who worked for the government agency responsible for food distribution. He had spent several years in London. "Lovely to meet you both," he said to us in fine Queen's English, and asked us questions about recent political developments in Washington. He knew more about primaries and gerrymandering and the latest filibuster in Congress than Ana or me.

"He's in IT, so he gets good internet access," Yolanda explained. "Not like us mere mortals, who have to stand in line and pay a week's salary to get online."

"It's not like that," Benny said, shifting uncomfortably.

"So what is it like?" Ana asked.

"Rick, you're sitting in your mother's place," Juanita said. "That's where she always sat. She loved looking out the window to the Morro."

I looked out that window. In the distance, where the city ended and the water began, rose the old white lighthouse of the Morro fortress. I knew of it from a hundred photographs, and from a book I'd read about the Revolution. Along with the nearby Cabaña, the Morro had served as a prison for political enemies of the Castro regime.

"You sure she wasn't looking north at Miami?" Yolanda asked.

"It's hard to tell the difference at this angle," Benny said.

I could tell Juanita was about to cut in again, so I spoke quickly. "Did you use to be close, *tía*? With my mother?"

Juanita smiled faintly. "Oh, yes. *Las hermanas Gutiérrez.* We ran the neighborhood. We played the best pranks. We got the cutest boys. And the way we danced? *Pa' acabar.*"

"You danced?" Ana asked.

"Who didn't? But we were something else. All the guys would ask us. If we didn't think they were good enough, we'd just dance ourselves, sister with sister. People would stop and watch and yell *agua!*" Juanita crunched wistfully on a banana chip. "We had some good times."

"Why did she leave?" I blurted out. "I mean, why did she leave and you stay?"

Juanita stared at me. A banana chip remained suspended in her fingers, halfway to her lips.

It was Yolanda who spoke, surprising me. "It's a personal decision, to leave or to stay. A decision everyone has to make for themselves."

Just like that, my question floated off like it had never been. It occurred to me that in this way Juanita was like her sister. They both wanted to forget the past.

And something else. For all her stories of Mom's youth

here in Havana, Juanita hadn't asked me a single thing about Mom's life. Not how she lived. Not how she died.

"Tell me," Benny said, looking at Ana. "What's it like, living in New York?"

"It depends," Ana said. "Are you the son of an investment banker? The daughter of Puerto Rican immigrants? Rich and white? Poor and brown? Rich and black?" She shrugged. "New York is a very different place, depending on who you are."

"Just like Havana, then," Yolanda said. "It all depends. If you're the daughter of a Party functionary or if your family's got a private business, or else if you're a black kid growing up in a *solar* somewhere."

"I thought that didn't matter so much in Cuba," Ana said.

Yolanda just stared at her.

"Benny grew up in a *solar* and he made it," Juanita said. "Free school, free university, free rent, do you get that in New York?"

"All my childhood friends are still in the *solar*," Benny said softly. "Worrying the roof might cave in on them while they sleep."

"It's all great on paper," Yolanda said. "There's no racism in Cuba, no sexism, and prosperity for all. But how many black faces do you see in the Politburo? How many women?"

"Maybe if there was no *bloqueo*—" Benny began.

Juanita slapped the table, a short, sharp sound. "*Basta ya!* Rick and Ana didn't come to Cuba to talk politics."

For a moment there was a silence. No one looked at anyone.

Then Ana said, "But really, New York is great. Nowhere like it. There's skyscrapers and Central Park, and if you ever visit we'll take you to Coney Island. . . ."

❧

After dinner, I handed out the gifts I'd brought. For Yosvany I had sunglasses and a Yankees hat. For Yolanda, a few CDs and makeup (selected by Ana).

For Juanita I had a hand cream and a couple of books. She caressed the cover of Margaret Atwood's latest story collection as if it were bound in fine leather. The other book I gave her was Mirta Ojito's *Finding Mañana: A Memoir of a Cuban Exodus.* It had been Mom's, a gift from Dad complete with the inscription *For María.* And it told the story of the Mariel boatlift during which Mom had left Cuba.

I'd taken it along on an impulse, thinking Juanita might find it interesting. But her eyes scanned the title and she nodded and put the book aside as if it didn't catch her attention.

Before we left for the Milocho, Yosvany put on the Yankees cap and tucked the sunglasses into the V of his shirt, even though it was twilight. Once on the street, he tugged at his cap occasionally and walked down the middle of the road like he owned it. Though maybe that was to avoid the precarious-looking balconies overhead.

"Tonight we party," he promised.

"Where's the club?" Ana looked uneasily at the empty street around us, held her camera bag close to her chest. "Do we take a taxi?"

"Not a taxi," Yosvany said. "They're a tourist rip-off. We'll take a *máquina*."

"A what?" I asked.

"A *colectivo*," he said. "An *almendrón*."

Once we got to Neptuno, the main Centro Habana drag, Yosvany showed us what he meant. Here the street was clogged with traffic, one American jalopy after another. "See how the cars are round like almonds?" He stepped into the street, stuck out his arm. "Pretend you're not tourists."

Ana and I exchanged a look. "How?"

"Don't talk," Yosvany said.

We didn't talk.

A portly older woman strode up to us. "Hi! Where are you from? Taxi? Cigars?"

Yosvany waved her off. "Try not to look so *yuma*," he said to us without much hope.

A car pulled up. Yosvany leaned in the window. "*Línea?*"

"*Veintitré',*" the driver responded—muttered fast, before he floored it and was off.

"You've got to know the route names," Yosvany said as he flagged down the next one.

The rattling car that pulled up—a Plymouth Fury, some corner of my mind recognized—was going the right way. An amorous couple perfumed like a Chanel factory crowded the front by the driver. We got the back to ourselves, a long, flat, unbroken leather seat. I piled in last and slammed the rusted door, which earned me a scowl from the driver.

"*Suave con la puerta!* Softly!"

The engine rumbled mournfully. We rattled up Neptuno for a long while, then past the grand steps of the University of Havana and into Vedado. An ugly, blockish skyscraper hotel swam past on our right—*Habana Libre* read a giant glowing sign up high.

Every once in a while the car stopped to let someone out or to pick up another passenger. The road was a river of light and traffic in the midst of low houses and dark streets. At last, when I could see a tunnel up ahead, Yosvany told the driver to stop. I fished about in my pockets for CUCs, but he gestured for me to stay still and handed the driver some bills. We got out.

"Give me thirty *pesos nacional*," Yosvany told me as we walked down a quiet, dark side street. "If you'd started waving around CUCs like a tourist, he would have taken five times that."

The side street ended in another major thoroughfare. A cool breeze ruffled our clothes. To our left, a second tunnel disappeared into darkness. But to our right . . .

To our right stretched Havana's seawall—the Malecón.

It ran four miles along the city coast, a concrete parapet that shattered waves into white foam and spray. People strolled down a wide promenade overlooking the water, couples and groups of friends, even here so far from the city center. Next to the promenade curved a motorway—the whole coast a golden scimitar of streetlights.

Inside the road rose the city itself, aglow against the night sky. The Hotel Nacional on its rocky hill, bathed in sharp lights. Residential areas half hidden in shadow. At the far end of the bay, the lighthouse of the Morro, the light pulsing periodically.

We crossed the road and approached a walled-off compound on the edge of the water. The left side of the compound was dominated by an imposing mansion with large red digits 1830 painted on its yellow facade. The rest of the place, what we could see through the gate, was a spacious outdoor patio brimming with people. A cheerful timba track played over booming speakers, "La Boda en Bicicleta" by Elio Revé Y Su Charangon. I shifted restlessly, surprised to notice how eager I was to dance.

Yosvany clasped hands with the heavyset bouncer at the ticket booth. He pointed at us and explained something. The bouncer nodded.

"It's two CUC each," Yosvany said. "My friend Carlos got you a discount."

We paid. A sign on the wall said entrance was three CUC. Which made me reevaluate my initial assumption—that Yosvany wanted us to pay his way.

The core of the Milocho was a round stone dance floor open to the sky. Right beyond it the water began, so you could stand at a low railing and look across a little bay that opened to the Florida Straits. Clumps of white plastic tables surrounded the dance floor, stretching away into a dimly lit garden. I made out some kind of decorative bridge and play castle in the distance.

The floor churned, a mass of couples dancing salsa, surrounded by a crowd of onlookers. About half seemed tourists, the rest Cubans. The locals here dressed well, in stylish, colorful outfits. The guys in particular stood out, some in tight red jeans, others with shaved eyebrows or elaborate punk-style hairdos.

We found an empty table near the back and sat down. Yosvany gestured at me surreptitiously.

"What?" Ana asked.

Yosvany glanced at her, then at me, and tossed his head toward the dance floor.

Oh. I turned to Ana. "You want to dance?"

She rolled her eyes. "I'm right here, guys."

But she gave her camera bag to Yosvany and took my hand.

I realized she was trembling a little. So was I.

We were about to dance casino in Cuba.

The song switched and half the people in the club got up to dance. We claimed a spot on the edge of the floor barely big enough to stand on, hemmed in by moving bodies—an airless box, suffocating, hot. Moisture covered our faces, and we hadn't even started dancing.

We didn't care. Like fools we grinned at each other and joined hands, and rocked the basic step, forward and back. Ana's hips moved with a life of their own, mesmerizing. I turned her in an *enchufla*. We did some simple figures—a *sombrero*, then a *setenta-y-dos*, turning round and round, tight against each other, my elbows hooked over hers. A heat suffused my chest, a frantic energy. I wanted to go on and on and on, dancing with Ana like this for—

But the song ended. Ana grinned and hugged me, and we headed back to our table.

Some Cuban girl had sat down with Yosvany and seemed to be having an intimate conversation with him, their heads so close they almost touched. A petite, athletic-looking white girl, she wore bright green slacks and a halter top.

Yosvany waved us over.

"Guys, this is Ingrid." He nodded at the girl. "Ingrid, this is my cousin Rick from New York"—for the city name he switched to exaggerated English, nyuu-york—"and his friend Ana."

"What's up." Ingrid turned back to Yosvany, her entire body toward him, leaning forward. "What do you say, *titi*? Let's go?"

Yosvany seemed not to hear. "So you dance," he said to me as we sat down.

I nodded.

"We'll get you a good teacher," he said.

I choked on thin air. Ana chuckled.

Yosvany grinned. "Hey, you're okay for a *yuma*. Your friend, though . . ." He nodded at Ana. "*Candela!*" He offered her his hand. "Shall we?"

As a wingman, Yosvany left much to be desired.

Ingrid didn't seem pleased to see them go either.

"So . . . ," I began. "How's it going?"

She got up. "I'm gonna go talk to some friends."

I'm a real charmer.

I shrunk back into my seat and watched the floor.

The music was Maykel Blanco's "El Bembé." Few couples could handle the song's complex mix of salsa and rumba, driven by sophisticated Afro-Cuban percussion. Ana and Yosvany had the middle of the floor to themselves. And they made use of it.

I'd seen YouTube clips of rumba—the Cuban street dance called guaguancó. A sexual pantomime where the guy imitated impregnating the girl and the girl evaded his advances, the dance had seemed crude to me, two hunched-over dancers circling each other and gyrating their body parts.

I'd had no idea.

Yosvany moved like a whip in the moment of unfurling, tense yet loose. His feet skipped lightly across the ground, kicking, pointing, stabbing heel down, a pattern too intricate to follow. His knees bent and swayed, elastic, human shock absorbers. His shoulders twisted and rolled and shimmied, now fast and sharp, now snapping into slow motion, like the abrupt slowdown of a John Woo movie. His arms . . .

But that makes Yosvany sound like some twitchy, uncoordinated marionette. He was the opposite. His shoulders and arms and hips and knees and feet, they moved independently and yet to one purpose, in counterpoint to each other, harmony emerging from chaos. His body an expression of playful challenge.

Even when he turned away from Ana. Even when he shimmied his shoulders bent low to the ground, a self-absorbed flourish. His every motion reflected her presence, like there was an elastic cord between them driving his movement. That cord stretched and stretched and stretched, and then he tossed his head at her or kicked out, or thrust forward his hips—and it snapped.

Ana danced simply, a side-to-side basic step that had her hips swaying to the beat of the music. Perhaps that was all she knew of rumba. But the grin on her face told me that she'd soon know a lot more.

When the song entered its salsa section, the two of them came together and lit up the floor. But I hardly even saw that part. My brain replayed the last minute in sharp, saturated color.

A tremendous envy came over me. Not the sticky, unpleasant kind that makes you resent people better than you. The kind that fills you up with a boiling impatience, a single desire—I want to be as good as *that*!

Yosvany and Ana returned, breathing hard and laughing. "You were right," Ana said. "Coming to Cuba was just what I needed."

"Ingrid left," I said to Yosvany.

He looked around for a moment. "There she is." Ingrid was at the other end of the garden, at a table with a bunch of ripped-looking guys in stylish clothes, chatting and smoking a cigarette. "Ingrid's good to hang out with. Her grandpa's in the Politburo, so she lives the good life. Parties, concerts, *farandulera* 24-7."

"Looks like she gave up on you, though," I said.

Yosvany snorted. "Watch."

He sauntered over to the other table. He said nothing to Ingrid, but clasped hands with the guys, clapped backs, gestured colorfully. Seconds later he was sitting down and deep in conversation. Ingrid sat off to the side, puffing on her cigarette, looking annoyed.

"Your cousin's a player, huh," Ana said. I couldn't tell if that was a criticism.

"I guess."

The music faded and the floor emptied. An emcee got on stage and invited couples up for the nightly salsa competition. A silence fell on the crowd, all eyes watching to see who'd dare take the floor.

I shivered involuntarily. They'd have to hold me at gunpoint.

Ana looked about openly. Searching for Yosvany, I realized, hoping to dance with him. But sometime in the past minute he'd disappeared, along with Ingrid.

Ana didn't look my way.

I was totally going to dance in that competition before we left Cuba.

(Yeah, I changed my mind. I'm complex like that.)

In the end five couples competed, and Ana filmed them. There were some good dancers, Cubans with nice body motion, and a European couple that blended hip-hop into their salsa.

I didn't see Yosvany again until the contest had ended. Ana had left to dance with some Cuban guy. Yosvany was coming from the back of the garden, where the decorative bridge and play castle loomed. Ingrid trailed a few steps behind him, color in her cheeks. Near our table they parted ways as if they hadn't been together at all.

Yosvany sank into his chair with a theatrical sigh. "See? That's how it's done."

"You went for a walk?"

He grinned. "*Me la tiré.*"

"What? Already?" I flushed. "I mean, there, in the castle?"

"It's a great spot," Yosvany said. "No one goes there. And there's a nice bench. Tell you what—I've got an idea. Take Ana there. Dance with her, tell her how special she is, how she makes you feel like no one in the world—"

"I told you we have different styles."

"You don't have to have sex with her," Yosvany said. "Just kiss her."

I would have told him about the agreement Ana and I had, that I wouldn't try to get into her pants. But then she came back to the table. And Yosvany said, "Hey, Ana. Rick's got a cool spot to show you."

She studied me. "As long as it's somewhere with a breeze."

I licked my lips, my mouth dry. Was I doing this?

What, exactly, was I doing?

We wound our way through the tables, to the back of the garden. Down a dim paved path, across the decorative stone bridge, leaving the crowd and the lights behind. What had looked like a castle from the distance was more like a water-side fortification, a stretch of faux-Oriental stone wall with walkways and a little tower, something out of a theme park playground. We made out the shapes of a couple standing atop the wall, so we descended instead, entering an opening in the wall that ran down into darkness.

Ana used her cell phone as a light, illuminating a narrow, rough-walled corridor. "You better not be an ax murderer," she muttered, switching to English now that we were alone.

"I'm out of axes," I said. "Blame the *bloqueo*."

We came out in a small grotto, an artificial cave walled in by jagged rocks on every side except one. We looked out across a small bay and to the Florida Straits beyond. Immediately below us, water lapped. If you craned your head to the right, you could see the edge of the Milocho's garden, and the lights of the Malecón stretching out beyond.

"This really is nice." Ana leaned out over the water. "I wonder if we'd get in trouble for swimming."

I looked down. The wall below us was craggy, and there was a wide ledge right by the water, room enough to leave clothes.

I kicked off my shoes, all nonchalance. I put one leg over

the edge, searched for grip with my toes.

Ana started. "We're doing this?"

I didn't say a thing, only swung the other leg over. I could be cool too, once in a while.

My foot slipped. I gasped, clutched at the wall. Stayed on somehow. Scrambled down to the ledge.

"I have a bad feeling about this," Ana said. But she followed me down, quick and sure on the wall.

There we were, in the dark. Two shadows on the ledge, the water lapping at our feet. Looking at each other.

Ana stuck out her foot, dipped her toes in the water. "Not bad."

"I saw you shiver," I said.

Ana pulled off her shirt. Her bra shone white in the gloom. She started to unbutton her jeans, then stopped. "Stare much?"

I turned away, blushing. Writhed out of my shirt awkwardly. Hesitated, then pulled down my jeans—trusting the dark to hide the boner raging in my boxers.

I was still struggling with one pant leg when Ana slid into the water—a lithe shape in my periphery, almost invisible except for the moonlight reflected on her underwear. I slunk down after her, clutching at the slick rocks to keep my balance.

Cold. A shock of cool against my skin.

Not a clean cold either—there was an oily feel to the water. No way I was putting my head under the surface. I didn't dive in, but climbed down. The bottom was shallow and painfully rocky under my feet.

Ana was fifteen feet away already, swimming on her back, arms arcing languidly through the air. She made a graceful turn and another, before heading back to me. She stopped a few feet away, floating on her back. "We should do that *Dirty Dancing* scene," she said.

"We can try," I said, dubious.

Ana came close, her face shadowed. I braced my feet on the bottom. She leaned toward me. I hesitated, then shot my hands forward, held her just above the hips.

Skin. Ana's skin, slick under my fingers.

She leaned in more. I sank into my knees, lifted.

For a second, Ana rose from the water. Then I lost my balance, toppled. We splashed down hard, both of us. Laughing, spluttering, casting about with our arms. Ana pushed off my chest, her fingers firm against me.

There was a rumbling. We froze, looked around.

There, a few hundred feet out, a motorboat. It had a spotlight on top, bright, shooting across the water in front of it.

"Police?" Ana asked, quiet.

We hunkered down. The spotlight traveled across the waves. Hit us, lit up the wall behind us bright. Ana gripped my hand, hard.

The light passed over us without slowing. The boat continued on.

"They didn't see us," Ana said.

I forced a laugh. "They probably weren't even police."

But that was the end of our swim. We clambered out onto the ledge and sat there for a while, drying in the warm night breeze.

"That was fun," Ana said.

"Yeah." My eyes drifted to her of their own accord. In the gloom, my mind painted sharp pictures out of every half-suggested curve . . . I wondered if she was thinking what I was thinking.

"We should have taken your cousin along," Ana said. "We kind of abandoned him."

Guess not.

Later, when we'd dried off and dressed and got back to Yosvany, he pulled me aside. "Well? Did you kiss her?"

"We went swimming," I said.

"What? You crazy? In that water?"

"I thought it might impress her," I said. "It seemed like a cool thing to do."

"You know what would have been a cool thing? Kissing her."

I muttered something to the effect that things weren't so simple.

"I give him a simple task and he goes swimming in the Malecón." Yosvany shook his head. "Next time, trust your cousin."

chapter ten

A REAL DANCER

"So you open the page and it's full of cats?" Juanita asked.

"That's right."

"And they do funny things."

"Sometimes." I buttered a bun of white bread. "Sometimes they just sit there, staring at you."

"*Dios santo.*" Juanita sipped at her coffee. "And people pay for this?"

"Advertisers do," I said. "It's the new age, *tía*. All about eyeballs."

"Eyeballs?" Juanita worked the English word around her mouth.

"Come, Mom." Yolanda stood at the sink, doing dishes.

"I've seen you on Facebook at Olivia's place. All you do is click on funny pictures."

"That's what Facebook is for," Ana stepped in loyally.

"I should introduce you to my friend Miranda sometime," Yolanda said to me. "She runs one of the smartest blogs in Cuba."

"Oh, yeah?" I asked. "What's it about?"

"The economy," Yolanda said. "And—"

"And a lot of *tontería*," Juanita cut in. "A waste of time and energy."

Yolanda looked ready to object, but Yosvany stuck his head in the door. "You guys almost done? I'm ready to go."

Of course he was. He'd been up two hours before me, after snoring so loud I couldn't sleep half the night.

"Two minutes." I scarfed up my food. The bread was stale, but there was a bowl of fruit to help it down—banana, guava, and the smoothest, sweetest papaya I'd ever tasted. *Fruta bomba*, they called it here, and the explosion of taste in my mouth justified the name.

"Where are you going?" Yolanda asked.

"I'm taking them to Pablo to learn salsa," Yosvany said. "I'll be in my room, guys."

I was ready to get going. I needed lots of classes if I wanted to dance in that competition at the Milocho.

"Really, Yosvany could teach us," Ana said. "He's very good."

"Yosvany won't be teaching anyone," Juanita said. "He's got a job."

"What does he do?" Ana asked.

"He waits tables and plays with the band at his uncle Elio's *paladar*," Juanita said. "He's saving up for a new guitar."

"So there are private restaurants here?" Ana asked.

"Of course," Juanita said. "You get a license and you're set."

"Unless they decide to change the law again," Yolanda said. "Then you lose everything."

"Changing circumstances require changing laws," Juanita said.

"Very good, Mom. That's very good." Yolanda looked at us pointedly. "That's why people like my friend Miranda are so necessary. Because some Cubans don't even know the hole that we're in."

❦

Here's the thing about life as a cat. Go somewhere new and everything's a threat.

A rubber duck? Holy terror!

A lawn sprinkler? Run in fear!

A plastic bag? OMG! Battle stations! Condition red!

Sometimes a cat can't get a break.

I didn't feel like this in Cuba. Sure, daily life in Havana was new to me, with plenty of surprises and learning experiences. But I could deal with it okay.

Talking to my newfound family, though? Land mines everywhere. Mr. Porcelain could have identified.

Later, out on the street, Ana brought this up with Yosvany.

"Your sister seemed in a bad mood this morning."

Yosvany waved his hand. "They're always going at each other."

"Different politics?" I asked.

"Something like that," Yosvany said. "I swear, you could say good morning to the two of them and they'd turn it into an argument."

"It's probably a sign they really care about Cuba," Ana said.

Yosvany snorted. "*Bobería a tiempo completo.* That's what it is."

It was in fact a sunny morning, windless, and the faint smell of rotting food hung in the air. The asphalt was already getting hot beneath my feet, promising a stifling afternoon.

"What's with those signs?" Ana pointed at a painted blue sign on a nearby door, like an anchor. "They're everywhere."

"That's a *casa particular,*" Yosvany said. "For tourists who don't like hotels. Everyone who's got a decent apartment runs one."

"I read about that," I said. "Raúl Castro freeing up the economy."

"Oh, yeah, we've totally got the free market. You can even buy foreign cars now." Yosvany laughed. "Two hundred thousand CUC for a new Peugeot."

"That money goes into the budget, right?" Ana asked.

"Yeah," Yosvany said. "Somebody's vacation budget."

Ana frowned but said nothing.

We'd barely reached Habana Vieja, the old city, before some hustler idled up alongside—a *jinetero* in local slang. "Taxi? Cigar? Taxi?"

Yosvany told him we weren't interested. It was only fifteen seconds before another voice cried, "Taxi? Girls? Cigars?"

And then, *"Amigo! Amigo,* hi!" And "Hi, my friend! My friend, where are you from?"

"I don't understand," Ana said. "It's not like we're not Latinos. How can they tell?"

Yosvany looked at her as if wondering if she was serious. "Your clothes," he said. "The way you walk. The way you look around. Everything."

Live music wafted from most restaurants, little bands playing son—the music that had preceded salsa, similar, yet more reserved in its cadences. A sound that I thought of as old people music. After a few blocks, I noticed something. "They're all playing songs from Buena Vista Social Club."

"Cuba is for tourists," Yosvany said. "That's what tourists want, so that's what we play, all day long. You've got some of the best musicians in the country playing 'Chan Chan' day after day to make money. Of course, we also have lots of good doctors and scientists and engineers playing 'Chan Chan' to make money."

"That's terrible," Ana said.

Yosvany shrugged. "The teacher I'm taking you to used to dance with the Conjunto Folklórico. Best company in Havana. Later they asked him to teach at a top professional dance school. But you can't put food on the table teaching Cubans, so he quit to work with tourists."

At the next intersection, we took a right. Our destination was halfway down the block, a three-story apartment building with a peeling green paint job. The scuffed outer door was locked. Yosvany stood in the middle of the street and craned his head back, looking at the balconies above. "Pablo!" he yelled, full throat. "*Oye, Pablo, consorte!*"

There was a long pause. Yosvany drew his breath to shout again, but a shape moved against the striped red awning of a third-floor balcony. A heavyset man peered down at us.

"Hey, Pablo." Yosvany waved.

"*Coge,*" the man called, and threw something.

I jumped aside. A yellow plastic duck smacked down where I'd been standing. It bounced and lay still on its side.

I picked it up, curious. There was a slit in the duck's butt. Someone had stuffed a key in there.

We went in, climbed a dark, dusty staircase. The smell of fried pork sat in the still air. Pablo stood in the door of his apartment, a man in his fifties, his skin the same dark shade of brown as Yosvany's, powerful arms crossed on a massive chest.

One glance and I knew him for a guy with style. Black-and-white jazz shoes. Cutoff jeans, an intense dark blue—no knockoff these. A sleeveless white tee constraining a substantial potbelly. A green baseball cap topped the ensemble.

"Brought you students." Yosvany clasped hands with the

man. "This is my cousin Rick and his friend Ana."

"*Gracias, hermano,*" Pablo said. "I'll remember this."

"I'll come by tonight." Yosvany waved at the two of us and started down the stairs. His voice floated up to us. "This is the best teacher in Havana, guys!"

Pablo looked us up and down. "Americans, yes? So you want to learn salsa." He sounded more amused than friendly. "Come in."

We entered a small, bright living room with a sliding glass door open to the balcony. A large mirror on one wall, a boxy TV with a DVD player by another. Three armchairs had been pushed out onto the balcony, leaving most of the floor bare.

The kitchen adjoined the living room, and it was the source of the fried pork smell. A slender young woman stood at an old, discolored oven watching meat sizzle. She was dressed all in white. White headscarf, white blouse, embroidered white skirt, and white shoes. The only bit of color to her was a necklace of small beads, blue mixed with white.

I'd seen people dressed like her all around Havana. Yosvany had explained they were new initiates into the Santería religion. I knew little about it other than that it was a fusion of a Yoruba belief system with Catholicism.

"This is my daughter," Pablo said. "Her name is Liliana, but you should address her as *Iyabó.*"

We introduced ourselves. Liliana nodded without much interest and said, "*qué bolá*"—Havana's equivalent of "what's up?"

"And this is Lalo, my grandson."

A little kid maybe five years old had come out of a bed-room down the hall. He was barefoot and bare-chested, his arms thin as sticks, and he had a gap-toothed grin ready for us. I got the sense he was the only one here genuinely happy to see us.

"My classes are ten CUC an hour," Pablo said.

Yosvany had told me to haggle. Looking at Lalo, so gaunt his ribs showed, I chickened out. "Okay."

As soon as I said that, I realized Pablo himself showed no sign he didn't get enough to eat. His clothes were new and his apartment looked decent. But it was too late. My budget would have to take the hit.

I'd told Ana I'd pay for our classes. I had more saved, and I'd be slowing her down, the beginner that I was. She'd agreed to let me pay two-thirds. "Someone gives me free money, I take it," she'd said. "But I won't have the destruction of your college savings on my conscience."

Pablo popped a flash drive into his DVD player and turned on the TV. Timba blasted forth, some old song about stepping on cockroaches—*cucarachas*. "Let's see you dance."

It was difficult, dancing under Pablo's gaze. You know that feeling when a painting's eyes seem to follow you around the room? Well, a dance teacher's eyes do. They see everything—every little movement, every mistake.

Then there was Lalo, watching us from the corner, his little arms crossed on his chest in imitation of Pablo. And

Liliana in the kitchen, observing us with cool, indifferent eyes.

Halfway through the song, Pablo stopped the music and looked at me. "You have some good moves and some complicated turns, and you dance on time. That is important. But you're as graceful as Frankenstein's monster. Except he's more flexible."

"Thanks." I grinned.

Pablo didn't. He turned to Ana instead.

"You dance mechanical, too elegant and classical, too perfect, understand? And you need more body movement."

I wondered what "too perfect" meant, but Ana nodded as if this were no more than she'd expected.

"We'll work on your salsa," Pablo said. "But I'll start you off with rumba."

I gaped at him. "Rumba?" My mind flashed to a vision of yesterday—Yosvany dancing with Ana, his body doing things I hadn't imagined possible. "You think I can learn rumba?"

Pablo's eyes weighed me. "Rumba exercises will free up your chest and shoulders."

Which wasn't exactly a yes.

"Can I film the classes?" Ana asked Pablo.

"Sure, if you pay me thirty CUC an hour."

She didn't film the classes, thankfully. The last thing I wanted was to star in *Unspeakable Horrors 2: Rick Gutiérrez Tries to Learn Rumba*.

To start off, Pablo ran us through body isolation exercises—

circling our torsos, moving our shoulders in rhythm to intricate drum music. None of it should have been hard, except for Pablo's favorite command.

"*Otra vez*," he said, and, "*otra vez*," and "*otra vez*." Again and again, and again, about a bazillion times.

Sweat stung my eyes. A soreness built in my shoulders. Then came a stabbing pain beneath my rib cage.

"Okay," Pablo said. "Now watch me."

The instant Pablo started to dance, he was no longer an older guy with a potbelly. An energy possessed his limbs. Even his substantial stomach moved in beat to the music. If Yosvany's rumba had been energetic and cool, Pablo's was funny and light. One moment he seemed a rotund clown, prancing on giant feet. Then he hunched over and wiggled his shoulders, arms pinned behind his back, like an overgrown chicken pecking at the ground. He made it look easy, effortless.

Then he said, "It's your turn."

In rumba, your knees were always in flex, so that you bobbed up and down like a jack-in-the-box. Okay, you weren't supposed to look like a jack-in-the-box—that was just me. But the principle was similar. With every step, your knees went flex, flex, flex.

There were other parts to the basic step. Arm movements. Chest movements. Shoulder movements. We never got to them.

We bobbed up and down. Up and down.

Both Lalo and Liliana had left to their own rooms early on. Sometime during the second hour, Lalo reappeared. He crept up behind Pablo's back and watched Ana and me bounce.

A grin spread on his face. He pointed at me. He sank deeper into his knees and started jerking his body, up, down, up, down, like a drunken monkey. He laughed.

Ana snorted.

I froze in place, midstep, flushing.

Pablo turned on the kid. "What are you doing?"

Lalo gave a little shrug.

"Go to your room." Pablo tried to sound stern, but I saw the smile curving his lips.

Lalo scampered off.

"As if you could do better," I muttered at the kid's back.

Pablo had been about to say something. Now he stopped. Looked at me, dead serious. "Come back here, kid," he called over his shoulder.

Lalo reappeared. Worry had wiped the grin off his face.

Pablo turned up the volume on the TV. Claves and congas and maracas thundered over us. "*Tira unos pasillos*," he said.

Lalo brightened. He strolled into the middle of the room and flicked his hand into the air stylishly, as if chasing away a fly.

Then, on the beat, he whipped his chest forward. Shimmied his shoulders like a pro. Kicked out his foot, curled that same foot behind him, spun in place, perfectly balanced. Raced across the floor in syncopated rumba steps, knees

flexing, stick-thin arms bending in and out, graceful as butterfly wings.

Then he tripped and fell on his backside, arms flailing.
But none of us laughed.

Pablo turned down the music. "If you learn to do that by
the time you leave," he said to me, "I'll call you a real dancer."

You know how in martial arts movies there's this hard-
ass old sensei who makes your life miserable? Except in the
end he's like, well done, young Padawan, and you realize he
was really rooting for you all along?

I didn't think Pablo was like that.

That night I lay on top of my sheets in my boxers and contem-
plated the impossibility of sleep. A sweltering heat had lain on
Havana all evening. Our window was open to the night sky
but no breeze stirred the curtains. The AC unit in the window
was broken. The steady beat of a salsa bell from some restaurant in the old city rang over the distant rumble of traffic.

Yosvany tossed and turned in his bed, his movements
punctuated by the occasional half-swallowed snore. Around
one in the morning the rattle of a truck woke him. I could tell
because of how still he went.

He must have known I was awake too, because he said,
"Hey, Rick."

"Hey," I said.

"Everything all right?"

Sure, I meant to say, I'm fine, I'm great, that standard

American nonresponse. "Havana is . . . very different from New York."

Yosvany snorted. "You've got a good eye, *primo*. Maybe you should become a detective."

"Do you know many people like Pablo?" I asked. "Working for tourists and hating it?"

"Most people feel lucky to work with tourists," Yosvany said. "People who get no tourist money, you can't imagine the way they live. I have a friend who peels tiles off walls in abandoned buildings, breaks bricks out of mortar to sell them on the black market. Lives in a shack in Marianao. Some days all he eats is rice, or bread with oil and salt."

"Your mom doesn't work with tourists," I said.

"Uncle Elio helps out," Yosvany said. "And besides, she's . . ."

"She's what?"

I could tell Yosvany was staring at me in the dark.

"Look, I will explain this stuff to you because you're my cousin. But don't talk about it with my mom, okay?"

"Okay," I said.

"Did you notice the sign on the door downstairs? The one that says CDR?"

"Sure." It had been a cute little emblem of a guy with a sword and a shield in the colors of the Cuban flag. I'd thought it just another communist peculiarity, like the many slogans painted on walls and billboards across town. "What's that about?"

"It's the Committee for the Defense of the Revolution," Yosvany said. "A neighborhood political organization. To keep things safe and clean and stuff, but also to make sure everyone's a good communist. And my mom runs it."

"Oh," I said.

That explained a lot.

"Mom still has friends in the army because of our grandfather," Yosvany said. "They come visit for New Year's sometimes."

"I see."

"Don't get the wrong idea," Yosvany said. "She's not this big communist or anything. I'm just saying, life is not so bad in Cuba if you know people. That's how it works here. Mom got Benny his job in food distribution, and now Benny helps out Elio's *paladar*, and the whole family gets by."

I made a guess. "That means you can't say anything bad about the government in public, not any of you."

Yosvany shrugged, a half-glimpsed motion in the dark. "You see why Mom and Yolanda get along so well."

How it must frustrate someone like Yolanda, knowing she was getting special treatment, having to stay quiet because of it.

"Don't get caught between the two of them," Yosvany said. "It's nonsense, useless, all this political crap. It never gets you anywhere. I don't know about New York, but in Havana it's better to live and have fun."

"I suppose," I said.

"I gotta get some sleep," Yosvany said. "In the morning I'm seeing this *jebita por allá*, need my energy, know what I mean?"

"Sure," I said.

I stared at the ceiling and imagined what my life might have been like had I grown up in this apartment.

chapter eleven

SNAG

We fell into a daily routine: class in the morning, then lunch with Juanita and practice at home, then a walk around the city. After dinner—a night dancing at the Milocho or La Gruta in Vedado or Hotel Florida in the old city.

Most days Yosvany had the gig at his uncle's restaurant, so we passed the afternoons on our own. After some initial awkwardness switching back and forth, Ana and I spoke Spanish between us—in part to practice, in part to blend in. Mom's language still felt a bit unwieldy to me, but I was starting to think in it. I was even acquiring a Cuban sound, I thought. Not that we fooled anyone on the street.

We strolled down the grand Fifth Avenue in Miramar,

with its embassy mansions and posh business centers. We took in the blocky gray tower of the Russian Embassy, like some Imperial headquarters out of *Star Wars*, a monument to the days the Soviets propped up Cuba's economy. We went swimming at Playas del Este, on soft white sand that warmed, not burned, your feet. On rainy days, or when storms came in off the ocean, we checked out indoor attractions. Galleries, the aquarium, the Museum of the Revolution—which included the yacht *Granma* on which Fidel and his rebels had arrived on the island, on their mission to topple Batista's regime.

They were nice days. I knew I'd remember them fondly, even if my plan of conquering Ana's heart wasn't making visible headway.

Every day I searched for hints that she might be interested. I found nothing, but I kept looking. Think one of those dog videos where flap-eared Spot is watching you eat dinner. You take bite after bite and give him nothing, and tell him you'll give him nothing, and still he keeps looking at you with those big, wet, hopeful eyes.

I remembered too well how it had felt, to stand with Ana's arms about me in the dark on that school stage, her forehead pressed against mine . . .

At least the dancing was going well. Pablo worked us so hard, I had to rub menthol gel into my chest to soothe the pain. But all those vicious exercises had an effect. I could actually circle my torso now, and shimmy my shoulders like I meant it.

All it took was a dance with a Cuban girl to dispel my illusions. Most of the better dancers never so much as smiled at you if you weren't good. Others nodded encouragingly, as if to say, isn't that charming, dear. Then there were the *jineteras* who smelled like a perfume shop and liked to dance real close. Real, real close.

And everyone had advice for me. Most Cubans seemed constitutionally incapable of seeing a *yuma* dance without offering some pearl of wisdom.

"Everyone is a salsa teacher," Ana observed. "Even if they can't tell their left foot from their right."

Not that all the advice was unhelpful. And it wasn't limited to dance either.

"You don't dance guaguancó to that music," Yolanda interrupted our practice one afternoon. "That's columbia."

She'd been leaning against the living room wall and watching us dance rumba—a very self-conscious rumba. I felt about as graceful as a headless turkey, and I suspected Ana wasn't doing much better.

"I didn't know you danced rumba," I said.

"Benny grew up dancing in the street. You do know rumba comes from the street, right? Might not be as pretty as the stuff your dancing teacher does, but you get *sabor* on the street, you get style."

"We've got a great teacher," I said.

But Ana said, "You're right. We should get out more. I want to see more of Cuba. The real Cuba."

At this Yolanda snorted. But before she could say more there came a knock at the door. She opened it.

A dark-skinned woman Yolanda's age stood on the threshold—skinny, almost gaunt, with watchful eyes set deep in her face. She gave Yolanda a subdued *qué tal* and they hugged.

"This is my cousin Rick from New York and his friend Ana. Rick runs that cat video site I told you about." Yolanda gestured at the woman. "Guys, this is my friend Miranda Galvez."

We made our hellos. "You're the blogger, right?" I asked.

Miranda raised an eyebrow. "I didn't realize I was famous in America."

"These two have a social conscience." Yolanda's tone was odd, not quite serious, not quite mocking. "Ana here just told me she wanted to get to know the real Cuba."

Miranda's eyes snapped to Ana, sharp and steady. "The real Cuba? As opposed to what?"

Ana hesitated as if sensing a trap, then shrugged. "All this tourist stuff. 'El Cuarto de Tula' on every corner. People yelling 'taxi!' in your face. Shops selling pictures of Fidel and Che and old American cars."

Miranda's face held no amusement. "You think that's not the real Cuba? What's not real about spending ten hours in the street to get a few dollars off some tourist so you can buy something to eat? Dinner's about as real as it gets, girl."

"I didn't mean to say—"

"No," Yolanda cut in gently. "But you did."

Ana was silent for a moment. She looked at the two women calmly, steadily.

Miranda sighed. "Look, we're as sick of Tula's room catching fire as anyone. All we're saying is, don't go around talking about the real Cuba when you don't have the first idea what it actually means to live here."

"We don't," I stepped in. "But we'd like to."

At this, Yolanda and Miranda turned to me in unison. I realized I hadn't simply stepped in. I'd stepped in it.

"That's exactly the problem," Miranda said. "You tourists come here and get the best of everything in Cuba, food like many Cubans never taste, hotels we can't imagine, night clubs, all that stuff. And that's okay because we need your dollars to survive. But then you want to poke your head into our kitchens, our bathrooms, our private lives? Why? So you can see how tough things are and go—oh, those poor Cubans! So you can go home and write a Facebook post or two and feel better about yourself?"

"Come, Miranda," Yolanda said, touching the woman lightly on the shoulder. "They mean well."

"Of course you do." Miranda's shoulders slumped; she sounded tired. "I'm sorry."

"Miranda risks her freedom with every blog post she publishes," Yolanda said. "It gives you a different perspective on life. Just yesterday she was walking down the street and—"

"No, Yolanda," Miranda cut her off. "I don't want to talk about that stuff."

There was an awkward silence. I searched for something to say and decided I didn't have anything valuable to contribute. My experience of online activism was limited to campaigning for a better class of lolcat. I felt small, listening to Miranda, imagining what her daily life must be like.

"I know there's not much we can do to help," Ana said quietly. "But is there anything?"

Miranda pursed her lips, glanced at Yolanda, shrugged. "We'll let you know if anything comes up."

"Okay," Ana said.

"Okay," Yolanda said.

"Okay," I said.

"Now, Miranda, just give me a second here," Yolanda said. "I need to explain the difference between guaguancó and columbia to these guys. It's too painful watching them flail about."

"You two are serious about rumba, huh," Miranda commented once Yolanda had finished her impromptu class.

"Rick here wants to be the Salsa King of Havana," Ana said.

I gave her a murderous glance. She seemed not to notice.

Yolanda just smirked. "Cousin, I don't meant to crush your dreams, but why not something where you have a little more expertise? The Cat King of Havana, maybe?"

In retrospect, I should have known that one would stick.

Yolanda's uncharitable lack of faith aside, I was starting to believe I might get good enough to compete at the Milocho. Then we hit a snag with Pablo.

It was Saturday morning. We arrived downstairs at Pablo's at eleven and waited for him to toss down the key. Except ten minutes passed, then fifteen, and he didn't.

Curious neighbors peered down on us. We watched an old man pull past a wooden cart, yelling his marketing *pregón—"frutas, vegetales, viandas, tamales, flores y hasta pescado frito!"* Eventually some guy approached to offer us cigars.

"Let's find a pay phone," I said. Yolanda had promised to get us a local SIM card, but you had to wait in line for one, and she hadn't gotten around to it yet.

Ana grabbed my elbow. "Look."

Pablo in his green cap, coming down the street. He waved at us and dug about in his pocket for his keys. He had a white plastic water cup in one hand. "You guys ready to dance?"

"Sure," I said.

Ana's grip on my elbow hardened. I glanced at her, surprised.

After a bit of fumbling, Pablo got the door open. We entered the staircase, him leading the way, and climbed.

That is, we started to. A few steps up, Pablo lost his balance. He flailed, then sat heavily on the stairs.

I reached to help him. "Sorry," he said, and got up.

A few more steps, and he sat down again. Water sloshed from his cup.

Except no. I realized it with a sting of dismay. That was rum, not water.

"Maybe we should come back another day," Ana said.

"No, no, come." Pablo levered himself up, grabbed the railing for all he was worth, and propelled himself upstairs.

We made it to his apartment without another hitch. He even managed to unlock the door with no trouble.

Inside, it was dead quiet, empty, bright with the morning light. Pablo put his cup on the table by the door and went into the living room. The armchairs hadn't been pushed out to clear the floor yet. He made as if to move one, but plopped down in it instead.

Ana's face was cold—as cold as I'd ever seen it. "Rick." She nodded at the door. "There's nothing for us here."

"No!" Pablo half rose, then fell back into his chair. "Stay. We'll work." It seemed like he was trying to summon the confident, no-nonsense tone he used in class.

"You can't work like this," Ana said. "We won't waste time on a drunk."

There was no missing the bitterness in her voice.

Pablo put one hand across his face. "My daughter, she left. She took my grandson, you understand. So I had a drink. This is Cuba. It happens sometimes."

I spoke to Ana in English. "Maybe we can come back tomorrow. I mean, shit happens, right?"

"No," Ana said. "*No, esto no se llama 'shit happens.'* I know guys like him. Coming back tomorrow won't help."

But I barely heard her. Because Pablo, he . . .

He'd plopped down on his knees, there on the stone floor. He swayed as he sat there, and put his hands in a wobbly prayer steeple.

"Get up." The words came out of my mouth before I knew I was speaking. "Get up, come on."

"Please," he said. "I need this. I have problems. When Yosvany told me you wanted two months of classes, I thought maybe things would get better. Maybe I could fix some things, with the money. Please."

"Get up," I kept saying. "Get up."

My face had flushed. My fingers dug into my palms. I had never felt as uncomfortable as in that moment.

This man who begged us on his knees, he'd once danced with the Conjunto Folklórico. He'd been among the best dancers in Havana.

It was Ana who ended it. "We'll come back tomorrow," she said. "If you're not sober, we'll leave for good."

Pablo got to his feet. He took a step toward Ana. He might have taken her hand if she hadn't backed away.

"Tomorrow," he said. "Yes. Come tomorrow."

We went downstairs in silence. Walked down the street in silence. Even the noise of Havana—the cars, the street vendors, the people—seemed muted. As if I'd just left a battle-field, my hearing dulled by exploding mortars.

I didn't want to talk about what had happened. I didn't want to think about it. I doubted Ana wanted to either. Clearly this brought back memories for her. And so we returned home without a word exchanged.

But the day wasn't over. In the hallway outside Juanita's door, an elderly woman stopped us. She was a regal lady who stood with poise, her back straight, her head up—gripping a cane in one white-knuckled hand.

"You're Rick?" she asked. "From New York? María's son?"

"Yes, hi," I said. "You knew my mother?"

"My name is Rafaela Pilar González," she said. "I've lived next door for forty years. Your grandfather helped us get our apartment."

My grandfather.

All I knew of Leonardo Gutiérrez Rivera—Mom's father—was that he'd worked for the government and that he'd raised Mom and Juanita by himself. I'd only ever seen one picture, a faded color photo of a smiling, thin, gray-haired white man.

I must have stayed quiet too long, because Ana elbowed me in the ribs (she was considerate that way).

"I'd love to hear your memories," I said. "Can I treat you to a coffee?"

Rafaela's eyes lit up. "Have you been to the Museo del Chocolate, by Plaza Vieja? They make a wonderful hot chocolate."

"Let's go there," I said. "Maybe in an hour?"

"I've got tourists coming today," the woman said. "But I'm

free tomorrow afternoon. And call me Rafaela, *niño, que no soy una vieja.*" I'm no old-timer.

"Tomorrow then," I agreed, excited.

If Juanita didn't want to discuss our family history, maybe this lady could help.

"You look like Leo," Rafaela said. "My husband always said meeting your grandfather was the only good thing that happened to him in Angola."

Angola . . . Cuba had been involved in some civil war over there. I hadn't known my grandfather had been part of it, though.

I might have asked about that, but there came a scraping at Juanita's door. Rafaela started as if at a gunshot. She waved at us and legged it down the hall with impressive speed.

Yosvany emerged, the visor of his Yankees cap pulled down over his face. "Hey, guys," he said. "What are you doing here? Don't you have class?"

We told him what had happened.

A minute later, he said, "Wait, you've been paying Pablo every day? You crazy? Once he gets money, it's off to party."

Another minute, and he'd left to see Pablo.

In an hour he was back.

"Give him until Monday." We sat in the living room, holding council. "I'll get him back on his feet. You'll see."

"We don't want to waste time on an alcoholic," Ana said.

"Pay him once a week, and you'll be fine," Yosvany said.

"Why do people treat drunks like children?" Ana asked.

"Because it works," Yosvany answered.

But I wondered. Maybe we simply didn't want to think of them as adults. Didn't want to consider what it must have taken, to reduce an adult to a sobbing mess on his knees in front of two teenagers.

chapter twelve

RICARDO EUGENIO ECHEVERRÍA LÓPEZ

Since we had the next morning free, Yosvany invited us to visit his uncle Elio's restaurant. "We've got a tres guitarist from Camagüey visiting today," he told us over breakfast.

It was a wet morning, alternating between periods of intense sunshine and downpours. During the latter, the streets ran with water and, in places, trash. We piled into a *colectivo* and trekked out to Vedado, where the *paladar* Tres Gaviotas sat in the shadow of Cuba's tallest skyscraper, the FOCSA building.

The *paladar* occupied the patio of a tan two-story

building, an airy space with simple wooden tables and a concrete floor, protected from the rain by a faded plastic awning. Only one of the tables was occupied when we arrived, by a young German couple picking at a salad of chicken and wilted cabbage leaves. Near one wall the musicians were setting up, five men with graying hair. Seeing us enter, the double bass player walked over. He was a stocky, muscle-bound type in a button-down shirt.

"Hi, *tío*," Yosvany said. "This is my cousin Rick and his friend Ana."

"Welcome." Yosvany's uncle Elio shook my hand, cheek-kissed Ana, turned to Yosvany. "We start in five. The Germans want 'Guantanamera.'"

"'Guantanamera,' *voy pa'allá*," Yosvany said.

"I'll get you some *refrescos*," Elio said before departing with Yosvany.

The band's take on "Guantanamera" was low-key and light. Yosvany's uncle sang lead even as he picked at his double bass. The tres player from Camagüey did a few intricate, playful solos. They moved on to "Cuarto de Tula" and "Chan Chan," playing gamely, with big smiles and apparent zest. Yosvany played the congas, tapping out rapid rhythms with distracted, nonchalant ease.

At the end of their set, Ana walked over to Yosvany. "Nice playing," she said. "Can you do something other than this tourist stuff?"

"Like what?"

"Like, Silvio Rodríguez? 'Mariposas' or 'Ojalá' or something?"

Yosvany looked at the others. The tres player nodded, but Yosvany's uncle shrugged. "I don't know the lyrics."

"I got this," Yosvany said.

Of course he did.

The tres guitar started into a contemplative, melancholy melody.

Yosvany had a low voice, rough at the edges but pleasant. He sang of love, of children killed by bombs and napalm, of a decent girl who must mind what people might say at church.

Ana gave a little sigh. "And he can sing too."

I can edit a mean cat video, I thought. I've made Reddit's front page on fifteen different occasions.

But when Yosvany came by the table later, I told him, "Nice singing." Because it had been. And because there's a difference between thinking douchey thoughts and being a douche.

I looked at my watch. "We're meeting Rafaela in forty minutes. Might be best to get going."

"Oh, I can't go," Ana said. "Sorry. Yosvany's taking me to a salsa party in Playa. No tourists, just locals. He says I can get some great footage for my film."

It was funny, I reflected in the *almendrón* to Habana Vieja. I'd come to Havana dreaming that I'd master dance and become this cool guy and sweep Ana off her feet. But if anything, leaving New York had robbed me of camouflage.

I now felt like the number one nerd of an entire country.

Filled with a restless energy, I walked fast through Habana Vieja to the Museo del Chocolate.

Rafaela Pilar González met me on Mercaderes Street outside the café. It was one of the posh restored streets in the middle of the old city, all bright colors and picturesque colonial architecture. Rafaela stood pressed against the wall to avoid the steady stream of tourists. She wore a fine blue dress and high-heeled shoes and had her hair up in a fancy do.

I regretted my jeans and T-shirt instantly. I hadn't thought this might be a special occasion for her.

Rafaela's face lit up when she saw me. "I was up all night thinking about you," she said. "There's so much you should know, *cariño*."

The Museo del Chocolate was a combination café and chocolate shop. Tourists waited in line to browse a veritable chocolate zoo of bear and turtle and rabbit figurines. There was no wait in the café, though.

A waitress slapped down two laminated menus before departing wordlessly. That kind of attitude would have rated scathing Yelp comments in New York. It seemed to be the norm at state-owned businesses in Havana. Not much incentive for good customer service if you're guaranteed a job for life, I supposed.

"This is such a wonderful place," Rafaela said. "The hot chocolate is amazing."

"Let's get some." Recalling this was probably a rare outing

for her, I added, "And please, order some food. Anything you like."

"I don't enjoy food much anymore," Rafaela said. "Nothing tastes the way it used to. But this hot chocolate . . . it takes me back. To when I was a girl in Holguín, and Fidel was just another boy's name."

"Uh-huh."

"There was a café called El Principe in Holguín. A friend of my mother's was a waiter there, Alberto, a big hairy man. He made me hot chocolate. I sat in the window sipping it while my mother and Alberto went outside to kiss." Rafaela chuckled. "They thought I didn't know. *Qué va.* I didn't mind, though. I watched the lights in the window, these bright neon lights. At home we didn't even have electricity."

"You didn't?"

"My village didn't get electricity until Fidel came down from the mountains. I was in Havana by then, married, but I remember the letters I got from my little sister. How excited she was to have that glowing bulb in her bedroom. A few months later they opened a school in the village. She got to learn math and literature and other things. That's why I never complained when my Eduardo joined the army. Fidel and the *barbudos*, they were bringing Cuba into the future."

"And today?" I asked, thinking of Miranda Galvez, Yolanda's friend. "Are they still bringing Cuba into the future?"

Rafaela blinked as if awakened, chewed her lip for a moment. "*Mira*, of course we have problems. Any country has problems. In the US, innocent people get shot in the street by the police, and poor folks die because they can't afford to go to the doctor." She shrugged, a small, conciliatory gesture. "But we're not here to talk politics. Let me tell you about your mother."

The waitress came to take our orders. Once she was gone, I asked, "What was she like back then?"

"I met her the day we moved in," Rafaela said. "A tall, thin fifteen-year-old, all bones. She wore this pretty white summer dress two sizes too big. I remember thinking, I hope she grows into that thing. She ran into us on the stairs—Eduardo and I were lugging up our furniture. She offered to help, though it was obvious she really wanted to run off. Eduardo said *claro*, of course she could help, so she worked with us for hours. The next day I took her for ice cream at Coppelia. She told me all about her school and her *novios*, and the stories she was writing."

"Boyfriends?" I asked. "Wait, she was writing stories?" Mom had taught literature, but she'd never mentioned writing any.

"Oh, yes," Rafaela said. "Exciting pieces with titles like 'In the Sierra Maestra' and 'Daughter of the Revolution.' Kids fighting against imperialist soldiers, setting booby traps, throwing themselves on grenades to avoid capture."

This sounded about as likely as Rush Limbaugh praising Obamacare.

"You have to remember, your grandfather was a colonel in

the army," Rafaela said. "And María adored him. All the way until 1980 she adored him."

My heart beat faster. That was the year of the Mariel boatlift, when Mom had come to the States. "What happened then?"

Our hot chocolate arrived. It was strong, dark stuff, less sweet than I was used to. Rafaela smacked her lips in pleasure. For a moment I saw the girl she must have once been.

"Some people thought it was politics," Rafaela said. "Others called it teenage rebellion. But what really happened to your mother was a boy. It was a surprise to us all. María always had boys circling her but she cared more for her stories than for the Josés and Oscars and Paulitos of the day."

"Until?"

"Until Ricardo Eugenio Echeverría López."

"Who was he?"

"Not much to look at," Rafaela said. "A bit plump, always red in the face. But he was a poet. Not one of the *pájaros* who write about birds and flowers. He was a poet in the style of José Martí and Salomé Ureña, all love of the fatherland and hot blood spilt on cool sand."

I blinked. This smiling old lady just used a homophobic slur without so much as a pause.

"Is something wrong, dear?"

"Uhh . . . so my mom fell for a revolutionary poet?"

"Yes. But his revolution wasn't Fidel's."

"Oh."

"His dad was in prison. His uncle's raft disappeared somewhere between Havana and Miami. He was a marked *gusano* already. So he walked about the place shooting off his mouth like he didn't care. María met him at the Malecón one night. They spent the next six months at each other's throats. She'd come to me sometimes, furious about this or that thing he'd said about Fidel or the army or the Revolution. Except as the months passed she came to me less and less. Until one day I saw them at the beach, kissing in the surf." Rafaela smiled. "I should have expected it. María had led a sheltered life. She wasn't ready to see the Cuba Ricardo showed her. And, well, she was a girl and he was a boy. Whenever a boy and a girl feel that strongly about each other, what does it matter if it's love or hate?"

I thought that perhaps Mom had understood more of Cuba than Rafaela credited her for. I could see it—Mom at my age, coming to grips with the realization that her father worked for an oppressive government.

"What did my grandfather do?" I asked.

"María wasn't a fool," Rafaela said. "She kept her change of heart to herself. She and Ricardo, they had one happy year together. He gave inspiration to her stories. She reined in his excesses, tamped down his outbursts, kept him safe. Then came the spring of 1980."

"Mariel," I said.

Rafaela nodded. "I remember it like today. April first, when those crazies crashed a bus into the Peruvian embassy and got asylum. Fidel announced he wouldn't stop anyone who wanted to join them. Within days, thousands of people were crowding into the embassy garden. Ricardo must have convinced María to go. She didn't tell me, but I figure that's how it was. They agreed to meet at a park in Miramar late one night and walk to the embassy together."

"They never made it," I guessed.

"When your mother got to the park, Ricardo wasn't there," Rafaela said. "She waited for an hour. He didn't come. But your grandfather did. He told her Ricardo had betrayed her. He said the boy had joined the army, had left Havana already."

I went cold. "And she believed him?"

"Of course not," Rafaela said. "She thought her father had beat Ricardo up, had forced the truth from him. But Leo had a letter for her, in Ricardo's handwriting. And, well . . . he'd been given a choice. Go to prison for his poems or join the army."

Even at the remove of decades, I felt this as a punch to the stomach.

"María went home with Leo that night," Rafaela said. "She didn't try to run away. She didn't care about leaving any-more. We all believed that. Even when I went to talk to her the next day, she just sat at her desk and stared out the window. For Ricardo she had only one word. *Traidor.*"

"Because he gave her up?"

Rafaela shrugged. "Because he joined the army and gave up his poems, I suppose. What do I really know? What did any of us know? We all thought María had lost her will to run away."

"But she did run," I said.

"Yes," Rafaela said. "Some days later she told Leo she wanted to go for a walk. He let her. He thought she'd seen reason, and anyway the embassy had been closed off at that point. But that was the day Fidel opened Mariel Harbor, told all Cuba to get out if they wanted to. We never found out how she got aboard, but María left on one of the first ships to Miami." Rafaela paused. "She never called. Never wrote. Never sent word of any kind. Not for years. It was hard on Juanita. It broke Leo. He retired soon after."

I clutched my cup of cold chocolate and marveled. Mom hadn't just up and left Cuba. She'd escaped under the nose of her despot father. There'd been a love story, and a betrayal . . . she'd lived a life fit for a *telenovela*.

She'd been eighteen. Only two years older than me.

All the years of my life she'd refused to speak of her past. Only now it struck me what it must have really meant, that denial of her homeland. How deep her resentment must have gone.

"There must be more to the story," I said. "Why did Ricardo give up on her that easily? Why did she give up on him?"

"There's always more to the story," Rafaela said. "But I don't know the rest. Leo died. Ricardo disappeared from our lives—I never heard of him after that day. I never asked.

I detested him for María's sake, the way I figured she detested him." Rafaela gave me a slow, measuring look. "But now I wonder."

"What? Why?"

"A boy called Ricardo comes from New York and says he's the son of María Gutiérrez Peña." Rafaela gave a little shrug.

I stared at her.

Ricardo.

As in, Ricardo Eugenio Echeverría.

No, that made no sense. My name was Richard—that's what my passport said. Richard, not Ricardo.

I tried desperately to remember who'd picked my name. Hadn't Dad told me some story about it? Maybe they'd used a baby name book. Maybe my grandmother in Leipzig had suggested it. . . .

"But . . . why?" I asked.

Surely Mom wouldn't name me after someone who'd betrayed her. Someone she detested.

Rafaela reached across the table, patted my hand with knobby fingers. "That's a question you stop asking, here in Cuba. One day someone's here and tomorrow she's gone, *se fue*, and there's no one left to answer."

chapter thirteen

MR. MODERNITY

That night Ana got home from Yosvany's fiesta charged up. "It was amazing," she said. "Some of these dancers . . . this old guy bounced around to salsa like he was boxing. A couple of kids, ten years old, did better casino than anyone in New York. And there was this rumbero, man, the way he could move. It was all locals, a totally different vibe, people having fun. I got some crazy footage."

"Sounds awesome," I said. And I managed to mean it.

Rafaela's stories had made me think. To consider the revolutionary poet Ricardo, and my mother the fiction writer, and their life on the verge of exile. They'd been two kids who believed in something. Who'd supported each other's passions.

The next morning, Pablo met us in the street outside his building in clean, pressed jeans and shirt—sober, business-like. "I apologize for last week," he said. "It won't happen again."

"Yosvany is a good friend to you," Ana said, her voice cool.

"Yes, and a good businessman," Pablo said.

Which made me wonder if Yosvany was getting a kick-back from the classes. I decided I didn't care, not as long as Pablo stayed sober.

And he did. Week after week, he drove us hard.

Our lives settled back into a regular beat. Havana started to feel like home. I no longer noticed the crumbling architecture or the potholes. My early cravings for burritos and pizza and a quality burger had faded with the weeks. I checked up on my website occasionally at the Hotel Parque Central, made sure my team of mods was keeping CatoTrope on track, but I forgot to miss broadband. My Spanish loosened up, words slurring together, vowels disappearing *a lo cubano*. On more than one occasion Cubans in the street took me for a local, asked me for directions with some half-swallowed cuban-ismo or other.

Before we knew it, we were halfway through our trip.

One night early in August we went to see Los Van Van in con-cert.

If you're a salsero that sentence has you frothing at the mouth. For the rest of you—Los Van Van is the most famous

Cuban salsa band in the world. They've been playing since the late sixties and they still rock it. Check out songs like "Agua" or "Tim Pop" or "Me Mantengo" and see if you can keep still.

Infomercial aside, going to a Van Van concert meant two things. First, ponying up twenty CUC at the door, a price that few Cubans could afford. Second, arriving two hours early to stand in line.

I offered to pay for Yosvany. For once, he accepted.

"We never get to hear these guys live," he said. "They play for tourists and *jineteras*."

Yosvany said this in apologetic tones. It wasn't that he was above milking a *yuma*. He'd told me stories of five European *novias* and the gifts they'd given him. "But family is different. I've got your back and you've got mine, yeah, *primo*?"

Best I could tell, he really meant it. That made me happier than I dared admit.

The night of the concert, Yosvany told us, "You guys go wait in line. I've got to run an errand."

To which Ana said, "You mean to say, would you please hold a spot for me?"

Yosvany grinned. "You're sweet, *niña*. I'll see you there."

"He can be kind of a dick," Ana said as we walked to the concert. She didn't seem to mind.

The show was at Casa de la Música Galiano, a movie theater converted into a dance hall. Galiano Street, a wide thoroughfare of grand old buildings, cut through the heart of Centro Habana. Groups of young people walked in the street and loitered on the portico-covered sidewalks. There was no line yet—we were early.

"Yosvany," Ana muttered as we took our spots in front of the closed gate.

But the line grew quickly. Within fifteen minutes, there were a dozen people behind us. Within a half hour, a hundred or more. Little clumps of tourists mostly, speaking Italian, Russian, German, and English. Right behind us stood two blond Swiss girls, their German so peculiar I had trouble understanding them at first (not that I was fluent—it had been years since Dad had made the effort to speak his native language with me).

Watching the growing crowd, I remarked to Ana, "At least we'll get a good table."

That's when someone brushed past me.

I turned to see a girl maybe eighteen years old, in a sparkly black jacket and a white miniskirt and skyscraper heels, lips painted a bright cherry red. She'd stepped in front of us in line and now stood chewing gum, thumbing through her smartphone with deliberate nonchalance.

Ana and I exchanged a look. She mouthed, "*jinetera*." I made as if to speak, but Ana shrugged expressively.

She had a point. Picking a fight with a prostitute didn't seem like a great way to start the evening.

Five minutes later one of the Swiss girls poked my shoulder. I looked out at the street.

A party of some ten women approached. Miniskirts, high

heels, gobs of lipstick, all of them.

Jinetera central.

The girl in front of us yelled out a rowdy greeting. The party of ten yelled back. They descended upon us in a tidal wave of bodies and perfume. They pushed us back, the whole line, to make room at the front.

"*Oye*," I said, almost involuntarily. "Hey, hey, there's a line."

The women ignored me. One, a girl who couldn't be that much older than me, eyed me. "You're cute."

"I can understand them," said one of the Swiss girls in German. "If I had to work here every night, I wouldn't want to stand in line either."

Which deflated my annoyance. I'd been seeing the *jineteras* as an irritant, much like a fly buzzing about your head. That's what it was like, going out in Havana: if you were alone at the bar for three minutes, one of them would slide up to you with a sly "*Hola, niño.*" I hadn't considered what it must be like, having that as your job.

It made me wonder how the girls in front of us felt about our stares and muttered comments. If they really didn't care or pretended.

Yosvany arrived shortly before the doors opened. He had a friend in tow, a stocky black kid with a shaven head, in a stylish striped shirt and tight jeans.

"Luis here is the best casinero in Havana," Yosvany said.

"What's up, guys." Luis clasped my hand, went in for the

cheek–kiss with Ana, smooth and cool.

"We got stopped on an ID check," Yosvany said. "I thought we wouldn't make it. Those damn police . . . *le pone el de'o a uno.*"

"They liked your pretty face," Luis said.

"At least I'm pretty," Yosvany said. "If we'd told him you were the *maricón*, not me, they would have let us go at once."

Luis only snorted. "I'm out of their league, and they know it."

Casa de la Música was a vast, cold, black cavern. You came in at the top, walked down a narrow path between an expanse of tables and two bars. The path descended to a dance floor hemmed in by more tables—and finally, at the far end, the stage.

When we entered, reggaeton blasted at earsplitting volume. We found a table near the dance floor and I got everybody a beer (these guys didn't card). By the time I got back to the table, the music had changed to salsa, and Luis took Ana to dance.

Yosvany and I watched the two of them. Luis was as good as Yosvany had said, his casino smooth and understated. Ana seemed ecstatic.

"Don't worry," Yosvany said. "Luis only goes for boys."

"Do you really think it's okay, calling him what you did?" I asked.

"What?"

"*Maricón.*"

Yosvany only looked at me, shook his head.

I thought he was ducking the question. But when Luis came back with Ana, Yosvany clinked beers with him and said, "Rick asked me a question and I didn't know. Do you mind when I call you *maricón*?"

I froze. Ana drew in a sharp breath.

Luis stared at Yosvany for a long moment, his face utterly expressionless. Then he laughed, teeth gleaming. "Not when it's a *comepinga* like you." His eyes stayed on Yosvany, unblinking.

Yosvany turned to me. "See?"

"Excuse me." Luis got up. "I've got to go say hi to a friend."

"You really are a *comepinga*," Ana said to Yosvany when he was gone.

"What? Why? He doesn't mind."

"Yeah," Ana said. "Like girls in the street don't mind when you whistle and tell them how hot they are."

Yosvany looked perplexed. "Exactly."

"Let me give you a hint," Ana said. "We do mind."

"Maybe you do," Yosvany said. "The *cubanas*—"

"Don't you think we talk?" Ana asked.

Yosvany shrugged. "They never asked me not to."

"Yeah," I said. This was familiar ground to me. "Because telling people to leave you alone works great."

"Especially when the people bothering you are guys twice your size," Ana said.

"I'm not twice Luis's size," Yosvany said.

"You didn't grow up hearing your friends make gay jokes and thinking—that's me they're talking about," I said.

Yosvany got up, an abrupt motion. "This is Cuba," he said. "Things are different here. Many of my friends at school are gay and you know what, they love me. We're like brothers. I'm going to dance."

"Did he . . . ," Ana began. "Did he really just . . . ?"

"Use the 'my best friend is gay' line? Yes, he did." I sighed. "I like Yosvany, but man . . . it's like he's from the fifties or something."

"All right, all right, Mr. Modernity," Ana said. "You grew up in Peter Cooper Village, not Cuba. Not even the Bronx, all right?"

"Huh," I said.

Ana took a long drink from her beer. "My father was like that, back in San Juan. Always in the street, always with two or three girlfriends at a time. My mom, she knew what she was getting into, marrying him. She figured she would get the macho out of him."

"Did she?"

"I think he wished she had, by the end." Ana shook her head. "When my stepdad moved in, I was afraid it was going to be the same. I mean, he even kind of looked like my dad, this big, tough Dominican guy. But they were nothing alike. I caught myself wishing my mom had met him first."

"Oh," I said.

Ana seemed to snap back to the present. "Besides, New

164

York is better, but not that much better. Not walking down the street, not at school, and sure not in the clubs."

The music faded then. Los Van Van walked on. We went to rock out by the stage.

I'd been to some good concerts in my life. Rock bands at Madison Square Garden, great jazz shows at Birdland and Blue Note. This was something else.

Not just the music—songs cheerful and bittersweet, relentless and leisurely, all with that syncopated Van Van songo sound. Not just the energy of the band. I was close enough to touch singer Mandy Cantero as he did comic rumba kicks in the middle of his signature theme, "El Aparecido," but that wasn't all.

It was that the music took hold of me, burst in through my ears and banged about in my skull and surged out to my limbs, and made me move. I felt as the dancer in some religious rite, possessed by spirits and helpless to resist. My feet rocked side to side in counterpoint to the beat. My shoulders shook with the cadence of the güiro. My arms swung now as in salsa, now as in rumba, now in patterns of their own invention.

Toward the end of the show, I noticed there was a girl dancing next to me. A white Cuban girl, short and cute, and alive with movement. I noticed her because she glanced at me once and then again, and smiled.

I angled toward her and danced with her—not salsa, not touching at all, just matching movement to movement and rhythm to rhythm. When the music entered a calmer section, we did dance salsa, for ten minutes as the band played mon-tuno after montuno, a marathon series of improvisations that kept the song going forever.

After, the girl hugged me, and held on for quite a while. I thought I might offer to buy her a beer.

That's when I saw Ana. She was dancing with some beefy white guy, looking like she was having a great time.

My mouth clicked shut.

The Cuban girl gave me a long look, then sidled off through the crowd. And I stood there wondering why I was such a fool.

❧

Once you spend time in the feline cinematography biz, you realize everything in life has a cat metaphor. An instructive lesson from the animal kingdom.

If at first you don't succeed? Watch that video of Mr. Por-celain going for the cornflakes.

Have a fight with your girlfriend? Cue Sugar and Spice tumbling all over the floor. They screech, scratch, roll in the litter box—then snuggle and lick each other.

Don't use an actual litter box. It's a metaphor.

The litter box, I mean. Not the snuggling. Or the licking.

Can't decide what college to go to? Set two shoe boxes side by side. Watch Ms. Pop-Tart lie down in one, get up, lie down in the other, get up, lie down in the first—then get kicked out because she forgot to save up for tuition (wait, are we still doing metaphors?).

Spending the summer in Cuba with your crush, who doesn't want to be your girlfriend?

That's a tough one. I may need to go meta on this cat metaphor.

Back in the early days of CatoTrope, I used to dream of five thousand page views a day. It seemed to me I'd be happy once I hit that level. A rising star in the field of brainless amusement, I'd kick back and bask in my achievements.

The day came when I broke through five thousand page views. Know what I did? Spent the day redesigning my site for search engine optimization. You know, so I could crack ten thousand sooner.

Of course, more views means more ad clicks, which means more cash. But still, the point stands.

When Rachel Snow had dumped me, I had been a klutzy geek. I'd decided to turn my life around. Half a year later I was . . . well, okay, still a geek and still klutzy—but damn it, I could dance. Kids at school had clapped me on the back and called me cool. One girl had given me her number, and another asked me to teach her salsa. Now in Cuba, I had cute girls hugging me tight and giving me suggestive glances.

Was I doing anything about it? No. I had Ana to moon over.

I'd had enough of it.

～

I made my way back to our table. I found Yosvany there, sitting back and downing his fourth beer (judging by the empties).

He nodded his head to the music, chillness itself.

"I've got to do something about Ana," I told him as soon as I'd sat down. "I can't keep waiting forever. I've got to know."

Yosvany lit up like he'd been waiting for me to say this. "*Coño, primo,* now you're talking."

"The problem is," I said, "what do I do?"

"Something big and stylish," Yosvany said. "Make an impression. If it works, great. If it doesn't, at least you'll know."

"Style isn't exactly my expertise," I said.

Yosvany clapped my shoulder. "Leave that to me. Tomorrow is the big night. Tomorrow, *le damos sin susto.*"

chapter fourteen

THUGS

I woke up the next morning thinking of Ana. I turned to ask Yosvany what the plan was, but he was gone, rumpled bed empty.

My first instinct was distress, that he'd abandoned me on this crucial day. The second was relief. Maybe I wouldn't have to go through with it. That relief propelled me to the bathroom for a shower.

The water heater had broken down. Juanita said it might get fixed. Not might get fixed tomorrow or next week—simply "might get fixed." In New York this might have reduced me to stuttering panic. Here the cool water was a refuge from the oppressive heat.

By the time I got dressed, Ana was in the kitchen drinking coffee with Yolanda. She didn't look up when I walked in. I felt a moment of dismay, but then took in Yolanda. She sat with her elbows on the table, leaning forward so that a curtain of hair hid much of her face. Even so I saw the bruise on her cheek, big and splotchy and reddish-blue.

"What happened?" I blurted. "Was it—" I stopped myself.

Yolanda glanced up, shook her head, a small motion. "Some thugs . . . they jumped me on the street last night."

"Are you all right?" I asked. "Do you need to—"

"She said it's nothing." Ana gave a little shake of her head. "Leave it."

"Really, kids, I'm okay." Yolanda paused, seemed to gather her strength. "Remember how you asked Miranda and me if there was some way you could help?"

"Tell us," Ana said.

"Anything," I said.

"I need you to—" Yolanda began, then swallowed. "My friend Lisyani, her mother's in the hospital. She needs some expensive supplies, maybe a hundred CUC."

"That's no problem," Ana said.

"Of course," I said.

I would have agreed to anything at that moment.

Yolanda hesitated. "You can come with me to Lisyani's. You wanted to see the real Cuba. This is part of it. Just leave the camera at home."

A few minutes later, when Yolanda went to get ready, Ana and I spoke quietly.

"Don't ask her questions," she said. "I don't know if it was Benny—"

"—yeah—"

"—I mean that's what Yosvany guessed, he was ready to rip Benny's head off, but Yolanda told him he knew nothing and to mind his own business. So I don't know. But she doesn't want to talk about it. Don't force it, okay?"

I tried to picture Benny enraged, violent—thin, geeky Benny with glasses pushed high on his nose. It was hard. But the failure of my imagination meant nothing.

"It's hard, when that happens," Ana said. "When it's someone you love . . . I mean, you're ashamed, don't want anyone to know . . ."

I nodded, and wondered just how well Ana knew the feeling.

Half an hour later we were on the street. The day was another scorcher. Yolanda wore a long-sleeved blouse. Her broad-brimmed hat drooped in a way that might have seemed comical under other circumstances, but it hid her face partway. Ana and I walked on either side of her as if on bodyguard duty.

"Are we going to a pharmacy?" Ana asked.

"Let's pick up Lisyani first."

Yolanda's friend lived at the far end of Habana Vieja. Halfway there, the silence began to wear on our little group. I decided to try and distract Yolanda.

"I talked to your neighbor Rafaela the other day," I said. "She told me about why my mother left Cuba."

"That's nice," Yolanda said.

"About how our grandfather tried to stop her."

Yolanda was silent for a moment. "I didn't know that."

"Really?"

"Juanita doesn't talk about that time." Yolanda shrugged. "Keeping silent is her way. You have to push her if you want answers."

I considered Juanita, my aunt, family stalwart and communist functionary. I wasn't sure how hard I dared push her.

"Make sure you really want to know," Ana said. "So your family's messed up. Most are. Does it really help to know all the details?"

I wasn't sure *help* was the right word. Here in Cuba, I almost felt like Mom was with me again. Like I could reach across the gap of decades and get to know her in a way that I hadn't when she'd been alive.

There was a blast of sound down the street. Lights flashed blue. Yolanda jumped with a little cry.

A block over, a police Lada rumbled down the street. A moment and it was out of sight.

"Sorry," Yolanda said. "Walking with foreigners makes me nervous. Sometimes the cops stop you because they think you're a *jinetera*."

I nodded as if I believed that explanation.

"It's around the corner here," Yolanda said.

We turned onto a small, quiet street near the southeast corner of Habana Vieja. Puddles of indeterminate brown liquid collected in potholes of various sizes. The buildings were a dilapidated gray, not a fleck of fresh paint in sight.

"Look, a park." Yolanda pointed at an empty lot at the far intersection. There were some flower beds and a bench, an unexpected sight on a street like this. "There are more and more parks in Havana these days."

"Really," I said.

"When a building falls down, they put a park in."

"Because of the *bloqueo*?" Ana asked. "Because you can't get any building materials?"

"Look at this country. The way things are run. You think if they took the *bloqueo* away tomorrow something would change?" Yolanda shrugged. "Well, maybe some things would. But less than you think. In the meantime, the *bloqueo* is the Castros' best friend. Gives them something to blame." She nodded at the nearest building. "This way."

Yolanda pushed open an unfinished plywood door and we entered a dim, narrow hallway. After Yolanda's tale of collapsed buildings, I gave the ceiling a worried look.

There was a vaguely chemical smell in the air. "The fumigator," Yolanda explained. "They come all the time and you have to leave while they spray, and then the house stinks for days."

Her friend's apartment was on the top floor. The door opened on the second knock. A forty-something white woman met us, a mop in one hand, a lit cigarette in another. She greeted Yolanda with an energetic cheek-kiss, then drew her by the shoulders into the light of her living room. She pulled off Yolanda's hat and studied the bruises on her face with a matter-of-fact clucking of her tongue.

"*Hijos de puta*," she said.

Yolanda pulled away as if embarrassed by the attention. "Guys, this is Lisyani. Lisyani, this is Rick and Ana."

"Nice to meet you," we both said.

We stood in a living room with old floorboards that sagged under every step. The paint on the walls, once a bright green, had faded in uneven patches. There was a ratty brown sofa and some chairs. Near the middle of the room, two upright wooden beams had been rigged to support the ceiling.

Between the beams there stood a plastic bucket with a layer of water in it. As I watched, a heavy drop splashed down from a wet patch on the ceiling.

"The kids wanted to see the real Cuba," Yolanda said.

Lisyani grimaced, gestured at the bucket. "This is it all right. Come, sit down."

Ana and I sank onto the sofa. It gave so much I thought I might fall through. Instead, my downward progress was stopped by a spring poking into my butt. Lisyani sat on the windowsill, which creaked alarmingly. Yolanda leaned against the wall, the only solid structure around.

"Aren't we going shopping for hospital supplies?" Ana asked.

"In a bit," Yolanda said.

"I don't get to chat with foreigners much," Lisyani said. "What do you think of Cuba?"

Ana frowned. I scratched my head.

"Come on." Lisyani took a long drag on her cigarette, blew the smoke out the window. "I'm sure you have an opinion."

Ana looked between Yolanda and Lisyani warily. "We do."

Lisyani smiled. "That's good. That's smart."

"I'm getting a feeling this isn't about hospital supplies," I said.

"A few weeks ago, when we talked about the situation in Cuba, you said you wanted to help," Yolanda said. "What did you mean?"

Ana had made that particular offer, so I let her field the question. She made as if to speak, then stopped. Seemed to consider for a while.

"Cuba is a very different place than I thought," she said. "It's clear the system isn't working. Everything's falling apart. But if you're asking if we oppose the Revolution, then that's not something I—"

"We don't care what you think about the Revolution," Yolanda said. "We care about our friend. About Miranda."

Lisyani cut her off. "I'm not sure—"

"Miranda?" Ana asked. "What's happened to her?"

Lisyani and Yolanda locked stares, as if arguing without words.

"Look," I said, "you're clearly no good at this hush-hush stuff. Tell us what's going on."

Yolanda shrugged at Lisyani. "It's your choice."

"That's the trouble with situations like this," Lisyani said. "Asking questions can't possibly prove something one way or the other. Yolanda, if you trust these kids, I trust you."

Yolanda nodded. Sighed. "This has to be a secret. You can't tell anyone—not Juanita, not Yosvany, not even Benny. You understand?"

We did.

"Okay," Yolanda said. "Yesterday, Miranda got kidnapped. They grabbed her off the street. Pulled her into a car right in front of us."

I stared at her. Miranda . . . that gaunt woman with those piercing eyes, gone. . . .

Unbidden, my hand shot up to my cheek, to the place where the bruises appeared on Yolanda's. "So that's where . . ."

Yolanda nodded. "I tried to fight them off."

"That's horrible," Ana said. "Did you call the police?"

Lisyani laughed, a short, bitter sound. But it was Yolanda who replied. "They were government. They didn't have uniforms or anything, but I recognized the guy in charge. He's MININT."

I took a careful breath. Even I knew about the notorious Ministry of the Interior. It had featured in some of Mom's bogey stories growing up.

So that's why Yolanda had been so jumpy on the street. That's why she'd worn that big hat. She was hiding from Castro's secret police. Perhaps taking the two of us along had been a disguise too.

I suddenly felt guilty for suspecting Benny.

"Was it the blog?" I asked.

"Did she post something big?" Ana asked. "Something counterrevolutionary?"

Lisyani snorted. "Counterrevolutionary. Right. Miranda used to write about gay rights and no one cared, no big deal, not with Mariela Castro fighting the same fight. Recently she started covering living conditions in Havana. The state of our hospitals. The collapsing buildings all across town. Her last post was about how she spent two weeks trying to buy a new sink for her apartment. If complaining about that is counterrevolutionary, you'd better lock the whole country up."

"She's not a household name like Yoani Sánchez," Yolanda said. "That would have given her some protection at least. But she hadn't had the time to build a following yet. Miranda Galvez means nothing to most Cubans. She can disappear and no one will care."

Ana started to say something, stopped, pressed her lips together. At last she said, "That's horrible. But what can we do?"

"When do you leave?" Lisyani asked.

"That's the problem," Yolanda said. "Not for another month."

Lisyani shook her head. "That's too long."

"Come on." Ana leaned forward, intent. "What do you want from us?"

I could pretend I was as eager as she, but the truth was, I

was shaking in my pants—literally. There were little shivers running up and down my body, as if I were out in the arctic cold instead of enveloped by the heat of a Caribbean morning.

"We need to get this out of the country." Lisyani dug about in her pocket, took out a little silvery USB stick. "It's a video I took of the kidnapping. The world needs to know Miranda was kidnapped by her own government. But it can't wait a month."

"Oh," Ana said.

I stared at that flash drive, my mouth dry.

"I thought maybe . . . ," Yolanda said. "I mean, I don't have any other *yuma* friends in town right now."

Lisyani bit her lip. "We might have to take a risk, approach someone—"

"I can do it," I said.

They all stared at me.

My legs were fighting to do the polka against my will.

"You don't understand," Lisyani said. "Who knows what will happen with Miranda in a month."

"I'll do it today," I said. "I'll upload it from my laptop."

"*Olvídalo*," Yolanda said. "The government watches everything you do online."

"You're forgetting who you're talking to," I said. "I'm Rick Gutiérrez."

Lisyani and Yolanda looked at me blankly.

"The Cat King of Havana?" Ana suggested.

I grinned. "Exactly. This is a challenge worthy of my talents."

"You mustn't do anything that could get you caught," Yolanda said.

"I don't think Cat Kings get diplomatic immunity," Ana said.

"But is this the right thing to do?" I asked her.

Ana considered for a long while. At last she nodded, a curt motion. And I saw that she believed I could pull it off.

That was almost enough to calm my chattering teeth.

Almost.

⁓

In a spy movie, a storm might have rolled in over Havana that afternoon. I might have taped my laptop to my body and put on a black trench coat over it. Ana might have said good-bye to me at the door, whispered "be careful" and given me a soft, ever so brief kiss on the lips. It might have left me with the aftertaste of peaches, that kiss.

I might have stridden down the cloud-darkened Havana streets, fighting my way against the gusts of the storm. A car might have backfired and made me jump. I might have watched every doorway for the shadow of a man and the glint of a gun. The mournful cry of a dog in the distance might have filled my soul with an existential longing for that day, long in the future, when I could lay down the heavy burden placed on my shoulders and come in from the cold.

It seemed, however, that we didn't live in a spy movie. We got delayed at the apartment because Juanita had fried up some banana chips—"You're not running off again without a proper lunch in your belly." Ana insisted she'd come along—"to make sure you don't do anything stupid." Yolanda had me put on khaki shorts and a backpack, and draped her prized DSLR camera around my neck—"so you look as *yuma* as possible."

So attired we descended onto the mean streets of Havana. The trip to the Hotel Parque Central—the closest place with Wi-Fi—featured some fifteen offers of taxis, cigars, and restaurants. Every time I started to worry about the video file sitting on my hard drive, another cheerful, "Hi, friends, friends, where are you from? *Sprechen Sie Deutsch?*" reminded me we looked a lot more like cash cows than secret operatives. At the corner of Neptuno and Galiano we passed a pair of cops, but they looked past us, smoking and chatting idly.

"It makes Havana look different, doesn't it," Ana said. "Knowing the things that go on."

"My mom said it was like this," I said. "She said you're always afraid, even if only a little. You can't quite trust any-one, not all the way. It was just words to me back then."

"In a way, I'm relieved it was those guys who hurt Yolanda," Ana said. "I know it sounds bad, but if it had been—"

"Yeah," I said. "I know."

There was a difference between getting attacked by an oppressive government and getting attacked by someone you loved.

Back at the apartment, we'd watched Lisyani's video in Ana's room with the door closed, just us three. The clip was shaky handheld footage. It showed three burly men wrestling with Miranda while Yolanda beat at them with her fists. Yolanda's face never showed clearly in the grainy video, but I recognized her stocky form. At last they shoved her to the ground and wrestled her friend into a Lada. The car sped off. Yolanda ran after it for a few futile steps, then slowed to a halt.

"I'd never felt so helpless," Yolanda had said to us. "One moment Miranda was right there, and then they took her, and I couldn't do a thing. It was like those guys didn't notice I was there. I don't think they even cared who I was. I mean, there's no way they did, or there'd be trouble by now, for Juanita and for me."

The Hotel Parque Central was a posh, recently renovated place. There was a spacious lobby inside, an open courtyard under a pyramid-shaped glass roof. It featured a long, well-appointed bar and restaurant; elsewhere in the lobby palm trees overlooked scattered tables. Everything looked new and clean and expensive, from the classical white columns rounding the courtyard to the wicker armchairs and the tiled marble floor.

The air here rang with foreign tongues. Every Cuban face belonged to someone in an employee's uniform. It made me wonder what it must feel like, living someplace like Lisyani's apartment and working here—serving *yumas* who treated this like nothing extraordinary.

We climbed to a second floor section that overlooked the lobby and found a comfortable couch. Nobody was close enough to eavesdrop or look over my shoulder. Ana went to buy a Wi-Fi card—these guys charged a princely five CUC an hour for dial-up speeds. I fired up my laptop and prepared the file.

I'd compressed the video so the one minute of footage only occupied a few megabytes. I'd written up a text document with instructions for publishing the video. Then I'd encrypted both files with Serpent-Twofish-AES, a jumbo pack that even the NSA should take a while to crack.

You might wonder—how do I know all this stuff about encryption? If so, you've never faced the wrath of a cat fancier. Calling a cat flop-eared shouldn't be a capital offense, should it? Didn't stop love_my_leo_73 from sending me death threats. That's when I looked into securing my data. I didn't want no crazy showing up at my door with foot-long grooming shears and a Cheshire grin.

Which is to say, encrypting the video wasn't a problem. But I needed to send the file to someone who could open it and publish it. Someone who would know the password without me having to tell them.

I explained this quietly to Ana while I got online.

"Do you know someone you can trust?" she asked.

"I know Lettuce Igorov," I said.

I'd texted him before we left for the hotel, told him to get to a computer. Now I logged into Gmail and messaged him. *Hey, dude.*

Five seconds later, there came the response. *Riiiick!!! Wazzupp???*

I blinked to clear my stinging eyes—my body's defense mechanism against a message like that. *Oh, the usual. Sun, sand, and girls, you know.*

It's more like Xbox, chicken wings, and vaseline over here.

Ana says hi, I wrote. *Because, you know, she's here. Next to me.*

Ana poked me in the ribs.

It's strictly for medicinal purposes, Lettuce wrote.

What's for medicinal purposes?

Hey, did I tell you about the BlueNuts? We're going on tour.

Ana says she doesn't want to hear about your blue nuts.

This time Ana punched me in the ribs. While I was wheezing, she took over the keyboard. *Ana here. Tell me all about your nuts.*

Ask Rick, Lettuce replied. *He knows. He's the captain of my fan club.*

I'll merge it with the cat site, I wrote. *You get a built-in audience, but you'll need to adjust your style. A lot more meowing.*

You can give me voice lessons, Lettuce said.

At which point I figured any government spook who had managed to get past Gmail's encryption would decide to stop wasting his time.

I looked up from the laptop. No one was watching us. A hotel security guy stood at the railing overlooking the courtyard, some thirty feet away. Everything seemed quiet.

My stomach gave a lurch.

Hey, listen, I typed, *we need a favor.*

What kind?

It's a surprise for someone. Which was, in a way, true. *Like that time we organized a birthday party for Rob Kenna and invited all those cheerleaders, remember?*

A long pause. *Sure.*

Good. He didn't ask what the hell I was talking about—so he must be getting it. *I'll email you a self-extracting archive with instructions. You'll need a password to open it.*

Okay.

The password is Rob Kenna's special name.

What? After a moment, *Oh. All right.*

"Who's Rob Kenna?" Ana asked. "And what's his special name?"

"I'll tell you later." I looked around meaningfully.

Ana nodded.

In truth, it wasn't just that I didn't want to risk being overheard. It was that some levels of profanity aren't fit for conversation with a girl you like—or fit for print either. Rob Kenna's special name involves poodles, pigs, and the creative use of human anatomy. Lettuce and I knew the name well because in tenth grade we'd spent a month playing a game called Name the Kenna. I'd won by a landslide.

I sent Lettuce the file. The lazy connection struggled with it, the progress indicator crawling along. But then it was done.

Got it, came Lettuce's reply. Five minutes later, *Dude.*

Yeah, I wrote.

No, dude.

I know, I know, I wrote. *It's a big favor.*

No, man, this is, like, an honor, Lettuce wrote. *Leave it to me.*

At which point Ana tugged at my elbow. A large man was coming toward us. He wore the dark suit of hotel security.

My heart raced. I minimized the chat window, fired up Facebook.

The man stopped at the foot of our couch. He was beefy and light-skinned, and wore a professional-looking, empty smile. "Good afternoon," he said in English.

"Hi," we said, both of us stupidly cheerful.

The man leaned toward us. His smile faded. His eyes shot from side to side, scanning the room.

Ana's hand found mine, squeezed it tight.

"You want marijuana? I can get you some. Cheap, cheap, okay?"

I sagged back on the seat. Sighed. Ana let loose a little laugh.

The man frowned.

"No, thanks," I said. "I mean, we're not in the mood."

Ana nodded. "Thank you for the offer."

"I have cigars," the man said hopefully. Then, looking at me, "*Chicas?*"

"No."

The man shrugged. Turned. Sauntered off.

"What a fancy place," Ana muttered.

I opened the chat window. There was a message from Lettuce waiting. *Working on it now,* it said—nothing more.

I deleted the video from my hard drive and overwrote it with random data to keep anyone from recovering it. Then we walked home, taking the scenic route. We strolled down leafy Prado and stopped to admire street art, two tourists out sightseeing.

"Do you think it will work?" Ana asked.

I shrugged. I'd told Lettuce to upload the video to You-Tube from an anonymous account, using Tor to cover his tracks, and then to post the link to every major Cuba-related blog. "It's the internet. One day it's all truth and justice. The next some dude posts a GIF of bacon taped to a cat, and, well, forget about it."

"Your competition?" Ana asked.

"I launched a cat-with-food campaign after that post went big. I made a bundle." I grinned. "You should leverage your competition, not fight it."

"You know, Rick, I used to think you were this hopeless nerd."

"And now?"

"Well, I don't think you're hopeless," Ana said.

That might have been a tinge of admiration in her voice.

When we got home, Yosvany pulled me into our room and shut the door. He looked tired but charged up, like he'd been running around doing something exciting.

"So?" he asked. "Are you ready for the big night?"

I had to think for a bit before I understood. It had been a long day.

When I did understand, there was no doubt. Not after what Ana had said to me earlier.

"Let's do it," I said.

A hopeless nerd would have chickened out. I wasn't that, not anymore.

chapter fifteen

ALL THE WAY

"If you want to go all the way with a girl, you've got to warm her up first." Yosvany perched on the edge of his bed and watched me seriously. "*No puedes meterle dedo si la jarra está cerrada, entiendes.*"

"Enough with the *dedo completo*," I said. "Pick a different metaphor."

"To drink wine you must first ease out the cork."

On a different day, I might have protested the comparison. But I needed a plan, and Yosvany had one.

☙

"Dress up, guys," I said to Ana and Yosvany after dinner. "We're going somewhere nice tonight. I've got a surprise for you."

Ana looked suspicious, but Yosvany came in on cue. "I like surprises!" Which seemed to cut off any protest she might have made.

Yosvany had predicted this. "If it's the three of us, she won't see it coming."

We dressed up. In my case, this meant pulling a rumpled dress shirt from my suitcase and running a comb through my hair. Yosvany found a pair of jeans somewhere that didn't sag below his underwear. Ana emerged from her room in a knee-length dress, intensely blue, sleek and asymmetrically cut, an angled line of buttons down the front.

By dint of much effort, I managed to keep my gaping to a minimum.

Yosvany whistled. "*Coño*, girl, don't give me a heart attack!"

I expected her to snap something witty at him, but she only smiled. "Let's go."

"Have fun," Juanita told us at the door. She winked at me. "Good luck."

"Good luck?" Ana asked in the elevator. "What did she mean?"

"She got stuck in the elevator yesterday," Yosvany said. "But I think they fixed it."

It was a comfortable evening for early August, with gusting breezes that converted the suffocating heat into a mere annoyance. We caught a *máquina* to Vedado, an enormous yellow Chevy with two rows of passenger seats, the three of us clumped together behind the driver. The *almendrón* creaked and groaned down Neptuno in the gloom of dim streetlights, passing scores of Cubans flagging down a ride.

I checked my watch. Eight forty. Twenty minutes to go.

The driver pulled over to the curb and put the car into park.

We couldn't possibly be picking someone up. The car was full.

The driver yanked his shiny new MP3 player from the rusted dashboard (in Havana, even the most decrepit old jalopy seemed to have one installed). In the sudden, ear-buzzing silence, he said, "Be right back." He jumped out of the car and disappeared into the nearest apartment building.

I stared after him, perplexed. Ana asked, "The hell?"

Everyone else in the car sat there as if nothing surprising had happened. Some chatted among themselves in low, unworried voices. Others poked at their cell phones. I cast a questioning look at Yosvany but he only raised his hands: What can you do?

A minute passed. Two. Five. The car's engine rumbled on, low, even.

I checked my watch. Hesitated. Leaned forward over the driver's seat and honked the horn, one long, mournful blast.

Nothing happened.

Another five minutes.

"Let's get another car," I said.

"No way." Yosvany gestured vaguely at the street. "It's too

busy tonight, and there's three of us."

"What's that guy doing in there?" Ana asked.

"Saving someone's life? Having dinner? Giving his girl-friend the ride of her life?" Yosvany shrugged. "Nothing unusual."

"In Cuba you're always waiting for something," Ana said.

"Go shopping with my mom sometime," Yosvany said. "You'll find out what waiting means."

At this point the building door clanged open and the driver strolled out. He got into the car without a word and went about plugging in his MP3 player.

"What were you doing, taking a dump?" Yosvany asked.

"I had to run up and down five stories," the driver replied. "Takes time."

At least we got moving again.

I bit my lip harder with every passing minute. We got to the Habana Libre high-rise at five past nine. "Come on," I said as we clambered out of the car. "We're late."

Yosvany's phone rang as if on cue. Okay, it actually did ring on cue, but Ana didn't know this.

"Yeah?" he answered. "Yeah, really? No. No, I can't. Listen, man, no—" He was silent for a while, as if listening to someone on the other end.

Knowing there wasn't anyone to listen to, I was impressed with the play of emotions on his face—annoyed, then worried, then resigned.

"Okay," he said at last. "Okay, *cabrón*, fine. I'll be right there." He put away his phone, looked at us, and sighed. "I'll have to miss the surprise. Sorry, Rick."

"What's wrong?" Ana asked. "Can we help?"

Yosvany shook his head. "The drummer for my friend's band just passed out drunk. They're playing in half an hour, so I'd better get on it. You go ahead."

"I hope his show goes well," Ana said as we entered the glitzy hotel lobby. "I can't imagine having to show up and play a concert with no warning."

"I'm sure he'll do great." If I didn't sound too worried, it was because Yosvany's plan for the evening involved a party in Centro Habana with his school friends and a bottle of Havana Club that I'd paid for. "We're taking the elevator."

We rode all the way to the top. "What's this about anyway?" Ana asked.

I shook my head, all Mr. Mystery.

The elevator opened on a dimly lit hallway. A short woman in a hotel uniform, clipboard in hand, blocked our way. She took us in. After a moment's hesitation, she smiled and spoke to us in English. "I'm sorry. The Turquino is closed for tourists tonight."

"It's all right," I said in Spanish. "We should be on the list. Rick Gutiérrez and guest?"

The woman watched me with narrowed eyes. "This event is for selected workers of the central—"

"Please," I said. "Check your list."

She did. A moment later, her eyebrows rose. She bit her lip. "This isn't salsa or reggaeton, you know."

"We know," I said.

The woman shrugged. "Okay."

Ana gave me a questioning glance. I pretended not to notice. Juanita had called some of her Party friends to get us on the list, but this wasn't the time to explain.

We pushed through large double doors into the Turquino. The dim expanse of a nightclub greeted us. There was a central bar and a well-lit stage at the far end. The rest of the space was small tables scattered across a dark floor.

The darkness wasn't a defect here, though. It was there to showcase Havana, twenty-five stories below.

Floor-to-ceiling windows looked out over a landscape that shimmered in yellow and black. A flat city, except for a strip of high-rises along the coast like a breakwater, a concrete mountain range, guarding Havana from the dark sea beyond. The city too was dark in places. Many patches of shadow hid amidst the brightness, where only isolated streetlights glowed like individual pearls sown on black fabric.

Too much shadow for a living city, it seemed—but then I was used to New York.

"Nice," Ana said. "Was this the surprise?"

I looked at the stage. Still empty.

"Not quite."

I supposed it had been silly to worry about being ten minutes late. This was Cuba.

A waiter seated us at a small table in one corner. We ordered sodas.

The people at the tables around us were Cubans, couples

in their fifties and sixties, the men in button-down shirts and pressed slacks, the women in fine dresses and high heels. Only a few brown faces, a drastic contrast to the usual mix in the dance scene. (This was one of the topics Miranda had blogged about, actually—how white the ranks of government functionaries looked in Cuba, compared to the population at large.)

Then a man with a guitar walked onstage. He sat down on a wooden stool, his guitar on his knees. He was an older white man, much like many in the audience, bald on top and wearing glasses. I would have passed him in the street without a second glance.

Silence fell on the Turquino, complete and total. Nobody seemed to breathe. Even the waiters and the bartenders watched the man with a stillness so perfect it seemed rehearsed.

My skin tingled cold. Beside me, Ana leaned forward.

The man's fingers caressed the strings of his guitar. Low mournful notes sang out into the silence. Graceful arpeggios, a simple melody, faint and haunting.

"No way," Ana whispered, recognizing the music—and the man.

Silvio Rodríguez sang. Of memory and butterflies he sang, of white wings fluttering in the dark, of visitors that would never come again, and of the souls of lost soldiers. His voice was as sweet and bright and rough and dark as the cries of his guitar. We listened to him and a blue unicorn wandered through the shadows around us, a blue unicorn that he'd lost and that he missed, and that we missed together with him. He sang about love and about war, about justice and about lies, and we listened, and in the end I wasn't sure if we'd been listening for ten minutes or an hour, wasn't sure if I'd applauded or not, wasn't sure of anything at all except that there was silence and before there hadn't been.

∾

"Once you get her emotional, take her for a walk," Yosvany had told me. "Compliment her. Tell her she's special. Make her feel like there's no one as beautiful and amazing as her in the world."

∾

Ana got emotional all right. The problem was, so did I. We walked down Twenty-Third to the Malecón and hardly spoke a word, either one of us. I was sure she could still hear the strains of Silvio Rodríguez's guitar inside her head the way I could.

We sat on the concrete lip of the Malecón and watched the crashing waves for a while. "I'd never seen an audience as focused as that," I said. "Not even at Carnegie Hall, and you know what those people are like."

"I don't, actually," Ana said. "But yeah. I think his songs meant a lot more to the locals than to us. For them it was like, I don't know, Bob Dylan playing a gig in your living room." She was quiet for a while. "My stepdad used to listen to Silvio, late at night with the lights out. I'd sit with him in the living room and we'd listen to song after song in the dark. Just now, at the concert, I closed my eyes . . . I could almost feel him beside me."

"I remembered that you asked for Silvio's music at Yosvany's uncle's *paladar*," I said, though of course it had been Yosvany who had remembered. "I figured you'd enjoy the concert."

"I used to love those songs so much," Ana said. "Now, though . . . I mean, it was a beautiful concert. I loved it. But I kept wondering—does Silvio mean all the stuff he sings? Does he really love this Revolution? Does he love what he sees on the street when he walks around Havana? Does he know what happens to people like Miranda?"

"So you no longer support the Revolution," I said.

"The Revolution was necessary," Ana said. "Batista was a shithead and Cuba was a mess."

"But?"

Ana sighed. "I'm no economist, but it's pretty obvious communism doesn't work. I mean, I knew about the Soviet Union and Cambodia and stuff, but I hoped Cuba was different."

"I'm no economist either, but I've learned a few things as Cat Guru of the Intertubes," I said. "When you're kidnapping people for being wrong on the internet, you've lost it."

Ana nodded. We sat in companionable silence for a while.

There came a rumble. A bright red convertible jalopy pulled up to the curb. Yosvany's friend Luis sat at the wheel looking stylish, almost macho in a tight-fitting white suit, a gold chain around his neck.

"What's up, guys?" he called. "You want a ride?"

Ana stared at him.

I realized I'd spent ten valuable minutes discussing communism with the girl I was supposed to woo.

Too late to back out.

"Tonight, the surprises keep on coming," I said.

Ana studied me through narrowed eyes. "I'm not sure I can handle any more."

But she got into the car.

⁊

"Your final goal is to overwhelm her," Yosvany had told me. "Shock her, wow her, give her an evening like she's never had. You do that, she's yours."

⁊

I was behind schedule.

Compliment her, I thought, as the car sped along the Malecón. A fine mist of water sprayed across us from a crashing wave. I searched inside me for brilliant, witty things to say, but the only thing I found inside me was my churning stomach.

"I remember you from the Van Van concert," Ana told Luis over the roar of the engine. "We should dance again sometime."

Luis smiled in the rearview mirror and gave her a thumbs-up. He pressed a button on the MP3 player in the dashboard.

197

Lively old son poured forth. Coincidentally, it drowned out anything else Ana might have tried to say to Luis.

Luis winked at me in the mirror. This guy knew what was up.

"Okay, this is getting weird." Ana watched the road ahead as she said this, didn't look at me. We passed the lit-up building of the Milocho on our right, going into the tunnel to Miramar.

"Uh," I said. "Ah." Then, deciding that wasn't enough, I added, "Um."

"What's this about?" she asked. "Don't tell me Luis just happened to be driving by."

"I wouldn't have come to Cuba if not for you." The words surprised me coming out, but I kept talking. It was easier while the darkness of the tunnel hid my face. "I mean, not this summer. You inspired me. When I saw you dance, how much you loved it . . . and then the way you helped me with the show for school, when you didn't have to . . . I realized you were a real friend. I knew that we'd have a great time if we went together."

Ana was quiet for a moment. We entered Miramar. In the yellow light of a streetlamp I saw her looking at me, thoughtful, maybe a little surprised.

"I wanted to say thanks tonight," I said smoothly, feeling satisfyingly devious. "Show you I really appreciate you being here with me."

Ana smiled then. "Thanks, Rick. I'm happy I came."

At some point we left the main road and wound through side streets populated by smaller family houses and tidy little gardens, uncommonly well-maintained for Havana. At last we pulled up before a low boxy building with tan brick walls, no windows and a single metal door—the kind of place that might have been a run-down bar in some forlorn corner of Brooklyn.

Luis put the car into park but kept the engine running, left the music on, only gestured grandly at the building.

Ana studied it for a moment. "Do I dare ask?"

I got out of the car, silent per Yosvany's advice, and went around to open her door. She slid out beside me.

I led her to the building's simple metal door. Held my breath as I pulled on the handle.

The door slid open with a creak. Inside, all was dark, pitch-black. I beckoned for Ana to enter.

"Okay," she said, "if someone jumps out at me, you're eating my fist."

But she went in. I followed her into the dark. The fresh, sweet smell of growing things enveloped us.

I closed the door behind us.

Perfect blackness. Not a sound, except for the two of us breathing.

Faint strains of fear rushed through me, but I suppressed them. I knocked on the door behind me—three sharp, loud bangs.

The lights came on.

For a long time Ana stood there beside me, staring about her. As did I, startled even though I'd known what to expect.

Flowers. Kaleidoscopic color, like a Photoshop palette made real. Vases wall-to-wall, on tables and stools and shelves and the floor. Enough flowers to blanket a New York intersection.

"Pick one." My heart gave a jump, painful in my chest. "Any one. It's yours."

Ana took a step forward, slow, hesitant, then another. She walked the aisles between the metal tables, wove her way around the vases on the floor, with their cargo of orchids and tall roses and a hundred other flowers that I couldn't have named at gunpoint. Here she paused to sniff a long-stemmed lily (or was that a daffodil?), ran her fingers over a bright yellow bud that looked like an upturned church bell.

Then she looked away from the flowers. Came walking back to me, calm and sure.

I felt blood rush to my face.

"This was Yosvany, wasn't it," she said.

My mouth popped open. No sound came out. No air went in.

You've got to lie to women, Yosvany had told me. The more lies, the better.

I gathered my strength to do that.

"How did you know?" I croaked out.

Ana's shoulders sagged. She turned away from me. Looked at the flowers once again. "You promised me you wouldn't do this," she said. "Not this summer."

I could only stand there.

"Don't you understand how it feels?" With every word Ana spoke, there was more force in her voice, something hidden boiling to the surface. "Every day you watch me, every day you're waiting for something from me. I came to Cuba to get away from everything, not to deal with . . . this."

"I only . . ." I cast about for words. "I thought maybe if I showed you how much I—"

"Rick, you're a friend." Ana looked at me earnestly. "Back in New York I thought . . . I thought there could be more, maybe. But these past few weeks, well, I've realized I don't really like you that way."

"Oh," I said.

Something inside me deflated. It was hope departing me like a turbulent fart. Not unlike the sensation of getting dumped, except worse—because there hadn't been anything between us to start with.

"Let's forget this, okay?" Ana asked. "We've got a few more weeks in Cuba. Let's dance. Let's have fun. How does that sound?"

I could have told her how it tasted. Like a mouthful of wet ash.

chapter sixteen

BED OF NAILS

On the way back, Ana told me her plans for finishing her film. At least, I think that's what she was talking about. She told me things and I sat there not listening, shrunk into the corner of the seat. I suspect she needed to talk as much as I needed to pretend I didn't exist.

People talk about heartbreak like it's this poetic thing, but there was an actual, physical ache in my chest. Like Ana had reached down my throat and squeezed until something went squish.

Except none of this was her fault. I knew that.

It was mine.

For pressing on when she'd said no.

For believing I could change her mind.

I'd imagined a hundred shared futures when she'd never even hinted at one.

I'd built a castle in the air. She had only let it fall to earth.

When we got back, Ana took the elevator up. I took the stairs. My thighs burned from the exertion. I didn't care.

On our floor, I passed Rafaela leaving her apartment. She started when she noticed me and waved me over. "Come here for a moment."

I nearly told her to leave me alone, but caught myself. Acting like an asshole wouldn't make me feel any better. "Hi, Rafaela."

"I've got news for you. I found Ricardo."

I looked at her without comprehension.

"Ricardo Eugenio. Your mother's friend."

"Oh."

Rafaela smacked her lips, perhaps disappointed at my reaction. "He's in Trinidad. Your mother's birthplace."

"That's great."

"I thought you'd want to know."

"I do," I assured her. "Thank you."

She nodded. "I can get you his address if you like. I'm not sure he has a phone number."

"That would be wonderful," I said. But really, it didn't seem very important.

I got away from Rafaela and went inside. Yosvany wasn't back yet. Thankfully, Juanita and Yolanda were asleep already, and Ana had disappeared into her room. I ate a wilted banana and went straight to bed.

Or rather, I went to Yosvany's room and lay on the sofa and stared at the ceiling. It's amazing, how fascinating every crack in the ceiling becomes in such situations.

Sometime long into the night, Yosvany came back. He smelled of rum but walked with sure, easy steps and sat on his bed with controlled grace.

"Well?" he asked. "How did it go?"

So I told him. It took an effort to talk, but once I did the words poured forth as from an unplugged toilet.

"I don't understand where I went wrong," I said in the end.

"I'm sorry, *primo*," he said. "But hey, at least now you know."

I couldn't believe how lightly he said that. "I guess."

"Don't worry," he said. "We'll find a girl for you. *Una jebita de pinga pa' kimbartela.*"

That's not it, I wanted to tell him. I didn't want someone to sleep with. I wanted someone special. But I could imagine him laughing to hear that. So I kept quiet.

Long after Yosvany fell asleep I kept quiet—held back all the things I wanted to say and shout and cry, until I'd become a turducken of misery. With that image firmly in mind, I finally fell asleep.

৵

I might easily have spent Sunday wallowing in entirely reasonable self-pity. I had a few seasons of *Person of Interest* on my laptop. That cure had helped with Rachel Snow, after all.

And indeed, for five brainless hours I made a good start on the project. But when I emerged in search of lunch—well after four in the afternoon—I found Yolanda in the kitchen. She stood at the window, staring out across Havana to the Morro.

I didn't recognize her at first. Gone was her long, smooth hair—she'd buzzed her head near bare, leaving a stylish bit of dark fuzz. She looked younger, a punk college kid, and she wore clothes to match. Ripped jeans, a bright yellow T-shirt.

When she turned to me, I flinched inwardly, expecting to see knowledge in her eyes, and maybe amusement—surely she'd heard of yesterday's disaster by now. But all I saw on her face was worry.

"Well?" she asked. "Do you think they'll recognize me?"

"Uh . . . who?"

"Those guys." She waved her hand impatiently. "The ones who took Miranda."

Oh. "I don't think so."

"Good." She went to the table, put her hand on the back of one wooden chair, squeezed. "Good. I haven't even talked to her family. I can't risk it. Those poor people—imagine what they're going through."

I felt very small, with my girl problems. "I'll go check my mail," I said. "See if the video has gotten any reaction."

"I'll come with you," Yolanda said.

I was glad for the company. We walked over to the Hotel Parque Central and talked all the way. Ana's name didn't come up even once. We settled in the same upstairs corner as before and got online.

I had an email from Lettuce. It said, *Check out this cool new cat video!* Attached was a self-extracting archive that asked for a password. After I put in Kenna's special name, a series of GIF images extracted to my desktop.

Screenshots.

A snapshot of a YouTube video. 4,357 views. Thirteen comments.

A prominent political blog, with a link to the video and a brief article about Miranda Galvez's abduction. Sixteen comments.

Reddit. Not front page but a top-rated post on /r/Politics. 120 comments.

Yolanda looked from image to image with avid interest. "What does this mean?"

"The word is getting out," I said. "Thousands of people have watched the video."

"Oh, great." Yolanda took my hand, squeezed it. "Great, great. Thank you, cousin."

"I can't promise this will achieve anything," I said. "You can post a video about the right way to peel a banana and it will get five thousand hits."

Still, it warmed me, hearing Yolanda's excitement. Made me feel like maybe this whole trip wasn't a failure after all.

When we got back, Ana and Yosvany were watching the TV in the living room. I said hi as if nothing had happened. "What are you guys up to?"

"They're playing an old Fidel speech," Yosvany said.

"It's been twenty minutes about oppression of the poor around the world, all big words and drama, not a single policy proposal." Ana gestured at the screen, where Fidel had at that moment raised an admonitory grayscale finger. "Let's go dancing. It's the Milocho today, isn't it?"

The prospect of dancing sounded about as enticing as napping on a bed of nails. "Sure! Let's go dancing," I said.

⌒

In the *máquina* to the club, Yosvany and Ana talked nonstop. He was setting up interviews for her with a few small-time salsa bands around town. "It'll give you a different perspective for the film," he said. "A musician's perspective. It's different watching the dance floor from the stage, seeing how people react to what you're playing."

"Awesome," Ana said. "Isn't this awesome, Rick?"

"Sure." I sat in the corner of the car, pretending I was reading something on my phone. "Yosvany's the best."

The Milocho was hopping when we arrived. On stage, the resident dance troupe was leading the crowd in a zumba-like routine set to a bombastic, reggaetonized Charanga Habanera piece—shoulders twitching, torsos swaying, hips thrusting. A sea of *yumas* crowded the floor.

Yosvany led us through the maze of packed tables around the floor. At every other table, someone got up to greet him, talk to him, clap him on the back, like he was a movie star at Comic-Con. I wondered what it was about him that made everyone want to be his friend. Even I couldn't bring myself to dislike him—despite all the crap he talked, despite the way Ana looked at him sometimes.

"Oh, hey," Ana said. "Pablo."

There he was, getting up from his table with a grin on his face. "My favorite students!"

If we were his favorite students, I shuddered to imagine how he treated his least favorites. Just Friday Pablo had called me a dancing kangaroo, and he hadn't been kidding.

Then Pablo's companion got up from the table, a short, portly white man in his sixties. "I'm Rodrigo. Please, sit with us."

"Rodrigo runs a big dance school for tourists in Habana Vieja," Pablo explained. "We're thinking about working together."

"Just considering some possibilities," Rodrigo said. "It's still early."

So that's why the enthusiasm. Pablo was trying to get a job.

"Pablo's the best," Yosvany spoke up. "I've seen him work and, man, he gets results. Like, take my cousin here. When he got here, the way he danced, *en candela*. I mean, I wanted to poke my eyes out."

"Thanks, Yosvany," I said.

"But now," Yosvany said, "he actually dances. And it's only been a month."

"Really." Rodrigo looked at me with interest. "So you're good?"

"Uh . . . *me defiendo.*" I shrugged. "Pablo taught us a lot."

"Pablo's amazing," Ana agreed, though I could almost hear her thinking *when he's sober.*

"I try my best," Pablo said, all humility.

At that moment the music faded out. This guy with a mohawk took the mic onstage. "Iiiit's salsa time! The famous! Milocho! Dance! Contest! It's now or never, ladies and gentlemen! Show us what you've got!"

"Excellent timing," Rodrigo said. "Do an old guy a favor, kids. Go dance in the contest. I'd love to see Pablo's students in action."

Pablo looked as though he'd woken up in the middle of the night to find a Xenomorph looming over him. "Unfortunately Rick injured his foot the other day," he said.

"Oh, it's fine," I said, staring right at him. "I'm feeling much better already."

Ana looked at me as though I needed to get my head examined. Then she shrugged. "Sure."

"Good luck," Yosvany muttered.

A few days ago, I would have shaken with cold fear. Tonight, I didn't care. I didn't need to impress Ana anymore. And, well, there's only so much knocking your knees can do in any twenty-four-hour period.

We walked out onto the floor. A scattering of applause met us. "Marvelous!" said the mohawk emcee. "Whooooo's next? Let's see a few more couples!"

I looked around, searching the crowd for who might

compete against us. But no one stirred.

"Come on, guys!" the emcee cried. "The winner gets Havana Club! The ultimate in Cuban rum!"

Two other couples emerged. The first was a lanky Asian guy and a white European-looking woman. I could tell from the way they moved that they weren't very good. But the second couple was Cuban and they were dancers. A muscle-bound black guy who moved lightly on legs like tree trunks, and a pale willowy woman who didn't merely walk onto the floor, but spun into place beside her partner. She was all in white. An *Iyabó*, a Santería initiate, like Pablo's daughter.

Watching the way she moved, I was sure we'd already lost the competition.

"Good, good," the emcee called. "We're ready. DJ, music, please."

With a triple blast of drums and horns, the music sounded. The song was "Agua Pa' Yemaya," a joyful anthem by Elio Revé. I could dance to this.

And we did. We came together with playful rumba steps, my hand in the air, waving a stylized hello. I took hold of Ana and spun her about, and rocked side to side with her, letting the music flow through us. Then some quick footwork, and we snapped into salsa with a sharp *dile-que-no.*

We didn't go for fancy patterns, arms flying all over the place. We didn't stress out over impressive spins or advanced body rolls. The song was dedicated to Yemaya, one of the Ori-shas worshipped by santeros. Pablo had taught us a couple of the traditional dance steps associated with Yemaya, but it felt wrong to try and force them in—not with a santera dancing against us.

Instead we danced simple casino all across the floor, weaving our way in and out among the other couples. Despite the upbeat music the dance felt almost leisurely, like we were alone on the floor, Ana and I—dancing and grinning at each other and singing along with the vocalist.

Abruptly, the song cut off. We kept going on inertia for another step, then halted.

The crowd applauded. Yosvany cried, "Agua!"

I looked at the stage. The emcee stood in a circle with the dancers from the house group.

"What a great show!" he pronounced. "Thank you, dancers. Let's hear what the jury has to say." He turned to talk to the others.

Ana squeezed my hand. "This was nice."

"Yeah," I said, that grin still on my face.

"Okay," the emcee said. "The jury wants to see another dance from two couples. This couple"—he pointed at the Cuban pair—"and the young couple over there!"

Ana and I exchanged a startled look. Another dance? My energy had already slumped.

"Each couple will get two minutes. You pick your own music. Who goes first?"

The Cuban couple looked to us questioningly. I gestured for them to go ahead. I needed to get my breath back.

A moment later, they started. The track was "La Suerte," a super-fast Charanga Habanera piece—macho lyrics, rumba fused with energetic salsa. The dancers launched into it with blistering footwork and lightning-fast turns. One intricate pattern followed another in quick succession.

"I think we're going to have a tough time," Ana said.

Just then the guy picked up his partner, spun her around his body, and then tossed her back over his head. She flew backward with her legs in a split, scissored them in and out with a flourish, landed in a deep crouch.

The crowd applauded. The music faded out.

"Well, that's that," I said.

"Come on," Ana said, tugging me forward. "Let's have fun."

There was no chance we could compete with the other couple in flashiness. I told the emcee to play Havana D'Primera's "Plato de Segunda Mesa," a tune of failed love.

I felt pretty sure I could express the appropriate emotions.

With the first roll of drums, I took Ana in the closed hold, my arm around her. We turned across the floor—cut a simple spiral path from one end to the other, as if we were doing the waltz. When the instruments hushed and Alexander Abreu's rough-edged voice entered with melancholy words, I spun her out so we ended side to side, shoulder to shoulder, my arm draped across her back.

We walked across the floor to the beat of the music, as if strolling arm in arm on a summer afternoon, easy and unconcerned. I turned Ana again and hooked my elbow over hers, and spun her under my arm to a flourish in the music, a simple accent. Then we danced simply again, in an open hold, gliding across the floor connected by a few fingers, our bodies like two wings of a butterfly now opening, now closing.

At last I drew her close and we spun about each other, smiling at each other, marking the cadence of the music with our feet.

The music faded. Applause rolled over us. Here and there a few voices cheered.

Ana and I hugged. For the moment, I didn't care what had happened between us the night before.

"Thank you, dancers," the emcee said. "Let's hear from the jury!"

"I think we can go sit down," I told Ana.

"Hold on," she said. "It might look like we're sore losers."

The Cuban couple joined us on the floor. They talked among themselves, smiling, laughing.

The emcee took a longer time with the jury than I expected. Then he turned back to us with a mysterious air.

"We saw some great dances tonight," he said in a stage hush. "This couple"—he pointed at the Cubans—"has excellent technique. They put on a great show." The audience applauded, as did I, making sure I had a smile on my face.

"However!" he exclaimed, and raised his finger like Fidel about to denounce imperialist Yankees. "You're not competing in acrobatics. Casino is a social dance! It's about partnership!

About music! About fun! That's why . . ."—his voice rose in a dramatic crescendo—". . . the winner of tonight's contest iiiiiis . . ."—he paused—"this young couple!"

He pointed straight at us.

I started. "Really?"

Beside me, Ana laughed.

It sounded like a mistake. But the crowd didn't seem to think so. They clapped and whooped. And the Cuban couple, they smiled at us and clapped too.

Ana hugged me. I hugged her back. We waved at the crowd. Then we headed for the stage to pick up our prize. I thought the emcee might card us, but he didn't hesitate a moment before handing over a large bottle of Havana Club.

By the time we made it back to our table, the music had started up again. No one paid us any more attention. No one except Yosvany, Pablo, and Rodrigo. They got up and clapped me on the back and hugged Ana, grinning and laughing.

"Well done," Rodrigo said.

"I guess you really did learn something," Pablo said.

"I knew you could do it," Yosvany said.

"Really?" I asked. "You did?"

"You didn't have much competition." Yosvany gestured at the Cuban couple we'd been up against. "Osmel's got technique but no ear for music."

"Oh," I said.

"But you danced well," Yosvany said. "Really, *primo*, you're not that bad anymore."

"Thanks." My cousin had a way with compliments.

"Ana, you were marvelous," Yosvany said. "Want to go again?"

Ana beamed at him. "Sure."

They'd hardly departed when Pablo got up too. "I'll get us some drinks."

I almost offered to share the Havana Club. Then I realized giving Pablo rum might not be the best idea. So I let him go and stayed behind with Rodrigo.

"It's rare to see foreigners dancing well," Rodrigo told me.

Watching the dance floor, I had to agree. The foreigners stood out not only because of their clothes or complexion. Flailing arms, wooden torsos, teetering steps—if you wanted to torture someone *Clockwork Orange*–style, you might peel open their eyelids and make them watch a bunch of *yumas* dancing salsa for hours on end.

"It's a matter of practice," I said. "There are many great dancers in New York. Non-Latinos too."

"Of course," Rodrigo said. "That's why I'm happy to meet you. Have you heard of *Casinero Mundial*?"

I shook my head.

"It's a TV program," Rodrigo said. "A big casino competition. This year we will film at the Cabaña fortress, in three weeks."

"You will?"

"I'm the organizer," Rodrigo said. "How would you like to participate?"

I thought I'd heard him wrong. "Us? On TV?"

Rodrigo nodded. "We invite a few foreign couples every year. People love it."

I'd thought I was past feeling fear today. Now it rushed over me like a long-lost friend. I had to clamp down on all sphincters to keep my pants clean. "Uhh . . ."

Yosvany's voice came back to me: *Really, primo, you're not that bad anymore.*

"Sure," I said. "I mean, I'll talk to Ana."

"Excellent." Rodrigo slid a card across the table. "Call me next week and we'll talk details."

When Pablo returned, I got up to find Ana and tell her the news. I couldn't wait to see Yosvany's face when he heard we were going to be on TV.

But they were nowhere to be found. It had been four or five songs, and I saw neither her nor Yosvany on the floor. I wandered through the Milocho's garden, weaving my way among the packed tables, pushing through the mass of bodies where necessary, searching, but no luck.

At last I found a quieter spot to the side of the stage and leaned on the white stone balustrade overlooking the water. That's when I spotted them.

They were in the back of the garden. Coming back from the faux stone castle, walking side by side, so close their shoulders touched. They glanced at each other from time to time. It looked as if they were struggling not to grin.

Ana stopped. It seemed she'd realized her blouse was

untucked. She glanced around, stuffed it hastily inside her jeans.

Yosvany said something. She laughed and swatted familiarly at his arm.

He leaned in and kissed her on the lips.

❧

I don't remember leaving the Milocho. I think I walked all the way home along the Malecón—staring blindly ahead, not feeling the spray of the waves—but perhaps I took a *máquina* at some point.

What I do remember is knocking on Rafaela's door, well after midnight. Knocking insistently until at last she cracked it open a hand's width and looked out balefully.

At least it started out baleful, that look, complete with a harsh, "Who is it?" Then she saw me and her expression softened. "Rick! *Mijo*, what happened to you?"

I guess I looked like something had happened to me. I guess something *had* happened to me.

"I'm sorry, Rafaela," I said. "I need the address. Ricardo, my mother's friend. Where does he live?"

For a long while Rafaela studied me, biting at her lip. Then she said, "Hold on," and disappeared, the door still ajar. Mere moments later, she was back with a slip of paper in her hand. She handed it to me through the grate. "I was going to give you this, but I thought you weren't really interested."

"I need to make a trip," I said. "Get out of Havana. Visit my mother's birthplace."

Rafaela nodded, but she didn't hurry to open the door for me. I got the distinct impression I was making her uneasy. For a brief, fleeting moment I wondered what I looked like—then the thought was gone, swept away by the dark torrent inside me.

"Thank you, Rafaela. Sorry to disturb you. Have a good night."

"Rick," she called after me before I was halfway down the hall. "One thing."

I looked at her without speaking. She shrank back into her apartment, but didn't close the door.

"When I last saw him, Ricardo was a dangerous man to know," she said. "This is Cuba, don't you forget."

PART THREE

Lolcats for the Revolution

chapter seventeen

NICE GUY

My bus to Trinidad was on the hottest day of the summer.

Every fan and air conditioner (they worked!) in Juanita's apartment was going. All the blinds were down. It was ninety degrees inside. I spent the morning sprawled on the cool stone floor by my sofa with a wet towel on my face. When I dragged myself to the kitchen in search of papaya juice from the fridge, I saw that the decorative candle Juanita kept above the dish cabinet had drooped to one side like a limp garden hose (actually that's not the first comparison that came to mind).

"Don't be ridiculous," Juanita said in the afternoon, when I rolled my suitcase into the living room. "Wait a day or two. It will cool down."

But I couldn't bear to stay in the apartment. Not knowing Ana was next door.

We hadn't talked since two nights ago at the Milocho. Ana and Yosvany had been back already when I got home, but she'd been asleep. Yosvany took me into our room, shut the door, and gave it to me straight. "Look, you tried, okay? But she's not into you. And, well, she's into me."

"You didn't hold off a day," I said. "Went straight for her, as soon as I was out of the way."

Yosvany sighed. "Be a man, *primo*. I told you my rule, remember? *Hay que chingar.*"

The images that came reeling through my mind . . . him and Ana in that stone castle, touching, kissing, and then . . .

I managed not to punch him. Partly because he was my cousin. Partly because spending years around Rob Kenna had taught me better than to pick a fight I couldn't win. Mostly because it was none of my business who Ana decided to make out with. Although right then that was hard to keep in mind.

Except Yosvany kept talking. "Look, I'd promised we'd find you someone. But you have to mix it up. Get style."

I stared at him. More accurately, I stared through him, trying to pretend he wasn't there.

"Like, it's how you walk," he said. "All mousy, shoulders slumped, always getting out of people's way. Straighten up, let others move aside for you. If you don't believe you're the best, no one will."

I tried to keep staring through him, but his words picked at my brain. I can't help it; I'm a sucker for self-help advice. Send me a link titled "Five Ways to Wiggle Your Eyebrows" and I'll spend the rest of the day in front of the mirror pretending I'm Jim Carrey.

"And then," Yosvany said, "you've got to pay attention to people. Even now I'm talking to you and I can tell you're thinking about your website or something. People can see when you're not listening. It makes them feel like you don't care."

I flushed guiltily, and then reminded myself I had nothing to feel guilty about.

"And here's the last thing," Yosvany said. "Once you straighten up, once you start paying attention to people, you've got to turn on the heat. Show people you like them, you know."

I scratched my neck.

"Smile, *primo!*" Yosvany said, exasperated. "And mean it, all right?"

So yeah. That was the pep talk Yosvany gave me after hooking up with the girl of my dreams. I walked like a mouse and didn't pay attention to people and smiled too little. Cheery.

Except, in a strange way, it did cheer me. It was what helped me fall asleep that night, hours after that conversation.

There's this trick Mom taught me. If someone points out

that you suck at something, you've got a choice. You can tell yourself you're a failure and feel bad about it. Or you can go, huh, so here's another way to level up (okay, that's not how Mom put it, but you get the point).

There was nothing I could do about Ana getting with Yosvany. But there was something I could do about carrying myself straighter and smiling more.

I still wasn't about to spend day after day watching Ana and Yosvany make out. So now I sat in the living room with my suitcase—perfectly still in my chair, sweat running freely down my body—and watched the wall clock tick the minutes away.

At the door, Ana caught up to me. She wore a light summer blouse—the fabric already dark with moisture—and stylish shades. "I'll walk with you," she said.

"It's hot out there," I said.

"Really? Huh."

Emerging onto the street felt like walking into some giant, world-encompassing furnace. The sun seemed an open flame against the skin. Even the shade offered little protection because there was no breeze.

The street was deserted. Not a *bicitaxi* in sight. Nobody wanted to pedal in weather like this.

I took a deep breath and started down the street, pulling my suitcase after me. Ana walked beside me. For a while, we proceeded in silence.

"I've done nothing wrong," Ana said eventually.

"I know."

"You've got no right to be angry with me."

"Of course not," I said. "Really, Ana, you're right. I get it."

"You're not acting like you get it," Ana said.

"I'm not feeling too happy," I said. "You can't blame me for that, can you?"

We walked for another block without talking. The suitcase handle was wearing a painful groove in the palm of my hand. Sweat stung my eyes.

"What gets me is that it's Yosvany," I said. "I mean, Yosvany of all people. You know his life philosophy? Like, there's only one thing he wants from you."

"So what?" Ana asked.

I stared at her.

"What, you think I want to marry him or something?" she asked. "We're leaving in a few weeks."

"Huh," I said.

"All that stuff he says about loving me, I know it's bullshit. He thinks he's clever, but he never met my dad."

"But if you see through it . . ."

"Why shouldn't I have some fun this summer?" Ana asked. "And Yosvany *is* fun. With him, I can forget all the crap that has happened in my life this year and just . . . be."

"I see." I wished this conversation were over already.

But Ana kept charging on. "Besides, you need to drop the nice guy act. You're not that nice."

"Gee, thanks."

"You invited me to Cuba hoping we'd hook up. Even after I told you that wasn't in the cards."

There was nothing I could say to that.

We came to the Parque Central. The area, usually mobbed by tourists, was quiet this afternoon. A lone *jinetero* ambled down the sidewalk in front of the Plaza Hotel.

"So what does this mean?" I asked. "We're not friends anymore?"

Ana flinched. "It means this is messed up. But we are friends. I mean, I think we are?"

"I think so," I said.

"Good."

"Good."

We reached the tourist bus stop in front of Hotel Inglaterra. My ride, a modern-looking blue Chinese bus, waited at the curb already. There were five minutes to departure. I loaded my suitcase into the baggage section. The open door of the air-conditioned bus beckoned. I decided there was one more thing I had to say.

"We got invited to dance on TV."

"Uhh . . . what?"

I told her what Rodrigo had said. "This show, *Casinero Mundial*, it would be a nice way to end our time in Cuba. Want to do it?"

"I don't think we're good enough for a real competition," Ana said.

I shrugged. "Yeah, but you want to do it?"

Ana snorted. "Wouldn't miss it."

"I'll be back in three days," I said, deciding on the spot to keep the trip short. "I'll see if I can pick up some moves in Trinidad."

chapter eighteen

TRINIDAD

Trinidad was a town defined by hills.

Tall green hills enveloped it and its narrow streets climbed toward one central hill, a steep incline that the bus pushed up sluggishly. The buildings downtown were old, colonial era, one or two stories tall with wooden doors painted green or blue. Enormous full-height windows opened to the street. The windows had no glass, each barred by an elaborate wooden grille.

The cobbled streets were clean of litter. I saw more tourists around than locals.

The bus left me on the edge of a sloping town square built into the hillside. Once on the street, I took a moment to compose myself. Straightened. Plastered a smile on my face.

I was in a new town. Ana was far away. It was time for a new start.

Beautifully restored colonial buildings rounded the square. An imposing church dominated the far side. Beside the church wide stone steps led farther up the hill. On these steps a band played a slow-moving rendition of "Chan Chan," what else. People danced and sat around and drank cheap beer (the Cubans) and cocktails (the tourists).

The *casa particular* Juanita had reserved for me was on the other side of the square, away from the noise. It was single-storied but built like a mansion, with enormous grilled windows and a massive door painted blue. I gave its heavy metal knocker a bang.

After a long while, there was a stirring inside. A sliding of bolts, and the door swung open.

A girl stood on the threshold. She was my age, short and a little plump in blue jeans. Beautiful in a classical sort of way—her face perfectly proportioned, her skin smooth and very dark.

She examined me with curiosity, then spoke up in American-sounding English. "Can I help you?"

I smiled at her, thinking of Yosvany's advice.

She smiled back.

I decided to stick with English. "I'm Rick. Juanita from Havana called about a room for me?"

"Oh, sure," the girl said. "Welcome. I'm Tania."

I dragged my suitcase into an enormous living room—
an antique wooden table and a few rocking chairs scattered
across a stone-floored expanse more suited to an art gallery
than a living space. Wooden beams supported a sloping roof
high overhead.

"You've got a nice place," I said, the way you might when
visiting someone's two-bedroom on Central Park West.

Tania only smiled and led me farther into the house.
Which went on and on. Beyond the living room was a long,
narrow dining hall with a carved table big enough to seat
twenty. Bookcases lined all walls except one, which opened
directly onto a great big white-tiled patio.

I wondered if this was the house of some government
minister. But the furniture, if antique, was simple and worn.
Many of the tiles in the patio were cracked. And the walls
looked like they could use a new coat of paint.

Tania told me to sit down at the dining table and left
through a side door. She reappeared with a man in his fifties.
On the heavy side, he had a lined, weathered face.

"It's the American," Tania was explaining, in Spanish.
"I thought you said he was this geek." (She used the English
word for "geek.")

I was still processing this—first, what the hell had Juanita told them? And second, hey, she thought I didn't look like
a geek!—when Tania turned to me. "Rick, this is my father,
Eduardo."

Eduardo smiled at me. "*Hola, Rick*," he said, and continued in rapid Spanish. "Juanita says you speak *castellano*."

"I do."

"I—" Tania stammered. "Um. Oh."

"Welcome to our house," her dad said. "We'll take good care of you."

"Even if I'm a geek?" I asked, grinning.

This time Tania didn't stammer, but grinned too. "Especially if you're a geek."

That grin, it made me wonder. Tania was cute . . . I didn't get all antsy looking at her like I did with Ana or Rachel, but hey, maybe . . .

Her father's watchful eyes lingered on me. They put an emergency brake to my train of thought.

Tania showed me to my room. It was small but clean, with its own bathroom and, best of all, AC. Everything in the room looked better, cleaner, newer than the rest of the house.

"We save our best for the guests," Tania told me.

At which I straightened up again. I kept forgetting Yosvany's advice. "Want to go for a walk? Show me Trinidad?"

On the inside, I marveled. Days ago I wouldn't have dared asked the question.

Tania smiled. "Sure. If you tell me about New York. The Statue of Liberty. The subway. Times Square."

"The first thing you have to know is, stay away from Times Square."

Tania leaned against the wall. "Why?"

"You know Obispo in Havana?" I asked. "How busy it gets?"

"I've never been to Havana," Tania said.

I stared at her.

"It's not easy for Cubans to travel."

"Well . . . ," I said. "Times Square is to New York what 'Chan Chan' is to Cuban music. You know, it's cool, except there's a million clueless tourists all over it."

Tania looked like she was holding back a laugh. "I know clueless tourists, all right."

I unpacked some things and put on a new shirt. Then we headed out.

Tania took me away from the city center, led me to quieter parts. Dirt roads replaced the cobbles, and the beautiful colonial houses of the center became dilapidated huts of stone or brick. Kids in ragged clothes kicked around a semi-deflated soccer ball in the dim light of a corner streetlamp.

"Did you study English in school?" I asked Tania. "You're really good."

"I learned from *Law & Order*," she said. "And *Game of Thrones*. And *Downton Abbey*."

"Huh. I didn't know they showed those on Cuban TV."

"I watch them on my laptop," Tania said. "It's like this whole other world, you know. Like nothing here in Cuba."

"You get cheap DVDs here?" I asked.

"Torrents," she said, in English.

This wasn't a word I was expecting to hear in the middle of Trinidad, Cuba.

"We're not in the nineteenth century here." Tania said this as a man on horseback clomped past us on the narrow dirt street. "Some people who work for the government have access to fast internet. Every week they download all the new shows to a portable hard drive. Then you pay them one CUC to copy anything you like."

"I guess it's sort of like a community internet."

Tania nodded. "We've got a lot of stuff like that. We use flash drives or copy stuff between phones with Bluetooth."

"You know a lot about it," I said.

"It's what I want to do. I want to study computer science in university." Tania glanced at me uncertainly, as if I might find the idea ridiculous.

I only asked, "In Havana?"

"There or . . ." Tania shrugged. "Yeah, I guess in Havana."

I wondered what she had been going to say.

"That's why I wanted to talk to you," she said. "My dad said you're a computer genius."

I felt a flush coming on. The last time anyone had called me a computer genius was when Aunt Lavinia asked me to "install the Facebook" for her.

"I run a pretty popular website," I said.

"What's it called?" Tania asked.

"CatoTrope. It's a content aggregator. About, like, funny cat pictures and stuff."

"Oh." After a moment, Tania added, "That's cool."

"There are some really interesting technical challenges," I hastened to say. "Content crowdsourcing, popularity algorithms, cloud storage . . ."

"Maybe you can take a look at my website," Tania said. "I'm writing one in HTML, for our *casa*."

I couldn't imagine what it would be like, trying to learn web design with hardly any access to, well, the web. "Sure, I'll help."

"I have this layout issue," Tania said as we returned to the city center.

We sat down amidst the crowd on the wide stone steps by the church. The band played old bittersweet boleros— "Silencio" and "Herido de Sombras" and "Siento La Nostalgia de Palmeras." Tania and I talked HTML, PHP, and Java-Script.

It was easy, talking to Tania. Most cute girls had this remarkable ability to tie my tongue in knots. But when Tania looked me in the eyes, it was a sort of simple, earnest gaze that put me at ease. Until I started wondering—as I talked about the best commenting practices—what it would be like to take her hand and pull her close and kiss her—

At which point I stopped talking midsentence. Because I'd remembered Ana, with a sudden lurching coldness in my chest.

"What's wrong?" Tania asked.

I still would have liked to kiss her. But I could tell that it was only a physical desire. With that coldness inside me, there wasn't room for anything else.

So what? Yosvany's voice sounded in my head. Just go for it.

I got to my feet instead. "I remembered that I need your help. There's this friend who lives in town. I have to figure out how to get to his address."

"Oh." Tania followed me up after a moment. "What is it?"

I gave her the address Rafaela had written down for me.

"It's a few streets over," Tania said. "I'll show you."

I could tell she was still nonplussed, though.

Ricardo's house was near the local Casa de la Música. But when we found the right building, it was a puzzle. There was no entry door, only a large green wooden gate. It was closed, with a sign above that said *Galería* painted in ragged white letters.

Tania looked at the sign dubiously. "Is your friend an artist?"

"He's a poet," I said.

"Should we try knocking?"

I looked at the door for a lingering moment. Behind it lived a man who was a living connection to Mom's secret past.

"I'll come back when the gallery's open," I said.

"You didn't tell me much about New York," Tania said on the way back to her house.

"Sorry."

"Maybe we can do another walk tomorrow." She smiled at me.

"Yes," I said. "Maybe."

Then cursed myself for hesitating.

chapter nineteen

POET OF THE REVOLUTION

The next morning after breakfast I ambled over to Ricardo's house. I ambled because my stomach was stuffed with crepes, honey, and fruit, and because the sun beat down ferociously on the stone cobbles of the old town, and most of all because I wasn't sure I was ready to face Mom's old boyfriend.

I mean, there I was—Rick Gutiérrez, purveyor of cat pictures—about to meet a revolutionary poet. A man once threatened with prison for his art. Okay, so he gave in and joined the army and left Mom hanging, but even so. Ricardo Eugenio Echeverría López had been an artist.

I stood before that large green gate again, now open. Within was a typical Cuban street gallery. Whitewashed walls set off colorful canvases mounted on simple wooden panels.

I saw no one inside. A beaded curtain concealed a doorway deeper into the house.

I hesitated, then entered the gallery.

The paintings were colorful and slapdash, thrown together by a careless hand. The subject matter: old American cars and old men smoking cigars. Also, old men smoking cigars while seated in old American cars. Just like every other gallery in Cuba, except I saw no picture of La Bodeguita del Medio, Hemingway's famous hangout in Havana.

No, there it was—a small square, squeezed in a corner in the back. The proportions of the facade were off. I guessed the artist had never actually seen the Bodeguita.

I bit my lip, a vague sense of dismay scratching at me. This didn't seem like the right kind of place for Ricardo.

"Yes, friend?" came a voice from behind me. "You like? I paint it myself."

A man had emerged from the curtained doorway. A pudgy, white, sleepy-looking face. Bald on top, gray stubble on the sides. A solid beer belly protruded from the man's faded green polo shirt. His trousers were a fashion statement—bright red sweatpants with a white stripe down the middle.

"I'm only looking," I said, in Spanish.

The man's shoulders slumped. "Okay."

"I was told that Ricardo Eugenio Echeverría lives here," I said.

A faint frown clouded the man's face. "You need something from me?"

Really? This guy?

"I . . . I heard you're a poet," I said.

For a moment, there was a stillness. Ricardo stared at me across the length of the gallery.

Then he rushed at me. One, two, three giant steps and he towered over me. I stumbled back into the wall but he kept going, his arms rising—

He stopped. Snapped to a halt as if he'd smacked into a wall Wile E. Coyote–style.

"*Que pinga tú quieres?*" he forced out, the crude words little more than a whisper.

"I'm Rick Gutiérrez, from New York," I said. "The son of María Gutiérrez Peña."

Ricardo took one single, heavy step back. His eyes never moved from me. "María . . ."

"You remember her?"

"I was a poet," Ricardo said. "Once." He turned away, an abrupt motion. "These days I paint. Cars and stuff. It's much easier. They pay you too."

He went to the largest painting in the gallery, a picture of a young Fidel munching on a giant cigar, green cap on his head. For a long time he stared at the picture.

"I wrote a few poems recently," he said then. "Would you like to read one?"

"Yes, please."

A shiver passed over me. For the first time in my life, I was excited about reading a poem.

Ricardo dragged closed the gallery's gates, leaving us in gloom. He slid the bolt home, then—a vague shape in the dark—headed for the beaded curtain in the back. "Come."

We passed through a dusty storeroom, then crossed a narrow patio open to the sky. A few cracked clay flowerpots lay on the faded tiles, filled with black earth. At the end of the patio there was a door missing, replaced by an off-white blanket hung from a rope. Ricardo pushed it aside to reveal a bedroom.

The room smelled of paint and cigarettes and mold. Yellow-brown rust streaks marred the walls. A wooden roof sloped overhead, the beams dark with rot. The bed was a narrow mattress, patterned with flowers—I could just about tell they had originally been blue.

I couldn't imagine living in this place.

Ricardo bent down by the bed and pulled out a round metal tin, the kind Danish butter cookies come in. He put it on the mattress and lifted off the top. It contained sheaves and sheaves of paper, thrown together in a chaotic mess. Pages torn from notebooks, paper tissues, printer paper, newsprint—all covered in handwriting.

Ricardo fished around, pulled out a notebook page that had been folded over several times. He unfolded it and handed it to me.

Ricardo's handwriting was spidery but clean, easy to

read—it seemed like it didn't belong on the crumpled, off-white page. His poem had but ten lines. I scanned them once, quickly, then passed over them again, searching for hidden meaning.

It was simple, that poem, the words graceful but straight-forward. They spoke of an evening in Trinidad. A tired man returning home, walking down cobbled streets, the setting sun warm on his face. He listened to some tourists argue with a taxi driver. He thought of the coffee he'd make himself when he got home. He caught the scent of orange blossoms in the air. It reminded him of his youth spent on the Isle of Pines. He smiled.

That was it. No revolution. No politics at all, nor even love or passion. Just a nostalgic trinket. A tourist piece, like the paintings in the gallery.

"It's nice." I handed the page back to Ricardo.

"Nice." He nodded. "Yes. It is nice." He watched me, as if expecting more.

"Well." I wondered what else I could say. "What was my mother like, back when you knew her?"

"I have to open the gallery," Ricardo said, and put aside his tin of poems.

I followed him back to the front. He opened the gallery to the street and leaned on the doorjamb, watching the tourists outside. "My friends," he called to an older couple who looked like American tourists. "Come in. Where are you from?"

I turned away from him. Made to go.

I'd taken a few steps down the street when Ricardo spoke

up. "María," he said. "How is she?"

I looked back at him. He stood in the door, staring at the street as if he hadn't spoken at all. As if it had been some disembodied voice that had asked the question.

"Mom died two years ago," I said.

I thought he might flinch, turn away, maybe even cry. But nothing shifted on that soft, pudgy face. Those distant eyes, they never even blinked.

❧

In the afternoon I helped Tania with the website for her family's *casa*—photos, room rates, a map, that sort of thing. We sat on her massive iron-framed bed, our backs against the headboard, and worked on her beat-up brick of a laptop. The door to the living room was open, but my skin tingled with the warmth of her presence. Every time her elbow brushed against mine, I thought I might bite my tongue.

I'd met geeky girls before, but none who listened to me like Tania did. She seemed to really believe I had something intelligent to say. So of course the most intelligent observation I made all morning was that she could include a cat picture on her site.

"Oh, that's nice," she said.

Okay, so the idea wasn't as stupid as I made it sound. Tania did have a cat, a cute gray creature that spent its days curled up on the roof, except when it was time to trip up some tourist lugging his suitcase across the patio. And people do like cat pictures with their browsing experience. But it was hardly the contribution you'd expect from a computer genius.

Tania didn't seem to mind. "That was good work," she said while we snacked on *fruta bomba* and fried bananas in the kitchen. "Want to go to the beach?"

Playa Ancon was a long beach ten minutes outside town, sandwiched between the water and a string of hotels. As we got off the bus a salty breeze swept over us, refreshing after days of stifling heat. We kicked off our sandals and walked along the fine white sand. The Caribbean rolled tranquilly against the shore, clear and blue.

We dropped our things in the shade of a tall palm tree and changed with towels wrapped around us. And, well . . . Tania in a swimsuit . . .

I hurried into the water to cool down. She came in after me. I tried to not stare too much at the way the water made her skin glisten. We swam in the shallows and splashed at each other and laughed.

Later we lay in the sun, slathered in sunscreen, listening to Mayito Rivera on the tinny speakers of my iPod. The wind brushed lightly across my skin and a languor filled me. I could have lain there forever. Except at one point the breeze carried some flowery scent to me, and that made me wonder.

"What do orange blossoms smell like?"

Tania shrugged. My eyes were closed, but I sensed the shift of her shoulders on the sand. "Why?"

I told her about Ricardo's poem. "That guy was my mother's boyfriend, back in the day," I said. "He was supposedly

242

this great poet, but I wasn't impressed."

Tania was quiet for a long time. So long I thought she might have fallen asleep. But when I opened my eyes to look at her I found her up on one elbow, looking thoughtful.

"You know the other name for the Isle of Pines?" she asked. "Isla de la Juventud?"

The Isle of Youth . . . that sounded familiar.

Oh.

A coldness passed over me. The Isle of Pines had been too commonplace a name to stick in my mind, but now I remembered. It was the place where Fidel had been imprisoned after his first failed attempt at revolution.

Later, once he finally succeeded, it was the counterrevolutionaries who got sent there.

"I wasn't going to say anything," Tania said, "but I asked my father about your friend. Ricardo. Before he moved into that house, he spent twenty years in prison."

I frowned, working through the numbers. "That can't be right." According to Rafaela, Ricardo had joined the army in 1980—right before Mom left the island.

But that poem. A youth spent on the Isle of Pines.

Twenty years . . .

⁊

As a cat video tycoon, I have long been fascinated with the power of a good title. The video is important, but even a brilliant video won't get shares if the title doesn't get clicked in the first place.

"Funny Cat Moment"? That's all right, you'll get a few clicks.

"Cat in a Shark Costume Chases a Duck While Riding a Roomba"? That's viral crack.

The video never changed. The outcome couldn't be more different.

It's like that with people too. Take Ricardo, for example.

Label him "failed poet who makes third-rate copies of second-rate paintings"? It's sad, but you don't exactly want to hang out with him.

Call him "freed prisoner of conscience who pens poems of defiance while disguised as a painter"? Now that's someone you want to get to know.

Makes you wonder who else you've met in your life and never realized.

❧

"I'd like to read more of your poems."

Ricardo didn't seem surprised to see me. He'd nodded when I came in, expressionless, and he nodded again at my request. He wore the same clothes from yesterday, and I got the impression he would again tomorrow.

He seemed perfectly at ease in this dinky gallery with his dinky paintings. But I had my suspicions now.

We retreated into the back and he brought out his cookie tin of poems. He didn't ask what kind of poem I wanted to read, but shuffled through the mess of pages and pulled out one, two, three of them.

"When I was younger, I wrote for others," Ricardo said. "These I wrote for myself. But if you're María's son . . ."

Ricardo's poems were simple. An ode to an evening spent sipping coffee on the porch. Five stanzas on a trip to the local agricultural market, people and tomatoes alike wilting in the afternoon heat. A portrait of the *pregoneros*, the street vendors who rumbled past your window in the morning, singing out the virtues of their goods.

They were simple things, Ricardo's poems, but that wasn't all they were. That man on the porch with his coffee, he saw the neighbor lady watching, *one who had all the right friends and none of the wrong ones*, and wondered what story she'd tell of him. At the agricultural market, as he weighed his scant purchases, he saw *yumas* pile fresh tomatoes and bananas and *fruta bomba* in their bags with careless indifference. And the cries of the *pregoneros*, they mixed with the solemn songs of children from the school next door. *Pioneros* singing praise to Che Guevara—their voices high and clear and free of doubts.

After some time I looked up from the pages in my hand. Ricardo stood before me with that metal tin in his hands, watching me. He hadn't moved since I started reading. He wore no expression, his face the sort of blank you can only achieve intentionally.

"You didn't join the army in '80, did you?" I asked.

He kept quiet for such a long time I thought perhaps he'd lost his hold on the present moment. "No."

"But the letter you wrote my mother—"

"How well did you know her?"

"She was my mother."

"And?"

Annoyance washed through me. "I knew her longer than you did, that's for sure."

Ricardo nodded, even, calm. "What would she have done if she knew I was in prison? Would she have left for Miami?"

I tried to picture it. Mom getting on a boat at the Mariel Harbor, knowing someone she loved sat behind bars on the Isle of Pines.

"She wouldn't even let Dad go to the dentist alone," I said. "She told me love meant being there for someone."

Ricardo's face twitched. I realized mentioning Dad hadn't been the smartest thing. But he said, "She would have wasted years fighting her father and the government and everybody. She might have ended up in jail herself. She didn't deserve that. That wasn't her dream."

"Her dream?"

Ricardo sat down on the edge of his bed. Gazed at the wall beside me. "Her father thought that I convinced her to leave for Miami. It was the other way around. I wanted to stay, to write my poems, to fight. She told me our voices would be louder in Miami. She'd write a novel of Cuba, and I'd write my poems, and we'd change the world." Ricardo laughed, a humorless sound. "She convinced me the world needed my poems."

246

"So you lied to her," I said. "You made her believe you were betraying her."

"She left, didn't she?"

"She never wrote that novel," I said. "She never wrote a single story after she left, as far as I know."

Ricardo's jaw shifted. He looked away.

I had to do something for him. The realization came over me as a certainty, almost inevitable.

This big man with his unwashed clothes and disheveled air and studiously indifferent face, he hadn't always been like this. Maybe even now he wasn't like this, not anywhere except on the surface.

"Your poems are beautiful," I said. "Do you have any of your old ones left? From before?"

Ricardo shook his head.

"It doesn't matter," I said. "Let me publish these." I gestured with the pages in my hand.

Ricardo looked up at me.

"I'll find them a publisher," I said. "Or I'll put them on the internet. I'll make sure a lot of people see them. They can make a difference."

Ricardo got up. Reached for the pages I still held. After a moment's hesitation, I handed them over.

"My poems are good for nothing except trouble," he said. "They never were. Twenty years on the Isle of Pines is all they got me. Make a difference?" Ricardo snorted. "The only difference they ever made was to me. And to your mother, I suppose."

"But people will want to—"

"I'm fine here. In this house. Free. I'm not going to lose this."

"Oh," I said, after a moment. "That makes sense."

It did. This was Ricardo's life.

He led me back to the gallery. Before he opened the door to let me out, he paused with his hand on the deadbolt. "The poems. You liked them?"

I nodded.

"I thought one day María might return and I would show them to her," he said. "Just her and no one else. I suppose I'm glad that you came, at least."

I left him standing alone amidst his work. The only work by which the world would ever know of him.

chapter twenty

A SPECIAL THING

It had been a sunny morning, but in the twenty minutes I had spent with Ricardo, a wind had risen and clouds had raced in to cover the sky. I had barely taken ten steps down the cobbled street when the first drops assailed the cobblestones.

I thought—that's refreshing.

Next I thought—okay, that's interesting.

Then—holy crap, do I walk or do I swim?

My clothes stuck to me and my sneakers squished and wet hair got in my eyes, but it was nice, walking through that downpour. Made me feel tough, like nothing could get to me.

I needed that feeling. Seeing Ricardo again had made me think. Sure, he'd been this zealous young poet once. But he'd become a man who stored his life's work in a tin under his bed. They'd sent him to prison and broken him, and released him to paint portraits of Fidel and Che for tourists to buy.

Before I met him, Ricardo had made me feel unworthy. Now I was simply glad I wasn't him.

He'd been my age when they locked him up. I doubted that he'd expected to spend twenty years in prison for running his mouth off.

Maybe it had all seemed like an adventure to him. The way sending the video of Miranda Galvez to Lettuce had seemed like an adventure. If he had it all to do over again, would he write those poems?

Maybe there was a lesson in there for me. I had no business playing at politics. I'd come to Cuba to dance and have fun.

Back at the *casa*, I left puddles across the length of the house. Tania laughed when she emerged from her room.

"Sorry." I ran a hand through my hair. "It's wet out there."

Tania did an eyebrow wriggle. "Looking sexy."

"I feel it." I grinned. "Hey, it's my last day in town. You want to go out with me tonight? You know, have fun with Mr. Sexy?"

Tania's smile faded. "Go out with you? What do you mean?"

I opened my mouth to backtrack, to say—oh, nothing, we'll just hang out like friends. But Yosvany's disdainful face flashed before my eyes.

"I really enjoy hanging out with you," I said. "I have so much fun when you're around. I don't know why." I paused, and a heat rushed to my cheeks. "I've never felt like this before. . . ."

The lie rolled awkwardly off my tongue. I couldn't speak the words *con la cara dura*—with a hard face, as Yosvany would say.

"I don't have foreign boyfriends," Tania said forcefully. "I'm not like that."

"I understand," I said, half disappointed, half relieved.

Tania smiled again, a small, shy expression. "But we can go out, this one night. Where do you want to go?"

My heart accelerated. "Somewhere with music. Where we can dance."

"I don't dance."

"It's okay." I couldn't believe I was about to say it, but, yes—"I'll teach you."

"I don't think that's going to work." But Tania didn't sound entirely opposed to the idea.

We left the house after dinner—once Tania's dad had gone off to see some friends. The rain had ceased, leaving the streets gleaming slick. There was a freshness in the air. Tania had on a pale blue dress that hugged her in all sorts of mesmerizing ways.

We walked arm in arm, and I wished for everyone on the street to notice us. I wished Yosvany were here to see me, and Ana—

Forget them.

We went to the local Casa de la Música. The stage was in the garden, a patio covered by a roof of loose vines. In one corner a band played son. The lead singer, a lively old man, ripped out verse after verse about a mischievous dog. The lyrics were outrageous, smutty double meanings subtle as a jackhammer.

I picked a table near the empty dance floor, got a mojito for Tania and a Bucanero for myself.

"I'm starting to enjoy Cuban beer," I explained to Tania, although the truth was simpler. With three more weeks left in Cuba, my funds were running low. With all the recent changes, I wasn't quite sure if my American ATM cards would work, or if they might get swallowed, never to be seen again.

"Beer is safer too," Tania said. "You don't know what water they use for the cocktails. Or if they wash the glasses."

"Oh," I said.

"It's Cuban flavor." Tania sipped her mojito, looked at me over the edge of her glass. "You foreigners can't deal with it."

I wondered if she was still talking about cocktails.

When there came a break in the music a heavyset, middle-aged white man went up to the band. They talked for a while, and I saw him hand the bandleader money. Moments later the band started into a portentous-sounding piece.

"Oh, no," Tania muttered.

The heavy guy began to sing. At once I recognized the tune: "Hasta Siempre Comandante," an ode to Che, and perhaps the most famous revolutionary song in the world. The singer had a good voice, deep and clear. His Spanish sounded native but European. He sang with all-out gusto, arms moving in grand gestures, a fervent enthusiasm on his face. The musicians behind him smiled as they played, but they seemed practiced smiles to me.

Tania sipped her drink with a pained expression.

"You're not a fan," I said.

"I think it's sad." Tania nodded in the general direction of the stage. "All these people who come here to live out their fantasies. Read *La Historia Me Absolverá*. Buy a hat with a red star. Sing a pretty song."

"Because they don't understand what communism is really like?"

"Because they've got nothing better to do with their lives," Tania said. "It's not just communists. We get people at our *casa*, they talk to us in hushed voices, ask us questions. They want us to tell them how bad things are, how Fidel is screwing everything up. And I'm like, guys, don't you have your own problems to deal with? If you've got two weeks of vacation, go to the beach and leave Fidel alone."

"Exactly," I said.

Exactly, Rick. Leave Fidel alone. No one wants you to bother with him. Not Tania. Not Ricardo. Not anyone. You're here to have fun.

Tania drained her mojito with a determined motion. She looked so cute it made me hurt inside.

The big man finished his song. The audience clapped long and hard, and he walked off with a grin. As soon as he'd left the stage, the band struck up again, a slow, leisurely son. Within moments a young black kid pulled a middle-aged white woman up from a table and took her to the dance floor. Another couple soon followed, graying Italian tourists. They embraced each other and did the side step and demonstrated an impressive ability not to hit a single beat of the music.

"Shall we?"

Tania studied my extended hand like I was offering her a steaming cowpat. But even as I was about to pull back, she took it.

Together we walked out to the floor. I put my arm around her.

Tania looked at me. No, more accurately she stared at me, her eyes unwavering, as if I was the only person left in the world.

That was a bit unnerving, but I told myself she was nervous. I whispered, "Just step where I step." I started in a basic salsa step.

Forward and back. Forward and back. Forward and back.

Tania really didn't know how to dance. She tripped over her feet and followed me sluggishly. I was afraid I'd have to manhandle her the whole song. But then she caught the idea and moved with me, not elegantly exactly, but easily enough. So I mixed it up, added a side step, later a rotating cumbia step.

It was a clumsy, awkward dance. I felt awesome.

Me, Rick Gutiérrez, teaching a cute Cuban girl to dance. Her grip tight on my shoulder. Her eyes on me, trusting and a little scared.

When the song ended, Tania hugged me, soft and warm against me. There was a grin on her face as we returned to our table.

"I didn't think I could do that," she said. "We're not a dancing family. They made fun of me at school, said I was the only black girl in Cuba who couldn't dance . . . not true, you know. I told myself I'd never get out in front of people and make a fool of myself. But tonight, with you . . ." Her grin widened. "I didn't care."

"I'm glad."

"A geeky dancer from New York, huh," Tania said. "You're a pretty cool guy, Rick."

I smiled. "You inspired me." I reached for one of Yosvany's corny lines, and this time it came easier. "Dancing with you I felt like I could do anything in the world."

"Oh, hey, I have an idea." Tania rose, an abrupt motion. "Let's go."

"Where?"

"You'll see. Come."

Tania led me along narrow cobbled streets, up the hill that overlooked Trinidad. Her shoulder bumped against mine as we walked. Then something happened and I realized we were holding hands.

I flushed. A warmth filled my body that had nothing to do with the weather.

Briefly, Ana's face surfaced before my eyes. I shoved it away. I wasn't doing anything wrong, was I? I liked Tania.

But not as much as I let her believe. . . .

I cast a surreptitious glance sideways at her. Her quiet smile told me nothing.

"It must be quite a contrast," she said. "Coming from New York to this . . ." She gestured at the street around us. The road was dirt here and streetlights were far between. We walked in shadows between badly maintained low houses.

"It's different here," I said. "Very chill. Especially if you have the right guide."

"Maybe one day you can guide me around New York," she said easily.

So easily.

Juanita had warned me about this many times. "Cuban girls want just one thing from a *yuma*," she'd assured me. "A ticket off the island."

Well, maybe that's what Tania wanted and maybe not. I wasn't about to make her any promises.

"I'd love to show you around if you come to New York," I said.

She squeezed my hand.

We left buildings behind and followed a winding dirt road up a grassy hill. At first I thought Tania had taken me here for the view—a lovely vista, Trinidad at night, patches of yellow light amidst whole neighborhoods sunk in darkness. Then I noticed a clump of people gathered in the shadows under some trees.

The people were standing on stairs. The steps led down, straight into the hill itself. I saw no sign, no indication what awaited inside—except that a burly doorman stood at the entrance, holding back the crowd.

"Las Cuevas," Tania said. "My friends are always talking about this place."

Five minutes later we descended narrow stone steps into the shadowed depths of a cave. The sounds of distant salsa echoed around us—an energetic, insistent cowbell beat carried through long dark corridors. Walls of rough rock loomed high overhead, dripping water down on us.

"Don't worry," Tania said. "I can't remember when we last had a cave-in."

I glowered at her. She snickered.

We reached the bottom and followed a corridor deeper into the cave. The music grew louder until we emerged at the base of a large cavern. Crowded plastic tables surrounded a well-lit dance floor. The DJ's booth was set high in the cliff face overlooking the cavern. A long bar hugged the opposite wall. There were lots of people at the bar and sitting at tables but nobody dancing.

"No one here likes Pupy?" I asked. The song was "Que Cosas Tiene La Vida," an older but popular hit, full of cheerful energy.

"Most of the good salseros have left Trinidad," Tania said. "My friends only dance reggaeton."

"Well, then." My heart sped up with premonitions of stage fright. "Let's go show them how it's done."

"Oh, no." Tania glanced around nervously. "This is too fast for me."

"Come on." I smirked. "You said you didn't care who watched."

At this Tania took a step back. "I did?"

"Yeah, remember?"

"No." Tania crossed her arms. "If you want to dance so much, ask my friend Lazara over there."

I couldn't tell if she was angry. Maybe the smirk had been a bad idea. "It's fine—"

"No, really, you must. Lazara!" She waved. "Lazara, come here!"

A young girl rose from a nearby table, maybe thirteen and stick-thin and dressed to impress—flowing white pants with flared bottoms and a stylish black T-shirt. She gave Tania a hug, looked me up and down.

"This is Rick from New York." Tania might have been presenting a can of sardines for the enthusiasm in her voice. "He wants to dance with you."

Lazara took my hand. She grinned at me with such open friendliness that I couldn't help smiling back. Whatever had bitten Tania wasn't Lazara's fault. She was a kid. I could give her a nice dance.

We walked out onto the floor. As the music hit an accent, I took hold of her and spun her about.

Lazara spun lightly, with perfect poise. At the end of the spin she kicked out her foot to a cymbal clash and shook her shoulders rumba-style.

I didn't humor Lazara with a nice dance. If anything, she humored me. She followed every move I led, seemed to antici-pate my steps, saved my balance when I tripped in the middle of an overambitious pattern. Even Ana wasn't this easy to dance with—Lazara moved under my hands as if she weighed nothing at all.

We finished the song with an elegant turn in closed hold—and both of us started, because people were applaud-ing. Tourists only, but still.

"That was nice," I said to Lazara as we headed to where Tania had claimed a table. "Thanks."

"For a *yuma*, you're an awesome dancer," Lazara said.

I knew that was a compliment.

At the table, Tania sat drinking a beer. I couldn't read her face in the dim light off the dance floor.

She nodded at Lazara. "Thanks, *niña*. We'll see you around."

"Oh." Lazara looked from her to me, then smiled uncer-tainly. "All right. See you later." She moved off.

"That was a bit cold," I said, sitting down.

Tania looked me straight in the eyes. Her voice came quiet, neutral. "Do you want someone else here with us?"

"Well, not exactly . . ."

"I thought you liked spending time with me," Tania said, still in that quiet tone.

My breath came fast, and not because I'd been dancing.

You've come this far, a voice said inside me. And besides, maybe she's only interested because you're from New York.

What would Yosvany say?

"There's no one else I'd rather be with." I flushed, pressed on. "Ever since I came to Trinidad, since we met, I've been feeling this wonderful thing, like—"

Tania took hold of my shoulder, pulled me close, and kissed me.

Okay, so Rachel had been a pretty good kisser. A bit on the wet side maybe and she'd had a habit of sucking at my lips that left them sore, but it had been good kissing times.

Tania, though . . . Tania kissed like she meant it. Her lips pressed soft and a little moist against mine, and her hands slid warm across my back, and her tongue, well, it did things I didn't know tongues could do.

When we finally parted, our faces inches from each other, Tania no longer looked like the cute young girl I'd met a few days ago. A change had come over her, nearly imperceptible and hard to describe. Like this relaxed, hungry energy.

"I saw you dancing with Lazara, everyone watching you two, and I couldn't stand it," Tania whispered. "Not for another moment."

We didn't stay in the club after that. On the way back to

the *casa*, on the dark Trinidad streets, we stopped often and long. When we entered the house, her father was already asleep—I wondered if he had any idea we'd gone out together. We walked quietly to the patio and up to my room.

I could have stopped at the door. I could have said to Tania—hey, listen, you know we're just having fun, right? I'm leaving tomorrow and I'm not coming back.

I said nothing. I kept quiet as we kissed in the dark of my room and undressed each other. Neither of us spoke while I struggled to pry the plastic off the box of condoms I'd brought all the way from New York.

The sex was sweaty and fumbling but nice—at least while it lasted, which wasn't very long.

Afterward, Tania snuggled up against me and spoke in my ear, "You haven't done this before, have you?"

I tensed in the dark. It had been so easy to tell?

"That's good," she whispered. "Your first time should be a special thing."

I lay there and said not a thing.

༄

It's supposed to be this life-changing event, losing your virginity. And I guess in a way it was.

Not because the act itself was earth-shattering, though. I mean, sex is great, but it's still just neurons firing, chemicals releasing, muscles spasming—it's this physical thing; you do it and you're still the same person living the same life.

The biggest thing about losing my virginity was this: I no

longer had to worry about losing it. Years of plans, hopes, fantasies, and expectations collapsed to the reality of that sweaty fumbling act. I no longer had to wonder—I knew.

It was the lifting of a weight I hadn't known I carried. And yet, freed of this weight, I felt no elation or triumph.

I only felt tired. And wondered if it could have been different.

❧

I woke to find Tania pulling on her clothes. It was early morning and gray light filtered through the curtains. The whole world seemed gray to me at that moment.

"I better get back to my room before Dad's up," Tania told me, and smiled.

Her smile was sweet and simple. Nothing hinted that the Tania I'd seen last night at Las Cuevas—the Tania who'd gripped me hard as she kissed me—was this same girl. It seemed a curious thing to me, that one person could be both.

I sat up against the headboard. "I'm going back to Havana today."

Tania's smile faded slowly. "I know."

"I can't change the ticket."

"Okay," she said.

"We've got a dance competition to prepare for."

Tania pulled her shirt over her head, tucked it in, then stilled herself. She looked me in the eyes for a long time, her face calm and serious.

I got the sense she was gathering her courage. That scared me.

At last she spoke. "Yesterday I decided I wouldn't regret sleeping with you. You're only my second guy, you know, and you seemed different . . . and today you . . . but I decided I wouldn't regret it."

I said nothing.

"Do you think we'll meet again, Rick Gutiérrez?"

I flinched. Opened my mouth to invent something. To spout one of Yosvany's lines. All that came out was, "Uh . . ."

Tania nodded, a slow motion. She didn't look surprised. That was the thing—she didn't look surprised at all.

For a moment longer she studied me. Then she turned for the door.

I thought I saw something glisten in the corner of her eye.

"If you ever come to New York—" I began.

But Tania left and closed the door behind her.

chapter twenty-one

REGRETS

It sucks waking up one day to realize you're a dick.

Most people do dickish things from time to time. Usually you find a way to dodge the blame. He started it, she had it coming, or I had a tough day, I didn't mean it, that's not really me. But sometimes you do something and look at it, and there's no way around it: you're a dick.

I had led Tania on so she would sleep with me.

I should have told her last night that I wasn't looking for anything serious. That I was leaving and not coming back. But I'd wanted to see what it was like, sleeping with a girl—wanted it too much to tell her the truth. So I'd stayed silent and allowed her to believe . . . allowed her to hope.

I wondered if Yosvany ever felt like this.

In the hours that remained before my bus to Havana I stayed in my room so I wouldn't have to face Tania again. When I finally came out with my suitcase, she was nowhere to be seen. Eduardo took my money and asked about my stay and said good-bye at the door with a pleasant smile and a firm handshake. I couldn't get out of his sight quickly enough.

It was an overcast day, relatively cool. I sweated profusely as I dragged my suitcase down the cobbled streets to the bus station. I half feared, half hoped Tania might appear at any corner. She never did.

Someone else came, though. I've no idea how he'd found out I was leaving, but there he stood outside the bus station. Baggy yellow T-shirt, worn, paint-flecked jeans. Ricardo Eugenio Echeverría López in all his glory. He squinted so hard in the morning sun that his eyes almost disappeared in his fleshy face. There was a familiar cookie tin in his hands.

He didn't move toward me when he saw me. Only looked at me, as if hoping. I almost passed him by. I didn't feel like talking to my mother's old lover this morning. But this could be the last time I saw him.

I pulled my suitcase to rest against the wall. "You came."

Ricardo studied his shoes for a while. The sneakers had once been white.

"I had forgotten what it's like, to believe you can make a difference," he said.

I blinked.

"I was once like you," he said. "Passionate. Sure of myself. I wanted to do the right thing."

Ah, yes. That was me all right.

"Here." Ricardo thrust the cookie tin at me. "Publish my poems. Let people read them. Tell everyone I wrote them. I, Ricardo Eugenio Echeverría López."

I stared at the metal tin. You've got the wrong guy, I wanted to say. I'm only here to have fun. To have fun, whatever it takes.

"It's too dangerous," I said. "You'll get in trouble."

At this Ricardo's eyes focused on me, as if he was only now fully seeing me there—and his voice came hard and sure. "I know the danger better than anyone."

"We can't risk—"

"*No te atrevas!*" Ricardo stabbed one thick finger at my chest, so hard I stumbled back. "You came to me. You made your offer. Don't you dare say no, now that I've made my decision. . . ." His words trailed off toward the end. He looked down at the tin in his hands. "It's my choice to make."

I took the poems.

Maybe it was a stupid thing to do. A dumb risk to take. A decision that wouldn't really help anyone. But Ricardo was right—the time to think about that had been before I made the offer.

Ricardo watched me secrete the tin away in my backpack. He straightened a little when I shut the zipper, and sighed.

"When you publish them, say the poems are for María," he said. "For María from Ricardo, with regrets."

Ana and Yosvany met me at the bus stop in Habana Vieja. They wore matching outfits—cutoff jeans, a white tee for him, a blouse for her, bright in the afternoon sun. Yosvany had one arm around Ana's shoulders, waved at me with the other. "Hey, *primo*, welcome back."

"Hey, Rick." Ana smiled, watching for my reaction.

"Hey, good to see you guys." It wasn't a big lie. Ever since Tania walked out of my room in Trinidad, I'd felt numb. The sight of Ana and Yosvany together barely registered. "What's new in Havana?"

"Pablo's furious you ran off to Trinidad," Yosvany said. "You don't want to hear the words he used."

"That's scary, coming from you," I said.

"He wants us at his place early tomorrow morning." Ana grinned. "We're on TV in two weeks."

My suitcase had lost one of its wheels somewhere in the bus's cargo hold. Half a block toward home, my arm ached like I'd been dragging a sack of potatoes across rocky ground. Maybe it was a good thing, because it distracted me from the spectacle of Ana with Yosvany's arm about her waist. He nuzzled her neck periodically, leaving the impression of a leech suckling on its victim. Judging from the possessive glances she tossed him, Ana didn't see it that way.

"Yosvany had a great idea," she told me. "I can use the TV show as the climax of my film. Rodrigo will get me some official footage to use."

"Yosvany has all the best ideas," I said.

"These past couple of days we've been going around Havana filming the competitors," Ana said. "Doing interviews, shooting their rehearsals. We're up against some amazing dancers."

"It should be fun," I said.

"Should be funny, at least," Yosvany said.

Ana gave him a dig in the ribs. They laughed, then kissed.

That was the general spirit of the walk home. When we got to our building, Yosvany finally released his hold on Ana. "I've got band practice," he explained. "We're planning to make a reggaeton CD. It will be huge. I'll see you guys later."

Which made me wonder if he'd only come to meet me to demonstrate his claim on Ana.

In the confines of the elevator, Ana and I managed to not look at each other. "Did you have a good time?" she asked eventually.

"I guess." A heat flared inside me, and I added, "Yeah, it was awesome."

"What did you do?"

"I met this girl." The words came out fast, before I could consider them.

"Really?"

"No need to sound so surprised," I said.

"No, I'm glad. What's she like?"

I paused, unsure how much I felt comfortable saying about Tania.

The elevator groaned to a halt. I dragged the suitcase into

the hallway and to the iron bars that enclosed Juanita's door.

Ana pressed the doorbell. "So?"

"Well . . . she's nice . . . ," I began.

The door opened. Yolanda stood on the threshold. Her whole body tense. Her face drawn tight. Not a hint of a smile on her lips.

"Hi, guys," she said loudly, then leaned forward. "Don't tell him anything," she whispered, a low, fierce sound.

A shiver rushed through me. Ana swore under her breath, one of Yosvany's favorite crudities. Neither of us was dumb enough to ask questions.

We went inside. There was no one in the living room. The smell of coffee came strong from the kitchen.

"Come," Yolanda said loudly, "you have to meet someone."

I left the suitcase by the door and we followed her to the kitchen. There, at the head of the dining table, sat a thin balding white man, perhaps forty-five. He wore pressed tan slacks and a white striped polo shirt and a small silver watch on his wrist, stylish and certainly not cheap. He sipped coffee from Juanita's best china with a vaguely pleasant expression that seemed alert and attentive.

"This is my cousin Rick from New York and his friend Ana," Yolanda said. "Kids, this is Maykel Valdes, from the government."

Valdes raised one hand as if to ward off Yolanda's words. "I'm just a man working to preserve the Revolution, like your mother." His eyes fixed on Yolanda. "And like you, of course."

Yolanda said nothing. Valdes nodded, as if she'd agreed. He turned his gaze to us.

Cold fingers squeezed my spine. This guy must know something about the video.

Now I recognized Valdes's look. It was the look a cat gave a mouse it played with—relaxed because it was in control; alert because it wasn't about to let lunch get away.

Another thought came to me: Yolanda had cut her hair for nothing.

"How do you like Cuba?" Valdes asked.

Ana and I exchanged a glance. She spoke first. "We've had a wonderful time."

"We came to dance," I explained. "Casino, you know?"

Valdes's eyebrows rose a little. "Are you good?"

I shrugged, then realized this was not the right time for modesty. "We're pretty decent."

"They can show you," Yolanda said.

"That's not necessary." Valdes hadn't taken his eyes off us. "You're Americans."

"My mother was Cuban," I said. "I wanted to see her home."

"I heard so much about the Revolution growing up," Ana said. "My father was in the Workers' Party in Puerto Rico."

Huh. She'd never mentioned it before.

"And how does the Revolution measure up to your father's stories?" Valdes asked.

Ana tilted her head. My fingernails dug hard into my palm.

"Some things are like he told me," she said. "Free medicine and schools and housing, that's wonderful. Other things, well, maybe my father was a bit optimistic."

I stared at her.

But Valdes only nodded. "So tell me, how do you keep in touch with home? By phone? Text? Email?"

I hoped Valdes couldn't see the cold sweat on my face. He knew about Lettuce. Or if he didn't, he suspected.

"We call and email occasionally," I said. "But really, we're too busy most of the time."

Valdes eyed me thoughtfully. "You've been on a trip?"

I realized I still had my backpack on. Then I realized something else.

Ricardo's poems were in that backpack. If Valdes asked to see . . . if he read them . . .

Visions of the Isle of Pines floated before my eyes. Rolling forests on a seacoast, and the scent of orange blossoms in the air, and me staring at it all from behind thick iron bars.

"I spent a few days in Trinidad," I said. "My mother was born there."

"I know," Valdes said.

The implication of his words came barreling down at me.

Valdes brought his coffee to his lips, downed it in three long gulps, and rose from the table. "Thank you for your help, Yolanda. Please say hi to your mom from me. She's been such a good leader for this neighborhood, an example for everybody."

Yolanda nodded.

"I can only hope that you will continue this tradition," Valdes said.

"Of course." Yolanda's voice shook only a little, but I heard it. I was sure Valdes did too.

He didn't show it, though. "Nice to meet you, kids. Enjoy the rest of your time in our country."

We saw him to the door. We watched him get into the elevator and listened to the motor work as it brought him downstairs.

Yolanda seemed rooted to the floor, unable to move even when he was long gone.

"Come." Ana took her hand. "Let's go inside."

We sat down in the living room. Ana brought Yolanda a cup of water. It took her a while to compose herself enough to speak.

"Someone recognized me with Miranda that day," she told us at last. "Now there was the article, and—"

"What article?" I asked.

"The *Guardian*, that British paper, did a piece about the video," Ana said. "They called Miranda Galvez a blogger kidnapped by unknown representatives of the Castro regime."

An article in the *Guardian*. A flash of triumph broke through my fear. "Lettuce did it."

"But they haven't let Miranda go," Yolanda said. "Valdes said it was criminals who took her, and whoever made that video and accused the government is a criminal too."

"They don't know it was you." Ana sounded like she was trying to convince herself. "Or they wouldn't be just talking."

"I suppose," Yolanda said.

Disorganized thoughts raced through my head. Maybe we should run. Get on the first flight to Mexico.

Ana seemed to read my mind. "We have to act like nothing's the matter. If we run, they'll know something's wrong."

There was a pause as we both considered this. Two and a half more weeks in Cuba. Seventeen days watching over our shoulders, worrying if we'd make it home. Seventeen sleepless nights waiting for a knock on the door.

"Please don't tell my mother. Maybe she won't hear about this . . ." Yolanda didn't sound like she believed it.

"You were trying to help your friend," Ana said.

"Think what this will do to her," Yolanda said. "She's been the head of our CDR for ten years. That's her life. If I get in trouble . . . I mean, she has known Miranda all her life, she'll understand. But it will break her."

I wondered how it had happened that Juanita had gotten so involved with the same government that had locked up her sister's boyfriend for twenty years—the same government that Mom escaped into exile. It was strange, to see a family split apart like this.

"The worst part is, we haven't achieved a thing," Yolanda said. "Miranda's still locked up, and God knows what they're doing to her."

Ana took her hand, squeezed it. "You did all you could. You had to, for your friend."

But I wondered. Would Ricardo agree?

∽

Then again, maybe Ricardo would indeed have agreed with Ana.

I reflected on this as I sat in Yosvany's room working through Ricardo's poems. There were perhaps two hundred pieces of paper in the cookie tin. Pages torn from a notebook, napkins, and tissues, a few sheets of printer paper, bits of newsprint, even the copyright page of a Dan Brown novel—I wondered how he'd come across that one.

Ricardo's handwriting covered every blank surface, some places flowing and elaborate with flourishes, others cramped and spidery. Some pages contained several poems, while other poems seemed to span more than one page, except there was no indication which excerpt connected up with which. I leafed through them with a mixed sense of trepidation and excitement. This would make for an interesting challenge.

Not a challenge I was about to engage in Yosvany's bedroom, though. Not when Valdes might return at any moment.

I took Ricardo's papers one by one and lay them down on the stone floor and photographed them carefully. Every ten sheets or so, I downloaded the pictures to my laptop and checked everything was legible. Then I encrypted the pictures and overwrote the data in the camera with zeroes. I wouldn't risk emailing the encrypted files—better to wait till I got back to New York.

As for the original papers, I tore them into shreds and stuffed them in a plastic bag. Technically speaking someone dedicated could piece the shreds back together, but I planned to dispose of that bag somewhere out of the way, when I was sure no one was following.

That's who I was now. Rick Gutiérrez, cunning spy and man of intrigue. Come to think of it, cat video entrepreneur was a pretty good cover identity.

I was still photographing the poems when Yosvany walked in the door.

I froze with my camera in my hand, some half dozen poems spread out on the floor.

He looked at me, at the poems, raised his eyebrows, shrugged. He walked past me and sat down on his bed, stretched his arms with a dramatic sigh. "So. Ana says you met a girl."

Oh. I'd managed to forget about Tania, this past hour. I sat down on the sofa, put aside my camera. "Yeah."

"Way to go, *primo*," Yosvany said. "So, spill it. What's she like?"

"Well . . . her name's Tania. She speaks great English and she wants to study computers—"

"I didn't ask for a biography. What's she like?" Yosvany mimed curves in the air with his hands. "You know?"

For a moment I wanted to tell him Tania was hot, the

cutest girl in town, and that I slept with her. But only for a moment. "She's nice. We had a good time."

"Tall or short? Thin, fat, curvy? A white girl?" Yosvany must have seen some reaction because he asked, "She's black?"

"What's that matter?"

"Just a little dark like me? Or really black? You don't want to date someone really black."

I stared at Yosvany.

"What?" he asked.

"Most people would call you black where I come from," I said. "Heck, they call me black sometimes, when they don't call me Mexican." I held up my arm in the light. "You really want to go around comparing pigmentation levels? Like, if someone's darker than you they're really black, but everyone else is okay?"

Yosvany gave me a flat look. "What are you saying, *primo*?"

"Doesn't it seem stupid to you? Like, if you say that crap, then I can use the same argument against you. Anyone can— you're giving them permission."

Yosvany shook his head dismissively. "You're like Ana, full of this American bullshit. It's different here in Cuba."

"Uh-huh."

I found it strange that I'd recently been worried what Yosvany might think of me. Sure, there were things I admired about him, wanted to learn from him. The way he always seemed sure of himself. The easy way he had of talking to anyone and everyone, like starting a conversation with a stranger was as simple as saying hi. His dance skills, of course—and, well, even some of his girl skills. But for everything that he knew and understood, he really was clueless about so much else.

Then again, that wasn't so hard to understand. I'd adopted Yosvany's attitudes with Tania not just because I'd been desperate to get with her, but also because I wanted to feel like a man, like someone Yosvany would approve of. If I'd had friends like him buzzing in my ear all my life . . .

"You need to relax, *primo*." Yosvany got up from his bed. "Put aside all those papers and go outside, enjoy yourself. Like I will right now, with my girlfriend." The last couple of words sounded almost vindictive.

For a while after he left I sat on the sofa, wondering. Go outside, he said. Enjoy yourself.

Read less, Rachel had told me. Turn off your computer. Get off your ass.

I was glad I'd taken Rachel's advice. My life had gotten more fun. I'd seen more of the world, become a person even I found more interesting, though I didn't like everything that I'd done along the way. But there was only so far I was willing to take this. I wasn't about to stop reading or watching TV, or running the best damn cat video site on the internet.

I enjoyed all those things. More, I learned from them. I learned things Yosvany never would if he spent all his days on the streets of Havana.

So I stayed there in Yosvany's room and took pictures of

Ricardo's poems. Later, when I was done—when thoughts of Maykel Valdes pressed down on me, alternating with images of Yosvany and Ana necking in her room—I played *Monty Python and the Holy Grail* on my laptop and allowed the Knights Who Say Ni to educate me on the value of shrubbery. And I had no regrets.

chapter twenty-two

LEAD AND FOLLOW

The next morning Ana had dark circles under her eyes. I guessed neither of us had slept much. We headed out for Pablo's after breakfast. The street outside Juanita's was quiet, only a lone *bicitaxi* rattling along. We kept quiet too, walking side by side in silence.

Pablo met us with zeal in his eyes. "*Qué vuelta?*" he greeted us. "Come in, let's get to work!"

He'd cleaned up the apartment. Every surface in the kitchen and the living room gleamed. The window was open to the street, letting in fresh air and ample sunlight. Pablo wore a new white T-shirt, basketball shorts, and rubber flip-flops—an unusually relaxed looked for him.

"You're competing in two weeks," he told us. "Rodrigo wants to film an interview with me as your teacher. That means one thing."

I scratched my head. "You'll be famous?"

"We'd better get good," Ana said.

"We'll practice four hours a day, six days a week," Pablo said.

"I suppose," Ana said. "As long as I'm free in the afternoons to shoot my film."

"I'm not sure we can afford four hours of class a day," I said.

"I won't charge you extra," Pablo said. "This is a great opportunity for all of us."

Pablo, offering to help for free. This was the same man who needed money so bad, he'd begged us on his knees.

A mysterious smile had crept onto Pablo's lips. "You kids have no idea what's waiting for you. Rodrigo's preparing a real surprise."

After recent events, I wasn't sure how I felt about surprises. But Pablo wasn't about to tell.

Four hours later, we wobbled downstairs on unsteady feet and ambled across Habana Vieja like retiree tourists taking in the sights. It was a pleasant kind of exhaustion. The sort that promised a dreamless afternoon nap once we got back, with no thoughts of Valdes to bother me.

But a few blocks from home, Ana touched me on the shoulder. "Don't look," she said. "There's a *bicitaxi* following us."

I woke up real fast. "You sure?"

"It was parked across from your aunt's place in the morning," Ana said. "I remember the guy."

I stopped, crouched to tie a shoelace, and used the pause to look around. I saw the *bicitaxi*. The driver was a skinny young kid. He had a phone in his hand and seemed absorbed in it even as he pedaled down the street, like his texts were more important than traffic.

His texts—or the phone's camera, pointed at us.

Maybe I wouldn't be taking that nap after all.

⌒

Over the next week we didn't see that same *bicitaxi* again. Every time we emerged on the street I looked left and right to check who was near, but I saw no recurring faces, except for a few of Juanita's neighbors now and then. Occasionally on the way to Pablo's I'd have us walk all the way around a single block, a trick I'd read about for figuring out if you were being tailed. We spotted no one.

"Maybe it was a coincidence," I told Ana after one such walk.

"Maybe," she said. A few steps later, she glanced over her shoulder for the fifteenth time that morning.

Every afternoon when I got back and locked Juanita's steel door behind me, a shiver of relief went through me. Except I knew that I'd have to go out again before long.

I forced myself to eat—everything tasted like cardboard, but I was doing too much exercise to skip meals. Then I lay

281

on the sofa in Yosvany's room and napped as long as I could. During what remained of the afternoon, I read books on my laptop to distract myself.

Ana, though—every day she left for the street again right after lunch. She texted Yosvany to get the address for the interview of the day, got her camera bag and, every time, asked if I wanted to come.

"We can't let them intimidate us," she said. "We haven't done anything wrong."

Tell that to my friend Ricardo, I wanted to say.

I admired Ana's energy and drive—and I had no intention whatsoever of going along with her. It wasn't just the fear. Wherever she went on those afternoons, so did Yosvany. If I heard him introduce her to one more person as his girlfriend, I might throw up. He always did it with this grand sweep of his arm, as if saying—check her out, she's my *yuma*.

Juanita gave me sympathetic glances the first few days, then cornered me in the kitchen one afternoon. "Relationships are hard," she informed me. "There was this boy I liked when I was your age. His name was Alfredo, and he—"

"*Déjalo, mamá.*" Yolanda stood in the kitchen door. "Rick will do fine without your advice."

I might have believed Yolanda wanted to protect my feelings, if not for how quickly she'd appeared when Juanita addressed me. She did her best not to leave me or Ana alone with her mother, as if we might inadvertently betray her secret. She stalked the apartment restlessly, hugging herself and gnawing her lips—I could only imagine what she felt inside.

One day I ran into Rafaela in the hallway. "Did you meet Ricardo?" she asked me at once. "How is he?"

I could tell she was hoping for a specific answer.

"He's a painter now," I said.

"Did he . . ." Rafaela drifted off. "Is he married?"

"He lives alone," I told her.

Rafaela nodded. It was a heavy nod, sad but satisfied, like this was what she'd expected.

And I realized my mother's relationship with Ricardo was more than a memory to Rafaela. It was a romantic story of the tragic kind, of doomed lovers severed by fate, destined never to be happy again.

I was tempted to tell her Mom had been happy in New York. I was tempted to say Mom and Ricardo had been kids taking dumb risks—that they should have known better. But I decided to let Rafaela believe the story she preferred.

And really, maybe Mom *had* loved Ricardo all those long years. There was the coincidence of my name to consider, for one thing.

The idea made me feel uneasy, disloyal to Dad, but that didn't make it impossible. If there was one thing I'd learned on this trip, it was that love was a messy thing.

❧

I said that we didn't see that *bicitaxi* again for a week. That's true. The next time we saw it was eight days later, in the evening on our way to La Gruta.

That afternoon Ana had gone all the way to Marianao for a shoot—a forty-minute trip. The dancers she was supposed to film hadn't been there to meet her. Nor had Yosvany. He didn't pick up the phone or answer her texts. She waited for an hour before coming back. Naturally she got caught in a downpour.

When Ana walked in Juanita's door, wet hair plastered to her skull, her outlook wasn't sunny. Picture a winter's day on the slopes of Mount Doom.

"Maybe something came up," I suggested, once she'd changed and sat drinking hot tea in the living room.

The look she gave me cast aspersions on my intelligence. "Of course something came up."

"What I mean is, maybe it wasn't his fault." I wasn't sure why I was defending Yosvany. "Maybe we should worry."

"*Qué va.*" Juanita passed through the living room, serene as a ship in harbor. "Yosvany's always running off after some shiny new thing. You can't count on that boy."

Which, judging from the tightening of her jaw, did approximately nothing to improve Ana's mood. It amazed me that Juanita failed to realize what she sounded like.

Or perhaps . . . perhaps Juanita knew exactly what she was saying.

"We're going dancing," Ana announced then. "Without Yosvany."

So Ana and I ended up walking down San Lázaro that

night. And we spotted that same *bicitaxi* crawling along behind us, the driver on the phone again.

"*Pinga*," Ana swore. She'd adapted a good deal of Yosvany's vocabulary since I left for Trinidad. "Let's go around the block."

We circled the block, not speaking at all, nor looking over our shoulders. But when we came to that same stretch of street once again, I glanced back.

The *bicitaxi* was behind us.

"Let's take a cab," I suggested.

But Ana was no longer by my side. She ran at the *bicitaxi* with long, furious lopes. "Hey!" she called. "*Oye, cabrón!*"

The driver started. He got up on the pedals, swung the wheel, turned the cab around with nimble ease. Ana was some thirty feet away, running hard. I thought she might catch up, but the guy accelerated fast, took off down the empty street like a rattling, clanging chariot.

Ana ran on for a bit, then slowed to a halt, panting. Turned and walked back to me.

I hadn't moved all the while. My insides felt dried up, inert, fragile.

"I wanted to see what would happen if I did that," Ana said, grim and satisfied. "It turns out, *nada*."

A few hours later, we stood outside La Gruta on Calle 23, trying to hail a *colectivo* to go home. A Toyota with tinted windows and dark green government plates pulled up. The passenger window rolled down. Maykel Valdes looked up at us.

chapter twenty-three

HOSPITALITY

"Get in the car."

Valdes's voice came flat, quiet, almost lost in the din of traffic. His small, deep-set eyes watched us calmly. Not a hint of pleasantness this time, his expression a cool mask.

His driver was a big man in a faded tan dress shirt. He stared ahead, beefy hands on the steering wheel. Under his armpit hung a compact black pistol in a leather shoulder holster.

Ana and I glanced at each other. She was ready to sprint down the street.

But sprint where? Twenty-Third was a commercial street, the heart of Havana's nightlife, brightly lit and crawling with police at all hours. And the police wouldn't be on our side.

"Where are we going?" Ana asked.

"You'll see."

"Let me text my cousin." I pulled out my phone. "So she doesn't worry we're late."

"Do what you like," Valdes said.

With numb fingers I stabbed at my cell. *Valdes told us to get in car outside La Gruta. Don't know what's going on.* I selected Yolanda's number, hit send, waited for the delivery confirmation to pop up. Cuba's cell network being what it was, it took a while.

We got into the back of the Toyota. The driver put the car into gear and we pulled out into traffic.

The car was relatively new, the brown leather seats clean of scuff marks and the seat belts functional, a rare thing in Cuba. The stench of cigarettes pervaded everything, though no one was smoking. The radio was tuned to Radio Rebelde, one of Cuba's main stations. A woman talked about the visit of a group of Venezuelan social workers to the province of Matanzas. She spoke with the kind of enthusiasm most people reserved for their team winning the World Series.

Valdes and the driver seemed content to let the radio do the talking. We did a U-turn and drove up Twenty-Third for a while, then took a left on Paseo. Heading toward the Plaza de la Revolución. I recalled vaguely that Fidel's office was supposed to be somewhere around there.

Except that before long the driver made a turn and another

and another. We entered a warren of dark side streets. Low residential buildings floated by in the gloom. Only here and there a lone streetlamp illuminated a stretch of pavement.

Something cold touched my wrist. I started, then realized it was Ana. We locked hands, her fingers clutching at me painfully hard.

My phone rang, a shrill, insistent tone. I reached for it.

"Leave it," Valdes said.

We drove on, while the phone rang and rang in my pocket, until at last it fell silent mid-ring.

I could imagine Yolanda sitting at the kitchen table, her fingers pale around her phone. She could do nothing to help us. We were gone, as her friend Miranda was gone.

We stopped at a well-lit intersection. There was a small café on one corner, a blue neon ice cream cone in the window. We parked across from the café, in front of a gray three-story building.

That building . . . every single one of its narrow windows had sturdy metal bars across it. The entrance was an unmarked steel rectangle. It was the kind of place that might swallow you and never spit you back up.

"Get out," Valdes said.

Ana still held my hand. A comforting feeling.

Valdes stood beside us while the driver stayed in the car. For a while, he let us take in the view. Then he said, "When we bring people here, they say they're sorry. But it's too late by then."

Ana and I said nothing. I had a feeling there was nothing we could say to make a difference, not with a man like Valdes. He had already decided what would happen here.

"Let's go," Valdes said at last, and I steeled myself. But he turned away from the building. Crossed the street to the café on the corner.

After a moment's hesitation, we followed him inside.

Four white tables, cold fluorescent lighting, white tile floor. Sugary bachata poured from a CD player. The air smelled of dishwater, not food.

The only person in the café was the waitress, a bored-looking woman in her fifties. She stood over a glass-topped fridge with some six tubs of different-colored ice cream—a wide selection by Cuban standards. When she saw Valdes, she livened and smiled, though the expression never reached her eyes. "Good evening, Maykel. What can I get you?"

Valdes gestured for the two of us to sit down. "A coffee for me. A scoop of vanilla for the girl, and mamey for Rick here. Isn't that right?" he asked us, unsmiling.

We stared at him. That was no accidental order. It's what we got at El Naranjal on Obispo, most days after practice.

Valdes sat down with us. "It's good hospitality to know your guests' preferences."

"Are we your guests?" Ana asked.

"I'd like to say so," Valdes said. "But good guests don't go peeking about in your cupboards and stealing your silver-ware."

"I don't know what you mean—" I began.

"I thought maybe I didn't need to spell things out," Valdes said. "You're not as intelligent as you appear. You were seen visiting Lisyani Blanco with your cousin Yolanda. We know you helped publish that video."

Neither of us said a word.

"Let's do a thought experiment," Valdes said. "Let's say I were to visit New York as a tourist and make a video of secret government operations. Let's say I were to smuggle this video out to China and have a Chinese newspaper publish it against the interests of American national security. And let's say I got caught by your FBI. What do you think would happen to me?" Valdes's lips twitched up in a half smile. "Maybe they'd send me to Cuba, eh? To Guantánamo? Would I ever see my family again?"

My palms, flat down on the table, were slick with sweat. I had difficulty finding the breath to speak. But Ana crossed her arms and looked Valdes straight in the eye. "In America, we don't abduct people in the street."

Valdes gave a short bark of a laugh. "If you believe that, *niña*, then you're even more naive than I thought."

"We sure don't abduct someone for blogging about the economy," Ana said.

"That's right. You only shoot people for walking down the street while black. But I'm not here to debate government policy. The point is, you're guests in our house and you've pissed on the carpet and taken a shit in the soup pot."

Valdes spoke the crudities with the same controlled ease as everything else, never raising his voice. But there was no missing the very real anger in his eyes, as he looked from me to Ana and back.

"We intended no disrespect to your country," I managed at last, though the words came out raspy. "My mother was born here."

"She should have raised you better," Valdes said.

Hot anger spiked in me, despite everything. I ground my teeth. Said nothing.

Valdes nodded at last. "The problem remains. What should I do with you?"

"Just leave us alone," Ana said. "You don't need a scandal, do you?"

Valdes stared at her. "Maybe we don't. Then again, maybe we need to make an example. A warning for meddling foreigners."

"We are Americans—"

"You think we're scared of *yanquis*?" Valdes asked. "You've tried to destroy us for almost sixty years, and we're still here."

"So you want to destroy diplomatic relations all over again?" Ana asked. I marveled at how strong her voice sounded, even as her fingers clutched hard at the edge of the table. "Demonstrate to the whole world that Cuba is a tyrannical dictatorship just so you can lock up a couple of American teenagers?"

Valdes took a long, deliberative sip of his coffee. "In a true dictatorship, they'd do a lot more than lock you up. If this were still Batista's Cuba, you'd disappear and never be seen again. There would be no scandal. Just two missing kids."

"We . . . my cousin Yolanda knows we're here," I squeezed out from lungs that refused to work properly.

Valdes gave me a look of withering contempt. "You're lucky," he said. "Cuba is a civilized country. We treat visitors with courtesy. And besides, your aunt Juanita has been a good friend to my boss. So here's how it will be." He leaned forward, and his voice fell to an intent hiss. "I will let you leave here today. But if you make another stupid move . . . if you so much as try to avoid my men . . . I will have no choice. If you speak of this whole affair to anyone, even after you leave this country, I will have no choice. There will be consequences for you and for your family. Do you understand?"

I nodded dumbly. I realized his words were meant to be a threat, but I only heard one thing—even after you leave this country.

He was letting us go. The relief was so powerful, I shook with it.

"All you did accomplished nothing," Valdes said, sitting back. "That's what I want you to remember. That's why I'm letting you go. Because the Revolution is strong. Because the noise you make doesn't matter. Because you don't matter."

He stared at both of us for a long, long time, as if waiting for a response. At last, I realized that I was nodding, my chin moving up and down, though I didn't recall deciding on the action.

"Forget all this nonsense," Valdes said. "Go to the beach. Dance casino. Fly home. And don't come back to Cuba. Am I clear?"

I would have simply nodded again. But Ana spoke up, surprising me. "This is Rick's country. His family lives here. You can't tell him to not come back."

Valdes looked at her for the longest time. "You know nothing about this country," he said at last.

It was clear it was all the answer he would give her.

Valdes got up. Even as the waitress brought the coffee and ice cream, he walked to the door. He stopped before leaving. "Don't eat here," he told us matter-of-factly. "You don't want to spend your last days in Cuba locked in the toilet."

⁓

For a while after Valdes left we stayed in the café, staring at the bowls of slowly melting ice cream, saying not a word. The mixed wash of relief and fear tasted foul on my tongue, seemed to choke up my throat. When we got up to leave, steam no longer rose from Valdes's coffee.

The waitress stopped us. "That's five CUC." Her flat voice showed no sign that she'd heard anything Valdes had said to us. She certainly didn't care that we hadn't touched the ice cream.

We paid up, of course. A service fee for intimidation by a government goon.

Valdes's car was gone. Without a word exchanged we started down the deserted street, in the direction we'd come from. The night air hung still and heavy around us, muffling all sound. Even our footfalls became muted, like the rhythmic ticking of some distant clock. The dark houses and gardens around us seemed entirely bereft of life, as though we walked through some evacuated town in Chernobyl.

The silence seemed appropriate, a match for the quiet inside my head. Not the quiet of peace, but the quiet of absence. The conversation with Valdes had frozen my brain like a modern website might freeze Internet Explorer.

"I'm sorry," Ana said at last.

"About what?"

"That stuff he said, about how we can't come back . . ."

It hit me.

I'd never get to come back. Never again see Juanita and Yolanda and Yosvany, never again visit the places Mom grew up, the people she knew . . . never walk along the Malecón at night and go dancing at the Milocho and stroll down Obispo on a hot Sunday afternoon.

I wanted to cry and throw up and laugh at the same time, a bizarre sensation. As if someone had reached inside me and ripped something vital out of me, and I couldn't function anymore.

I wondered if this was how Mom had felt, the day she decided to leave on the boat to Miami.

Perhaps Ana realized what I was thinking, because she spoke again, with forced cheer. "I doubt it's official, like a ban or anything. I mean, maybe he's only trying to scare us."

"There are consequences for everything," I said. "I only wish I'd met Ricardo earlier. Then I would have known."

Ana was silent for a moment. "Would you do it all again?" she asked. "If Yolanda asked you to help her friend?"

"You heard him. We accomplished nothing."

"But would you do it?"

There it was. An easy question on the surface, yet when I opened my mouth to say—no, of course not—the words died in my throat.

Because when I thought about Cuba, about the time I'd spent here, it wasn't only the dancing that came to mind. I thought of the collapsed buildings on every other corner. I thought of the *jineteros* on Havana's streets, making a living the only way they knew. I thought of Mom and Ricardo as kids, walking down the Prado hand in hand, not knowing what was about to happen to them.

Something else occurred to me. If I published Ricardo's poems, if I used the inscription he'd requested—for María from Ricardo, with regrets—sooner or later they'd trace them back to me. To my family. And there would be consequences.

I had a responsibility to Ricardo. But I also had a commitment to my family. The inscription would have to go. And I couldn't put the poems on my site. I'd have to find another publisher. If MININT talked to him, I'd have to hope that Ricardo would keep his mouth shut about me.

"So we do what Valdes says," Ana said. "Dance. Go to the

beach. Leave the country. And leave this fight to Yolanda and her friends."

I heard the judgment in her voice, but that didn't change the truth.

"It's the responsible thing to do," I said.

chapter twenty-four

TO FEEL NOTHING

The last days before the competition passed quickly. Pablo kept us too worn out to think—he grew more agitated by the day. "What's the matter with you kids?" he'd ask. "You've lost your spark."

We couldn't tell him, of course. The days after the car ride were almost a relief, though. The previous week we'd suspected someone was watching us. Now we *knew* we were being watched. The certainty of it was liberating.

It wasn't fear that got me, that final week. It was living my last days in Havana and knowing I might never return.

I sat down for breakfast with Juanita, and she told me next year I had to come for Yolanda's birthday. We'd rent a cabin on the beach and grill food and lounge in the sun. I nodded and smiled and said that sounded nice. She laughed with someone on the phone or sang boleros doing the dishes—and I couldn't understand how someone right next to me, someone breathing the same air, could possibly be so cheerful.

As for Yosvany, all he talked about these days was his reggaeton CD. His band had gotten studio time, and he talked of winning a Latin Grammy already. Neither Ana nor I saw much point in dampening his spirits.

"I like him," Ana said. "I mean, *cantidad*. But it's not his political acumen that gets me going, if you know what I'm saying."

Which was a conversation that I stopped right there. But still, despite everything, I knew I'd miss my cousin.

Yolanda had freaked out the night of our conversation with Valdes. We'd only remembered to call her when we got to Avenida de los Presidentes. By that time she'd taken a cab to La Gruta and asked everyone within five blocks if they'd seen us. She'd been about to go home and tell Juanita everything, hoping her government friends could help. When we finally met up on Twenty-Third that night, she sat us down in a small street café, her expression quiet, grave.

"I'm so sorry," she said. "I made a mistake getting you guys involved. You have to promise me one thing—for the rest of your time in Cuba, don't take any risks. Not a single one, okay?"

We didn't tell her that we'd already made that same decision.

The morning before the contest, we walked to Pablo's for one final practice. In the stairwell to his apartment, the sound of raised voices made us stop—Pablo's voice and his daughter Liliana's.

"—give me a chance, *mija*. I'm working things out—"

"Yeah, with Jimmy and Dionisio and those guys every night, don't you think I know?"

"Yes, with Jimmy and Dionisio, playing dominoes!"

"Ha!"

"Come back and you'll see. I'm working hard every day, training those *yumas* for a TV show—"

"Oh, stop already—"

"It's true! You should see them now that—"

"Grow up, *papá*. I've got to go."

Ana tugged at my arm. Up to that point I'd stood frozen on the stairs, listening, not sure whether to go up or retreat. But she pulled me forward decisively.

We reached the top to find Pablo and his daughter still there, faced off outside his apartment door. Liliana wore the same white outfit as the last time I saw her, and it looked damp with sweat. Her son Lalo hugged her waist and studied the floor between his mother and grandfather.

"There they are!" Relief washed across Pablo's face. "Morning, guys."

"Morning," Ana said. She strode right up to them, leaving me to catch up.

"Hi," I said with my usual eloquence.

Liliana acknowledged us with a tight nod. "I'm off, *papá*. We've got shopping to do."

"Come in for a minute," Pablo said. "Watch Rick and Ana dance."

"I don't want to bother them," Liliana said.

"It's no problem," I said.

Liliana shook her head. "I only came by for the mail. It's a busy day."

"Well, then, promise us one thing." Ana smiled cheerfully, as if she really believed Liliana's words. "You'll watch us on TV."

Liliana's eyebrows rose. She glanced at Pablo, nodded. "Fine. Let's go, Lalo."

The boy cast a look over his shoulder, waved at his grandpa uncertainly. Pablo didn't wave back. When they were gone he didn't move from the door, didn't say a thing, didn't look at us—only stared at where Lalo had been moments ago.

After a moment Ana touched his shoulder. "Come, Pablo. Let's dance."

"I . . . ," he began, then seemed to gather himself. "I can't today."

"The contest's tomorrow," I said.

"I'm sorry," Pablo said flatly. "I've got plans."

Ana and I exchanged a glance. Minutes ago Pablo had been ready for a class. I think we both knew what kind of plan he'd come up with.

"These things take time, Pablo," Ana said. "They will

learn to trust you again, if you only—"

"Shut your mouth!" Pablo barked.

I jumped. Ana herself barely even drew back, though I suspected that was surprise more than anything.

"I don't need advice from a couple of kids who've seen nothing of life," Pablo said.

Ana looked at him. It was a steady look and calm.

I realized I'd been wrong. She wasn't surprised at all.

"You're right. I haven't seen much of life." Ana spoke quietly. "But I know this. Your daughter, she wants to believe you. She wants to believe you so bad it hurts. But she's afraid."

I listened to her. Something ached deep in my chest.

Pablo grunted. He turned away, walked to his door.

That ache in my chest, it worked its way up my throat. "You made a promise," I said. "Back when we started out, you promised that you'd keep it together."

Pablo stopped halfway through the door. Didn't turn to look at me.

"Hold off until tomorrow," I said. "Come see us dance. You owe us that."

He went inside and shut the door. The lock turned.

Ana sighed.

"You okay?" I asked.

"Oh, yeah." Ana gestured dismissively. "People make their own choices. There's nothing you can do about it."

I nodded, though I didn't buy her nonchalance. "Want to go back and practice on our own?"

"Maybe later. Yosvany's playing at the *paladar* this morning. You want to come?"

That pang in my chest again.

"Some other time," I said.

We both knew there would be no other time on this trip. Or possibly ever.

∾

By eleven o'clock that night, Ana and Yosvany still hadn't returned.

It was a hot, windless evening, and the electricity was out in our building. I sat bare-chested in the dark of the living room, hoping to catch a breeze from the open windows, and stared at the door. I felt like the star of one of those dog-waiting-for-owner videos—not a fitting pastime for the Cat Guy, perhaps, but I couldn't make myself turn away.

When Juanita had asked, I'd covered for them, said Yosvany was taking Ana to a concert. In fact, Ana and I had been planning to practice.

A hundred scenarios floated before my eyes in the dark, a hallucinogenic sequence. The two of them held up by thugs on a dark street in Centro Habana, or locked up in some police cell, or disappeared behind the gray walls of Valdes's workplace, never to emerge again.

There was also a different kind of vision. The two of them in some bedroom, going at it loud and hard, in Technicolor and Dolby Surround. Oblivious that I was freaking out.

At eleven fifteen, I picked up my cell and dialed Ana's

302

number for the seventeenth time. The tone rang. Rang. Rang. Clicked off.

It was time to tell Yolanda.

My cell buzzed.

A message from Ana. It contained the address of an intersection in Miramar and one word, *come*.

I caught a rolling coffin of an *almendrón* across town. My destination proved a well-lit corner in a residential part of Miramar, home to a mansion-sized night club.

Kids my age were chilling outside, smoking and drinking and chatting among themselves. Even out on the street, the music rattled windows.

I steeled myself, paid the entrance, and went in.

Dark corridors. Choking cigarette smoke. Cold, cold air from industrial-strength AC—my damp T-shirt became an icy towel about my torso. Kids lounged about by the walls. I scanned the faces in the dark but saw no sign of Ana or Yosvany. A door off the corridor led to a dance floor; I went inside.

Noise. Louder than anything I'd ever heard. The music blasted at you like a cannon going off in your face three times a second.

Disco lights flashed on and off in a rapid, dizzying sequence. Lasers painted green patterns on the black-box walls and floor, and on the milling kids. Teenagers all of them, the youngest club crowd I'd seen in Havana, swaying and gyrating, thrusting their chests in and out to the reggaeton beat. Many of the kids danced in couples. The girl bent forward at the waist, swaying. The guy behind her, his crotch up against her butt, thrusting in rhythmic pantomime. A subtle, nuanced dance, reggaeton.

I looked for Ana and Yosvany in the crowd.

Not here.

I left the dance floor, kept going down the corridor outside. It ended in a bar area. The music here, still louder than at any bar in New York, must have been too quiet for the locals—only a few kids were at the counter drinking.

In the corner, at a plastic table with six Bucanero empties before her, sat Ana.

She looked up unsteadily when I approached. "Hey." Her makeup was smudged. She'd been crying.

I sat beside her. "What happened?"

Ana didn't answer for so long I thought she never would. She picked up a can of Bucanero, rattled it, looked at the bar as if weighing the difficulty of getting up. "Remember when I started going out with Yosvany? How I said I just wanted to have fun? That I knew what he was like?"

"Aha."

"Well, I was right about the second part."

I considered this. "I'm sorry."

And I was. To my own surprise, I felt no vindictiveness, no urge to say I told you so.

"I thought I wouldn't care." Ana's voice shook. "But that's tough, you know?"

I thought of Tania my last morning in Trinidad, standing

there in the middle of my room. "Yeah."

"I guess it takes practice, learning to feel nothing." She tipped over the empty can of beer at her fingertips. "This stuff does help, though. You do feel less. I wonder if my dad . . . I wonder if that's why . . ."

I had no wisdom to offer her, so we sat in silence for a while. Ana bumped her shoulder against mine once, as if by accident, then again. Then she leaned against me.

It occurred to me that Yosvany would call this a prime opportunity. Comfort Ana, pat her back, see if this could become something more.

Maybe a few weeks ago I would have felt tempted.

Eventually Ana spoke again. "So I showed up at the *paladar*, looking for Yosvany. But his uncle Elio was like, what are you doing here? Said Yosvany asked for the key to his house and he figured we, well . . ." Ana glanced at me, looked away. "Well, we used the house sometimes, you know. So we could—"

"Yeah, yeah," I said quickly. "No need to draw me a picture."

"Except going to the house wasn't the plan today. I understood at once what was up. Elio must have realized too, because he got this look. I told him—oh, yeah, d'oh, I forgot, what a dumbass. And I ran out of there, grabbed a cab. Because you know these machos, I was sure the first thing Elio did was call Yosvany, give him a heads up. So I rushed across Vedado, thinking maybe I'll catch this girl bolting out of the house.

Except I was wrong." Ana laughed, a short, sharp sound. "I forgot Yosvany turns off his phone in bed."

I pulled away from her a bit. I didn't want to know what Yosvany did in bed.

Ana kept right on. "I walked in on them. Kenny G playing, this song he said made him think of me. An empty Havana Club on the floor. And the two of them on the kitchen table. You want to know the best part?"

I really wasn't sure I did, but Ana told me anyway.

"The girl was Celia, this white dancer chick. Yosvany introduced us a while ago. I shot her dancing for my film. We'd been hanging out for weeks, the three of us—and all the while he was banging her." Ana crunched her fist around the nearest beer can. "Classy guy, your cousin."

"I'm sorry." Then, piecing it together, "Wait, you shot this girl for your film? Is she . . . ?"

"Yeah. She's dancing in the contest tomorrow."

"With Yosvany?"

"What? No, with her partner." Ana snorted. "I told Yosvany he better not show up tomorrow, or I'm gonna slug him on national TV."

"Well . . ." I considered what I was about to say, decided I was okay with it. "We don't have to dance tomorrow. Not if you don't want to."

"You kidding? We're gonna show up and we're gonna win this thing. Show that skank how it's done."

"Sure." Ana had shown me some footage of the other

306

couples practicing. I rated our chances on par with those of the Jamaican bobsled team in the Winter Olympics. "We'll leave them in the dust."

Ana draped her arm across my back, an easy, familiar gesture. "You're a great guy, Rick." She leaned her head on my shoulder. "Trustworthy, not like that *comemierda*. And you're a hunk too."

I sat perfectly still for a moment, wondering. Maybe . . .

But I knew this wasn't real.

I put my arm around her shoulders, gave them a squeeze. "We'd better get home."

"I'm not a drunk," she spoke up then, straightening forcefully. "I've just had a hard day. You know that, Rick. You know that, don't you?"

"Of course," I told her. "Let's get back, okay?"

"Yeah, yeah." She slurred her words a bit, gave me a sly little smile. "Take me to bed, Rick Gutiérrez."

I did. Ana to her bed and me to mine.

Though not before she hugged me goodnight, long and tight. Then I too wished I knew how to feel nothing.

chapter twenty-five

CASINERO MUNDIAL

Yosvany didn't come back that night. Next morning at breakfast Ana avoided my gaze.

"Forget yesterday," I said to her. "Let's just dance, all right?"

Then she did look at me. She smiled and nodded and passed me the honey. I suspected that was all we'd ever say about Rick the hunk and his chances with Ana Cabrera.

We danced a few songs in the living room, then got ready to go. Casino was a street dance, not ballroom. I wore clean blue jeans and a V-neck instead of a tux. But Ana . . .

When she came out into the living room, I thought they might need to call the fire brigade to put me out. She had on this tight little dress, red on white, down to mid-thigh. Tongues of flame curled along the curves of her body, broken by a neat black belt.

I opened my mouth, closed it again. "Where'd you get that?"

"A leftover from my wilder days," Yolanda said from the couch.

"Make us proud, *niños*," Juanita said.

"I'm already proud," Yolanda said.

Ana and I knew what she meant, even if Juanita didn't.

We were supposed to meet Rodrigo at the Cabaña fortress, where *Casinero Mundial* would start shooting at eleven. From Juanita's kitchen window you could see the enormous fortress straddling the canal into the Port of Havana, with its long white stretch of aged stone wall.

The weather had shifted overnight—the morning was cool and clear. We walked to the Prado to catch a cab. I tried to enjoy the fresh breeze, but my stomach had shrunk into a pulsating sac of nerves.

I was about to dance in front of a whole country.

When we got on the road and Ana told me there was a car following our cab, it barely registered. I checked out the gray Mitsubishi at the far end of the block—government plates, tinted windows—and shrugged. "Valdes's guys."

"Business as usual, huh," Ana said.

Except then we passed through the tunnel and approached the Cabaña—the gray stone fortress imposing ahead of us— and got stopped at a roadblock. A full-on checkpoint with two green army jeeps flanking the road and soldiers holding submachine guns.

One soldier—a young, thin, clean-shaven kid—stood in the middle of the road, flagging us down.

The driver, a chain-smoking older white guy, cursed as he pulled over. In the back Ana and I exchanged a look.

"Is this usual?" Ana asked him.

"Say that you're my friends," the driver said. "I'm not supposed to carry tourists."

He stopped next to the soldier and rolled down his window.

The soldier peered at the two of us in the back of the car. Up close I realized he was no more than a year or two older than me.

"The Cabaña is closed for tourists today," he said. "They're shooting a TV show."

"It's okay," I said. "We're here for the show."

Brakes shrieked.

The gray Mitsubishi ground to a halt beside us. The door burst open. Maykel Valdes sprang out.

The soldier clutched at his gun. "What—?"

"I'm taking over here." Valdes quivered as he strode up, as if he couldn't hold himself still. He pulled a small plastic pouch from the pocket of his sports coat, showed it to the soldier. "Search the car."

The soldier stared at Valdes's ID, straightened. "Understood." He waved an okay to a couple of his comrades who'd been watching the exchange tensely, then turned to the driver. "Pop the trunk." To us, he said, "Step outside."

The driver had gone white as milk. He was probably wondering if he'd been transporting two of the CIA's youngest recruits in the back of his Lada. He got out.

Ana and I looked at each other. So maybe we wouldn't have to dance today after all.

We got out, stood beside the car while the soldier searched the trunk.

"What's the matter?" I asked Valdes.

He only nodded at the soldier, gestured at us. "The *yumas* too."

The pat down wasn't too bad; the TSA got more intimate with you. The soldier checked my bag, found only our dance shoes, and shook his head at Valdes.

Valdes studied him for a moment, as if wondering if he could trust the guy. He shifted his gaze to us. "Didn't I warn you to behave yourselves?"

"I don't get it," Ana said. "You told us to go to the beach and to dance casino. That's why we're here. To dance casino."

Valdes looked slowly from me to Ana and back. "You're here to dance? Today, at the Cabaña?"

"Yeah," I said. "For a TV show. *Casinero Mundial*, you know?"

"You're on *Casinero Mundial*." A light seemed to have gone on behind Valdes's eyes.

"That's right," I said.

"You're here for the contest," he said.

"We got invited after winning a competition at the Milocho." I reached into my pocket, drew out the participant pass Pablo had given us. "Look."

Valdes took the slip of paper. Studied it for a long while. "If this is some kind of trick . . . ," he said after a moment. "If you mean to make a scene on TV or something . . ."

"We're here to dance," I said.

"Besides, it's not even a live transmission," Ana said.

Valdes nodded. Shook his head, a small motion. Then he laughed. He actually laughed, an amused snigger that went on for a while. "It's fine, then. In a way it's almost perfect. You two dancing at the Cabaña, today of all days."

The soldier stared at him, perplexed. Ana and I shared his confusion.

"You can go," Valdes said. "But I'll be watching you. Do you understand?"

We nodded.

The cab driver waded in. "I don't know these people." He waved at us defensively. "I'm going home."

Valdes rounded on him, stabbed his chest with one bony finger. "You will shut up and take them to the Cabaña."

At which point we got back into the cab and the driver took us to the Cabaña. He didn't talk, didn't even smoke, only kept checking the rearview mirror. Valdes's Mitsubishi followed us a few car lengths away.

Within minutes, we reached the fortress entrance, a

formidable stone gate. It was accessed by a bridge across a moat that I suspected had been a drawbridge once, ready for fast removal in case of an attack. The current version was solid, paved in brick, with decorative wooden balusters. It made the Cabaña look like the tourist attraction it now was, instead of the prison where Che Guevara had executed enemies of the state.

We got out. I was reaching for my wallet when the Lada screeched into motion. The driver did a violent U-turn and raced away.

"Poor guy," Ana said.

"None of this makes sense," I said. "Why would Valdes flip because we're going to be on TV?"

"Maybe he thought we were going to do some kind of political protest. But why's the army here?"

Ana pointed at the parking lot that adjoined the fortress walls. There, some half dozen figures in fatigues lounged around four jeeps. As we watched, Valdes pulled up next to them in his Mitsubishi. The soldiers looked at him with curiosity, but no one made a move toward his car.

We didn't get much time to consider the mystery. "There you are!" came a familiar voice. Pablo emerged from the fortress gate, clad in a bright red polo shirt, pressed white slacks, and jazz shoes polished to a shine. He had puffy eyes, but there was an alert tension to him. "We're waiting for you."

I checked my cell. "I thought we had fifteen minutes."

"Do we need to do makeup?" Ana asked.

"Rodrigo wants to talk to you," Pablo said.

We entered the fortress. The Cabaña was a large complex of tan stone barracks separated by cobbled roads. The barracks housed various museum exhibitions that Ana and I had explored on a previous, touristy visit. Pablo led us past them at a hurried pace.

"Remember to smile when you dance," he told us. "Pay attention to each other and to the music. Don't let me down, all right?"

There was a tightness in his voice that made me think he really cared.

"We'll do our best," Ana promised him.

Pablo led us to a wide open square at the edge of the fortress, where an array of cannon set in the Cabaña's sturdy walls faced out across the canal and toward Havana proper. I knew this from last time, that is—now the cannon were hidden behind a mass of people sitting five rows deep around the square. School kids in uniform, adults in white T-shirts and blue jeans or else red tops and white slacks, it was a color-coordinated army of an audience. I wondered if they'd been brought here by the busload. They sat talking to one another, orderly for a crowd in Cuba.

In the middle of the square a wooden dance floor had been erected. Three television cameras overlooked it, ancient-looking boxy things. Each one had its own platform, an operator sitting behind it.

Some twenty couples clustered near the center of the

314

floor. A few older men that looked like officials stood in front, Rodrigo among them. Dressed in a summery white outfit, a microphone in one hand, he glistened with sweat.

Rodrigo spotted us and waved, a grand, welcoming gesture.

"You said he wanted to talk to us," I said.

"Yes," Pablo said. "Rodrigo will talk and you will listen."

"We've got to change our shoes," Ana said.

So we stood there at the edge of the stage and changed our shoes and everyone on the whole square watched us. My face burned. My fingers fumbled endlessly with the laces on my sneakers.

At last it was done and we lined up behind Rodrigo. The other couples moved to make room. A few of the dancers were our age, the rest in their twenties or thirties. Many nodded at Ana familiarly. One, a tall white girl in a reflective green dress, gave her the evil eye and Ana pretended not to notice.

That would be Celia, I decided.

Rodrigo tapped the microphone. Looked at the nearest camera, got a nod from the operator. Raised his hand to quiet the audience. "Good morning and welcome to the fifth annual *Casinero Mundial* contest. Contestants from every part of Cuba and two visitors from New York have gathered here today to celebrate that wonderful Cuban tradition, the dance of casino. A round of applause!"

The crowd clapped and cheered. I felt a hundred eyes watching me and Ana, wondering about the *yumas* here to dance for them. I leaned toward Ana. "I'm getting nervous."

The dancer behind me snorted. "Too early, man."

I wondered what he meant. Then Rodrigo went on. "Before we start the contest, I would like to say a few words. When a group of friends first got together to create the dance of casino in the year . . ." Fifteen minutes later, Rodrigo was still going strong. ". . . and so it is with great pleasure that I look forward to watching these fine young men and women demonstrate this uniquely Cuban art to us all today."

He paused to take a breath. In that instant, someone started clapping. A moment later, applause rolled across the square.

Rodrigo looked startled for a second. He scratched his head, then nodded as the applause faded. "Thank you for your attention."

Clapping, once again.

"Can applause sound relieved?" I asked Ana. "Or is it my imagination?"

She checked her watch. "I guess we might even start on time."

Rodrigo waited for the crowd to quiet. "Now my fellow jury member, the respected Fernando Rivera, would like to say a few words."

To the audience's credit, there were no boos. Another white-haired man took the mic.

"My back hurts from all this standing," I said.

"I guess they take their lead from Fidel," Ana said.

But it wasn't so bad. No more than ten minutes later, or maybe fifteen, the speeches were done. The judges cleared off the stage and took their seats around the platform. Technicians rushed up to pin a large white paper sign to my back. Our participant number was 16. Then, before I could so much as close my eyes and take a deep breath, Rodrigo's amplified voice rang out again.

"Dancers, take your positions."

Ana and I ended up near one corner of the stage. We looked at each other. Ana smiled, a tremulous expression. I forced my lips to follow suit.

Then I noticed something off to the side. "Check out Valdes."

He stood right beside the platform. Arms crossed over his chest. His eyes locked on us.

"Ignore him," Ana said.

"Yeah." I put my arm about her in the closed hold.

My teeth chattered. I'm not being poetic here. My jaw clicked open and shut like one of those cartoon talking skulls.

It wasn't all Valdes's fault. We were about to dance casino in front of the Cuban nation. A whole country of people who couldn't watch a foreigner dance for five seconds without stepping in to give advice.

But Valdes . . . why was he here, watching us?

The question nagged loud in my skull, and so I missed the first bar of the music when it came with a blast of horns. Ana squeezed my shoulder and I rushed into motion—stepped too fast, off time, struggled to correct. Settled into the basic step, back and forth, back and forth, breathing hard.

Ana grinned for all she was worth. Her eyes said, Come on, Rick. Dance!

The song was "Seis Semanas," a lively Van Van number with a retro sound. In the periphery of my vision I saw other couples turning, spinning, executing intricate patterns. I had to get going. But I had this feeling, like when you're doing a test at school and you get hung up on the first question, and fifteen minutes pass and you've got to forget it and move on but you can't, and then you're losing it because there's only half an hour left and you still haven't solved a single problem and—

Ana spun away from me. I hadn't led the move—she'd decided to take things into her own hands. She separated from me, danced an intricate shine, fancy footwork all over the place.

I gritted my teeth, forced my body into overdrive. A rumba step, side to side. A shoulder shimmy, fast and hard. A jumping step—

I tripped. My arms wheeled.

Ana and I stared at each other, both of us falling back to the basic step. My face burned.

I'd tripped. On TV.

Ana's lips cracked open. She smiled. It was no fake dancer's smile this time, but a grin wide across her face.

For a moment, I was surprised, affronted, mortified.

Then a laugh burst from me. With that laugh, relief flooded me.

The contest was over. We'd never stood a chance, not against people who'd danced casino since they were five—but now we were truly done. There was nothing left except to enjoy ourselves.

Ana and I came together and circled each other in a simple turn. I let go of her and we did an improvised *pilón*—stomping the ground in a relaxed cadence, our arms pounding imaginary sugarcane. Then I went to Ana and spun her under my arm, drew her close and rocked side to side with her.

Simple stuff, nothing flashy, and yet it felt nice, satisfying. Like our time in Cuba, all the work we'd done, it had taught us something.

Eventually the music faded. Applause rolled over us, and cheers. We came to a halt, stood side by side, my arm around Ana's waist. Across the platform dancers smiled at each other, wiped sweat from their faces, whispered comments to their partners.

"That was fun," Ana said.

"Yeah."

I didn't dare look in the crowd for Pablo's reaction.

After a while Rodrigo clambered onto the stage. Ana tensed. So did I.

I told you I thought the contest was over. I did believe that, really. But it was also a bit of a lie. I believed two things at the same time. One that the contest was over, so I could stop worrying and get on with dancing. The other that maybe, maybe, just maybe . . .

Rodrigo brought the mic to his lips. It was the moment of truth.

"I remember when I first learned to dance casino, on a rainy day back in the summer of 1982 . . ."

Okay, so maybe it was like the ten minutes of truth.

"The jury has selected ten couples for the second round," Rodrigo announced a while later. "Couple three, couple six, couples seven, eight and nine, couple thirteen, couple fifteen, couple sixteen, couples nineteen and twenty."

"Sixteen," Ana said. "He did say sixteen, right?" She turned me around to check the sign on my back.

I pumped my fist, smiled at Ana. She smiled back.

At the same time, I wondered how bad the other couples must have been.

I didn't care. I felt like I could dance now. I could rock this.

"Dancers, positions," Rodrigo announced.

Moments later music sounded again. "Báilalo Hasta Afuera" by Pupy—a fast, energetic piece, with a difficult, heavily syncopated rhythm. I thanked Pablo silently for playing the song during practice. Ana in my arms, I snapped into motion.

We did well, this second round. Hit a lot of accents in the music. Did some complicated patterns, flashy and fast. So maybe I was a bit tense, a bit caught up in my head thinking what move to do next—but we did well.

Except well couldn't possibly be enough. In a calmer moment, when Ana and I danced in a close hold with my elbows hooked over hers, I took in the rest of the stage. Wherever I looked, I saw dancers killing it. Smooth body motion, perfect accents for every break in the music. That girl Celia and her partner had footwork to do a tap dancer proud. All of them looked like professionals, and I knew we didn't.

When the song ended, the audience clapped long and hard. Long enough for Ana and me to compare notes.

"We stick out like ketchup on a white T-shirt," she said.

"I wonder why they let us through to this round," I said.

At that point the applause quieted and Rodrigo got on stage again. But not to announce the results.

"Today at the *Casinero Mundial* contest we have a great honor," he pronounced. "A visit by someone of very special significance to us all here."

I became aware of movement in the audience. People everywhere turning to one side, craning their necks to see.

The object of their attention—perhaps a dozen men entering the square, a few in green uniforms, others in sweatpants and T-shirts. And between them two figures.

One, a burly guy in an Adidas running shirt, supported the other. A tall man but frail, in a checkered gray button-down shirt, bent forward over a cane.

Lanky frame. White beard. And that face, intent, as if listening to something he couldn't quite make out . . .

I shivered.

"*Compañeros y compañeras*," Rodrigo said. "Here to watch the final round of *Casinero Mundial* is the historic leader of the Cuban Revolution, Fidel Castro Ruz."

chapter twenty-six

SALSA FOR FIDEL

Cheers thundered.

"No way," Ana said, in English.

I could only stare. Fidel made his slow way to a string of empty chairs not far from our corner of the stage, followed by every eye in the square. Every eye—but none of the cameras. Maybe they'd been told not to film the tired way Fidel walked or the way his security detail surrounded him. Only when he sank into his seat did the cameras swing around to focus on him. Then he raised his arm and gave a little wave, smiling with grandfatherly affection.

The crowd went wild.

Now it all made sense. The soldiers guarding the road.

The well-behaved audience—probably handpicked for the event. The way Valdes had acted.

I felt trapped in a dream. Me within a hundred yards of Fidel. The bogeyman of my childhood. A man who'd seemed like a mythic figure to me—technically speaking real, but no more part of my everyday world than Darth Vader.

"I thought Fidel doesn't even like dance," Ana said.

"It's a photo op." I understood this much. "They roll him out for the cameras to prove he's not dead."

"Huh. Then I guess we know what happens next," Ana said.

I stared at her.

"We go to the next round," Ana said.

"And so with our very special guest in attendance, I announce the participants of the final." Rodrigo stuttered over the words a bit, and spoke quickly. Perhaps Fidel's gaze sped him along. "Dancing for the title of best casinero in the world will be couples three, seven, nineteen, and twenty." He paused for a breath. "And of course our friends from New York, couple sixteen."

Amidst applause, the cameras swiveled toward us.

Ana squeezed my hand. My teeth clicked shut on my tongue. I tasted blood, coppery and hot, and winced. Imagined what I would look like on TV sets across Cuba. And maybe on a screen somewhere in a dark room in Langley, Virginia. Some analyst studying the faces of two Americans appearing on TV with Fidel Castro.

We were the photo op. Kids from New York dancing for Fidel.

A vision of Mom's face flashed before my eyes, disgusted, cold . . .

I brought a hand to my mouth as if to cough, spoke under it. "We can't dance, not for that guy."

"I know." Ana's mouth barely moved. "But how do we get away?"

My eyes had acquired a life of their own, searching the audience for someone, anyone who could save us. Strangers everywhere, smiling, laughing, nodding. Rodrigo clambering off the stage. The other finalist couples, looking excited, except for one pair, who seemed to be arguing over something heatedly.

Maybe we weren't the only ones who minded.

Pablo didn't mind. He stood off to one side of the stage, looking thrilled, waiting for us to dance.

Rodrigo was preparing a surprise, he'd told us. How excited he'd sounded.

I'm sorry, I wanted to tell him. We can't do this. Not this.

And then I saw Valdes. Not far from where Fidel reclined in his chair. Standing with his hands in his pockets. Watching me.

Our gazes met. He smiled, the faintest curve of his lips.

I looked away.

The speakers buzzed. Electric guitars riffed a forceful intro—it was Pupy's "Me Están Llamando," an intense, complex piece with intricate Afro-Cuban percussion and lyrics full of Santería references.

I turned to Ana, took hold of her unmoving form. Swayed my torso in rhythm to the music.

"We have to dance," I said.

About us, the other dancers spun into life, all of them—even the couple that had been arguing. Because of course they had no choice.

I rolled my shoulders, pretending this was part of the plan, just our groove, chill and relaxed.

"We could bomb," Ana said. "Dance bad, make a point."

"No, we can't." I pushed Ana forward, into the basic step, back and forth, back and forth. "Dance, Ana. For Pablo. For Juanita and Yolanda." I nodded off to the side, toward Valdes—a small, curt gesture. "For my family."

I saw her understand. A transformation in her eyes, so swift and subtle no one else could have possibly seen it. Understanding, acceptance, determination.

In that moment, I crushed on her so hard it hurt. But there was no time for that. Ana relaxed in my arms and smiled—a machine-gun, drive-your-enemies-before-you grin, ear to ear. And we danced.

Of course we danced. Because we understood why Valdes had laughed, outside at the checkpoint. As soon as we told him we were here for the contest, he'd realized this moment would come. And he was here to make sure we went through with it.

If it was just us, we might have made a different choice, maybe, if we'd dared. But we had no right to screw up my family's life because we wanted to make a point. A point that would achieve exactly nothing, in the big scheme of things.

So we danced like there was nothing else in the world. We danced like two kids living the high point of their salsa vacation, clueless about the dour old man sitting in the audience. We danced like we didn't care that we'd lost Valdes's game—like we didn't realize we'd lost—like we didn't even know we'd been playing.

The cowbell pulsed in my chest, fierce and hot. The congas possessed my feet, swift and intense and relentlessly, furiously precise. The horns drove me on with their insistent mambos, motifs repeated again and again until they got inside me and I lived them.

Ana was right there in the music with me. Moving to the same beat, possessed by the same spirit, ready for every signal, always there when I reached for her. Her body undulated in symmetry to mine, whipped forward in an accent when mine did, flowed through the air in such harmony that at one point I was no longer sure if I led the dance or if she did—and it didn't matter.

We mixed in rumba when the music fit, and mambo, and mozambique. For once the movements came to me naturally, in harmony with the exalted cries of the chorus. We danced like we never had before, and I knew that I'd happily spend years looking for this feeling again.

When the music ended and applause rolled, Ana and I hugged. It was hot in that embrace and uncomfortable, our clothes soaked through with sweat, and yet I couldn't let her go. Her arms too clung fiercely around my back. We were like the heroes of some disaster film as the credits rolled, the survivors of a shipwreck maybe, clutching at each other, not ready to face the world again.

"What a spectacular demonstration of casino that was!"

Rodrigo's amplified voice pushed in between us, levered us apart like a crowbar. He'd taken the middle of the stage again, and waved for all the dancers to gather around him. We walked over to form a semicircle behind Rodrigo with the others. Ana pulled at my hand, led me to the far end of the semicircle, away from Celia and her partner.

I glanced over at Fidel. In that instant, I was certain I'd find him staring at me, pinning me down with sharp, merciless eyes—but he wasn't looking at the stage at all. He'd leaned to the side to talk with some gray-haired man.

"It is a wonderful day here in Havana," Rodrigo sermonized. "To see such fine young men and women from across our island as well as the city of New York, all here to share dance in the spirit of goodwill and friendship. But unfortunately in each contest there must be a winner, and today is no exception." Rodrigo drew an envelope from his pocket dramatically, opened it with his thick fingers. "And so. In third place today, couple seven, Juan and Lily."

Cheers and applause. I dug my fingernails into my palm.

"In second place, couple three, Yunier and Celia."

Ana groaned, swore something under her breath.

My heart beat faster. Could it be?

No way, I told myself.

"And in first place, the winners of this year's *Casinero Mundial* . . ." Rodrigo drew out a dramatic pause. "Couple nineteen, Yasser and Anita."

I flushed. We hadn't even placed in the top three. Hadn't even come close to winning.

Then a chuckle escaped me, unexpected.

The winning couple came forth to be congratulated by Rodrigo and answer some questions. The rest of us stood about in the back, looking awkward.

Ana smiled at me. "We did well."

And she was right. We had danced well. So well that, if the Rick of six months ago had seen it, he would never have believed it possible. But honestly, not well enough to win. Not against this crowd.

I was no Salsa King after all.

Ana squeezed my hand. I realized Rodrigo was heading our way, the cameras tracking him. He came up to us with this big toothpaste-ad grin. "And now some special congratulations for Rick and Ana, our guests from New York. What an accomplishment, to make it to the final round of this exacting competition! How do you two feel?" He stabbed the microphone at us.

"Umm," I said.

"We feel great," Ana said. "It's an honor to be here with so many excellent dancers."

"And a double honor with our very special guest in the audience today," Rodrigo said.

I glanced toward Fidel again. The old man was still engaged in conversation. If he'd heard Rodrigo's words, he showed no sign of it.

I opened my mouth to say something bland and inoffensive but nothing came out. At that moment, I couldn't summon a single word. Couldn't think of a single way to answer that wouldn't endorse Fidel on national television, or cause Valdes to come after us.

"It is a special opportunity to be here today." Ana smiled, all sugar and cream. "I feel a bit like the pianist Van Cliburn when he went to Moscow in the middle of the Cold War to compete in the Tchaikovsky Competition."

Rodrigo opened his mouth, then shut it again. I could tell his reaction was the same as mine—Van Who in the What Competition?

"It is important for artists to rise above the disagreements of politicians," Ana said. "Bring nations together in friendship, things like that."

"Bring nations together in friendship." Rodrigo seemed relieved at a line that he recognized. "Yes, yes, that's good. Thank you, Rick and Ana."

Once he was gone and the cameras with him, I nodded at Ana appreciatively. "Quick thinking. You made it sound like we're generally friendly without supporting Fidel or anyone else."

Even if some CIA goon reviewed this footage, this wouldn't get us marked as enemies of the state.

"I feel like I've eaten something rotten," she said. "Let's get out of here."

Now that the winners had been announced, the event wound up within minutes. The cameras shut off. The audience got up and streamed toward the exit in a mass. By the time I looked around, Fidel and his clique were already gone, as was Valdes.

The dancers milled about the stage and congratulated the winners and clapped each other on the back. Then, couple by couple, people drifted off into the crowd.

Pablo met us offstage. He bounced from foot to foot like he'd won the Powerball. I thought back to the day we first met—to the big, serious man who'd resented having to teach us. If someone had told me he could look this thrilled for us, I wouldn't have believed it.

"How'd you like your surprise?" he asked. "*Empingao, no?*"

"Oh, yeah," I said. "*Empingao.*"

Pablo didn't seem to notice my lack of enthusiasm. "You guys killed it. I can't wait for my daughter to see you on TV. Never seen *yumas* dance like that."

"Thanks," I said, without much feeling.

"We couldn't have done it without you," Ana said, a flat, rote response.

Pablo grinned. "I hope you kids had as much fun as I did."

I realized he expected a response. He wanted us to share in his enthusiasm.

I felt tired and sore and cold. I felt used and defeated. More than that, I felt a coward.

Yet I knew we'd made the right choice, there on the stage. And I wasn't about to let that choice go to waste, not any part of it.

I pictured Pablo working at Rodrigo's new dance school. I imagined him reconciled with Liliana, together with his grandson Lalo once again. And I didn't need to force a smile—it came to my lips on its own.

"You're a great teacher," I said.

"He's right," Ana said. "Don't give up on it, all right? We *yumas* need someone like you to show us the way."

Then we found a cab and went to the old city. We treated Pablo to ice cream at El Naranjal and drank coffee and talked and laughed. I would rather have hidden from the world in my room, and I was sure Ana felt the same. But this day wasn't about us.

☙

When we got back to the apartment, Yolanda met us at the door, frantic, excited. She waved us in, slammed the door shut, put her back against it. "She's free! They let her go."

"Wait, what?" I asked.

Ana said, "Oh, Miranda?"

Yolanda nodded. "I heard from Lisyani. Miranda's home."

"Great." I felt a little lighter; at least some good news today.

"Is she okay?" Ana asked. "Can we go see her?"

Yolanda shook her head. "She's shaken up, wants to lie low for a while. But she's all right. She says the food was horrible and they didn't let her sleep much, but they didn't hurt her." Yolanda leaned forward, lowered her voice. "Apparently they kept asking her about the video. About how it made it out. About the BBC News segment."

"A segment on BBC News?" Ana asked. "Really?"

"Miranda thinks that's why they let her go," Yolanda said. "They got scared of the publicity."

"I'm so happy." Ana hugged Yolanda.

I hugged her too.

I knew something, though. The plan had worked but not without a cost.

Valdes knew about Yolanda now. He'd be watching her, and our entire family. Because of him, I couldn't come back to Cuba, not anytime soon.

Today he'd gotten a photo op out of me and Ana. On the other hand, we'd helped Miranda get free. Valdes and I, we were 1–1. But the game was only beginning.

For the first time in my life, I knew that I could make a difference.

When Rachel Snow had called me out as a geek, she'd had a point. But there was a power to being a geek.

I had an idea for my new website. It would be part anonymous blog, part discussion forum. Lots of funny pictures and videos. Some not so funny. The video of Miranda Galvez would go up there, with instructions for anonymously uploading others. The site would be a WikiLeaks for Cuba—except more exciting, with memes and music videos, and tropical-themed cat GIFs to draw eyeballs. I would call it Lolcats for the Revolution.

It was time I earned my title as Cat King of Havana. Even if I had to go into exile to do it.

chapter twenty-seven

NOT DONE

Our last morning in Havana I took Juanita out for pizza, just the two of us. Cuban pizza was spongy, cottony bread with melted cheese on top, but I'd found one place at the Meliá Cohíba hotel that would have done all right in Manhattan (and charged Manhattan prices). Juanita dressed up finer for pizza than many New Yorkers would have for Per Se—a long pale silk dress and a pearl necklace and red earrings that stood out like small bright berries in her silvery hair.

After, we strolled along the Malecón back toward Habana Vieja. The sun blazed upon us. A breeze blew in over the water, sent waves crashing against the seawall so that the cool spray of the Caribbean refreshed us. "I read the book you brought me," Juanita said.

It took me a moment to remember what she was talking about. "The one about Mariel."

She nodded. "I wasn't going to. But I saw the inscription, *For María. . . .* Why did you give it to me?"

"I thought you might want to know what it was like, leaving on the boatlift."

Juanita nodded. "It's strange the way a book gets inside you. Maybe you start out disliking some character but you hear her thoughts inside your head and eventually you begin to understand her."

I waited for Juanita to say more, but she never did. So I spoke instead. And asked her the one question I'd been holding inside these past weeks.

"What really happened in 1980? With my mother?"

Juanita's stride wavered. She recovered and kept going, her eyes inscrutable behind sunglasses. "You know, don't you? María must have told you about it."

"She didn't say much."

"It was a painful time," Juanita said. "Maybe it's better to leave it in the past."

Better for who, I wanted to ask. But I only said, "Please, Aunt Juanita. I don't want to go home with so many questions."

Juanita was silent for a long time.

"What do you want to know?" she asked finally.

"So Mom fell in love with Ricardo, the poet. They were going to leave Cuba. Claim asylum at the Peruvian embassy and get out."

"That kid was good for nothing. Head in the clouds, full of ideas. He had no idea the risk he put María in. The risk he put our family in."

Juanita's voice came hard yet brittle, with a tremor to it. I kept my eyes carefully forward, afraid that looking at her might startle her into silence.

"He opposed the Revolution," I said. "He thought Fidel was hurting the country."

"Of course he did. His family was rich before the Revolution, and close to Batista." Juanita snorted. "If Fidel had failed, he'd never have needed to work a day in his life."

I could have told Juanita about Ricardo's place in Trinidad. The rust streaks on the walls. The rotting roof. The missing bedroom door. I could have asked her if she thought that was what Ricardo deserved.

I could have asked her if she still believed in the Revolution. I could have pointed out that Juanita's own daughter had more in common with Ricardo than with her.

I did none of these things. They would have hurt Juanita to no purpose. It was hard for me to imagine that she'd never thought such things herself.

Instead I said, "There's one thing I don't understand. Grandfather had Ricardo locked up before he could meet Mom at the embassy. But how did Grandfather find out? Who told him?"

It took me a few steps before I realized Juanita had stopped. I turned.

She walked to the seawall and leaned on it, gazed out at the sea. When she spoke, it was so quiet I had to come close to hear her.

"For thirty years I hoped María would come home. Thirty years waiting for a visit, to see her face, to hug her and hold her close. *Las hermanas Gutiérrez* together again." Juanita's fingers clutched at the concrete seawall, so hard I was sure it hurt. "Six letters she wrote me. Three phone calls—one when Yolanda was born, another for Yosvany, and another for you. Three phone calls over thirty years. Sometimes I thought to get pregnant again, just so I'd hear her voice. Your mother was a hard woman, Rick."

I thought of Mom sitting beside me at my writing desk, her shoulder warm against mine. Her head bent over a math problem that she couldn't make head or tails of—but tried to anyway.

On the road behind us, a large wedding caravan drove past. Horns honked. A lively Strauss waltz blasted from someone's speakers. The bride stood upright in a red convertible *almendrón*, a plump figure in a cloud of white lace, waving to everyone on the Malecón.

"María told me her plan the night before," Juanita said. "We were close, as close as two sisters can be. She knew I wouldn't go with her, knew I was a revolutionary at heart, and besides, I had a boyfriend here—but she wanted to say good-bye. That was María's mistake. She wanted to say good-bye."

I meant to keep my mouth shut. I really did. But the words

escaped me, quiet and flat. "What was your mistake?"

"My mistake was thinking I could hold on to her."

Juanita fell silent then. I sensed she would say no more even if I pushed.

I didn't push. I'd heard all I needed to. I went to stand beside her instead and put my arm around her. Together we looked across the water toward Miami.

👀

In theory, packing for home should have meant three minutes of tossing all my stuff in the suitcase and locking it up. In practice it became a tropical treasure hunt. That pile of Yosvany's T-shirts, did it hide my electric razor somewhere? That fine selection of papers, CDs, shorts, and books on the table, did it include my flashlight? And Yosvany's room demonstrated effectively that the best camouflage for socks was more socks.

By the time I finished, it was almost time to leave. I was struggling to zip up my overflowing backpack when Yosvany came in. I hadn't seen him since the incident with Ana and Celia—he'd been staying at his uncle's, by Juanita's edict. Now he didn't knock, didn't say hi. He swept in, ripped off his shirt, and plopped on his bed, arms outstretched. "This place smells like ass."

"Don't worry," I said. "You'll get used to it again."

We looked at each other for a while. Me on the sofa holding my backpack. Him stretched out on his bed like he didn't have a care in the world—but his eyes on me, focused, bright.

That would have been the moment to tell him everything I thought of him. What a dick he was for hurting Ana. But it would have accomplished nothing. Yosvany was not the kind who'd listen to advice from his nerdy *yuma* cousin. It would only have pushed us apart.

And he was my family. After my conversation with Juanita, I wasn't about to forget that.

So I opened my mouth to say I'd had fun this summer—when Yosvany spoke up. "Bad luck with Ana, huh."

"Bad luck?" Family's family, but there's only so much you can take. "You really are a *comemierda*, Yosvany. You were with the most amazing girl I've met, and you know what, she liked you, she really did. And you spat on that."

"You've got to be bad with girls," Yosvany said. "If you're good, they get bad with you. *O jodes o te joden*. I know, cousin—I've tried it both ways."

"So you're gonna be a dick all your life," I said. "Never trust anyone, and never have anyone trust you."

"You can't trust a woman." Yosvany shook his head sadly. "Everyone knows that. This famous writer, he once said to his mom—I trust you as a mother, but not as a woman."

Yosvany quoting a writer, now that was something new.

"It sounds like you're going to have a lonely life," I said.

"It sounds like you're going to have a painful one," Yosvany said.

I sighed. "Tell you what, Yosvany. Let's leave this for the next time we meet. Maybe then we can figure out who was right."

"Maybe next time will be in New York." Yosvany pushed up from the bed with newfound energy. "We'll go clubbing in Manhattan."

We clasped hands.

"Sure," I said. "Take care of Yolanda and Juanita."

"Of course. And you . . ." Yosvany glanced away. "Well, look after Ana, will you?"

The sudden awkwardness in Yosvany's manner surprised me. "I don't think she needs looking after. But I'll do my best."

"I'll send you a copy of my new CD when it comes out," he said.

"Okay," I said.

Yosvany grinned. "One day you'll realize how much I taught you this summer, *primo*."

"Oh, you taught me things, all right," I said.

We stood there looking at each other. This cool, ripped Cuban kid and his skinny nerd of a cousin.

I hadn't magically morphed into Mr. Ripped this summer. If I was cooler than when I'd arrived in Cuba, I still wasn't about to make the cover of any teen magazine. And yet our last handshake seemed more equal than our first.

Yolanda had airport duty. Juanita said she had a neighborhood meeting to attend, but really I think she didn't want to cry in public. She fed us a late lunch and packed us ham sandwiches—still hot from the toaster oven—and never stopped talking for a moment, as if words could hold off the need to think and feel.

"Make sure to exercise on the plane to avoid an embolism," she said, though she'd never flown, and "Speak well of us in New York," and "Tell your father to come with you next time."

She hugged Ana and me for thirty seconds each at the door. I wondered how long she might have hugged me if she'd known there might be no next time.

The truth was, I didn't want to let go either.

Yosvany came into the hallway, but didn't approach us. Ana ignored him. I waved him good-bye.

Yolanda had gone down already to get the car. Ana and I dragged our suitcases out of the apartment and into the elevator. For one last time I cranked its manual lever. The metal cage shook and creaked and descended. Juanita watched us from the door until the very last moment—immobile, a statue, her hand locked on the doorjamb.

In the darkness of the shaft, I found myself wishing the elevator would break down for once. But it never did.

We rode through Centro Habana in the family Lada, windows down, breathing in that Havana special—fresh Caribbean air mixed with diesel fumes. Up front Yolanda drove one-handed, her elbow jutting out the window. She peppered us with questions about the TV show, about our flight, about our plans for the last week of summer break. Ever since the news about Miranda, she seemed changed: taller, relaxed, comfortable with herself.

Me and Ana, we were different. We kept looking back,

scanning the road for cars with government plates. At any moment I thought we might hit a roadblock and Valdes would pop out like Freddy at the end of *A Nightmare on Elm Street*, yank us off to that gray building with barred windows near Plaza de la Revolución.

But Valdes didn't come. We got to the airport and stood in the check-in line for an hour, and no one seemed the least bit interested in stopping us or asking us questions.

Yolanda left us before passport control. She hugged us both and made us promise to write, and said not a thing about what we'd gone through this summer. Instead she smiled at us when it was time to leave and said, "Thank you for everything."

"I'm happy we could help," I told her. It wasn't exactly true, not knowing the cost of that help. But it wasn't exactly a lie either.

"Don't give up," Ana said. "Things will get better."

Yolanda nodded. I could tell she wasn't so sure. She turned and walked away.

I looked after her. I must have looked after her for a very long time, because eventually Ana touched my shoulder— carefully, as if afraid she might startle me. "Shall we?"

In the line to passport control my stomach did its usual imitation of a blender on pulse. The official in the booth barely looked at us, though. He checked our passports, mumbled something under his breath, and buzzed us through.

Later, as we sat on the tarmac waiting to take off, I

realized—they were done. Valdes, the rest of them, they didn't need to shoot us or torture us or lock us up. Fear was all they needed, fear for ourselves and our families.

All they thought they needed.

As acceleration pressed me into my seat, as the gray buildings of the airport blurred past outside, I closed my eyes. I wanted to feel every bump and rattle along the runway. These might be my last seconds on Cuban soil for many years.

Cuba might be done with me. But I wasn't done with Cuba.

epilogue

RETURN OF THAT CAT GUY

Back when Rachel and I were dating, we made a music video set to her rendition of "The Cat Came Back." The clip featured a Creative Commons–licensed feline escaping disasters ranging from neighborhood dogs to a computer-generated apocalypse. It was loud, it was hectic, it was colorful—and it got like seven hundred views.

Pearls before swine.

Right after Rachel dumped me, I'd watched that clip over and over again. Partly to hear Rachel's voice—and partly because I'd admired the scrappy hero of the song. I'd wondered if I would ever escape the nuclear winter of Rachel's dumpage as the cat escaped all his troubles.

Now, though? I'd have liked to see that cat deal with Maykel Valdes—or Ana Cabrera for that matter.

"It's hard to believe we're going back to our old lives tomorrow," Ana said to me halfway to Cancún.

"Are we?" I asked her.

She stared at the dense white clouds outside the porthole. "My dad hasn't moved out," she said at last. "Mom didn't say much on the phone, but I bet he's still drinking."

I searched for something reassuring to say, but Ana gathered herself and spoke again. "I can't fix their lives, can I?" She paused. "You can love someone but . . . what they do with your love isn't up to you."

And it occurred to me that Ana too wasn't leaving Cuba entirely unchanged.

That old cat? He had nothing on the two of us.

∽

Ana and I talked for hours, that long trip home. On the plane, at the airport in Cancún, on the evening flight to New York that night. At first in Spanish, then—somewhere over the Gulf of Mexico—switching to English. We answered some questions over salted peanuts, settled a few things while rattling in turbulence, came to understand each other a little better waiting in the bathroom line. Ana and Rick, two friends, nothing more, nothing less.

This isn't a soap opera so I'll skip over those conversations.

Here's the last question Ana asked me, though.

We were getting ready to land at JFK late that night. The lights of the New York skyline tilted this way and that out the window. The captain came on the intercom, told the crew to take their seats. Ana adjusted her neck pillow, gave me a quick glance, then turned to look at me straight on.

"Tell me one thing," she said. "Are you sorry you ever met me?"

I studied this girl before me. Deep-set eyes that had never looked at me with desire. Lips which had never said the words I'd hoped to hear. I thought of the nights I'd spent tossing in bed, thinking of her. The days I'd gone without wanting to eat . . . the moment when I'd first seen Yosvany kiss her . . .

"This year might have been a lot easier if I hadn't," I said.

Ana winced.

"Easy isn't always good," I said.

Ana looked at me as if she expected more.

I smiled. "You want me to thank you for breaking my heart? Well, thanks, Ana. It was a blast."

She laughed. We both laughed.

But I meant the thanks.

Without Ana I would never have danced casino while Mandy Cantero and Los Van Van rocked the night so close I could touch them. I might never have met Ricardo Eugenio and learned the true story of Mom's last days in Cuba. Years might have passed before I walked down Obispo with music playing on every corner or strolled along the Malecón on a breezy morning, or met Juanita, Yolanda, and Yosvany, my family.

As we glided down toward the runway, the lights of Long Island streaming past, I said to Ana, "I was messed up when we met. Confused. I was in for rough times whatever happened."

"Then I'm glad I'm what happened," Ana said.

"Me too," I said, with no reservations.

Yet half an hour later, as I stood in the passport line watching Ana talk to the immigration lady ahead of me, a weight sank down on me. It felt familiar and strange, like a childhood toy that you find in the closet years after you last played with it. It was the weight of solitude.

I'd spent two months in that small Centro Habana apartment with Ana and Yosvany, Juanita and Yolanda. Aside from three days in Trinidad, I'd hardly ever been alone, not even when I wanted to. Now I'd left my family behind. Ana and I would go our separate ways at Penn Station. We'd still go dancing, maybe even perform together eventually, but it wouldn't be the same.

From today I'd live with Dad again—and sure, I was excited to see him. But living with him felt a bit like living alone. The two of us sharing the same space, each of us in our own world.

It didn't matter, I told myself. I'd always been comfortable as a loner.

But somehow I couldn't make myself believe that anymore.

Ana and I collected our bags, went through customs,

and left the security area. The Arrivals Hall was packed with people waiting for friends and family. We weren't expecting anyone, so I craned my head looking for the AirTrain sign— when Ana tapped me on the shoulder. "Uh, Rick? I think that guy wants something from you."

It was one of those black-suited limousine drivers, a stocky man with sunglasses and a white sign that said—*THAT CAT GUY.*

I blinked. Looked at the driver again.

Lettuce! No wonder I hadn't recognized him—he'd lost some weight and had a beard now, close-cropped.

He strode over with measured steps, all pompous formality. "Your car's here, sir."

"Oh, great, take my luggage." I shoved my suitcase at him, nodded at Ana. "Hers too. And hurry up if you want a tip."

Ana stared at me with wide, horrified eyes.

"A tip?" Lettuce asked. "How about the tip of my boot up your ass?"

I laughed, clapped him on the shoulder. Lettuce grinned, pulled me into a hug.

"Easy on the ribs," I said when he let go. "You've got ripped, man!"

"You mean I've got from fat to pudgy," Lettuce said, but he sounded pleased. "Joe cooked for us on tour. He loves this raw, healthy stuff. Disgusting."

"I remember you," Ana said. "You're the guy with the band. The nuts guy."

"The BlueNuts guy," Lettuce said. "That gets you more

action than Cat Guy, by the way."

"Only at the Third All-American Peanuts Symposium,"
I said.

Outside under the night sky, the August New York heat
enveloped us like the smelly breath of an overgrown Labra-
dor. I'd always hated the sensation, but now it reminded me
of Havana.

On the way to the parking garage, we caught up about
Miranda Galvez. "It worked," I told Lettuce. "She's free,
thanks to your help."

"The internet doesn't know that," Lettuce said. "There was
another article today, in *Le Monde*. You know what that is? A
newspaper in Paris? In effing French?" He shook his head.

"And we're not done," I said. "At least I'm not."

I told them about Lolcats for the Revolution. I hadn't
mentioned the idea to anyone, not even to Ana. It had seemed
too risky to talk about it in Cuba or on the plane. I was surprised how confident my explanation sounded now, even to
myself. With every word the project seemed more and more
real. I could almost picture the website already. A big banner
up top—a fluffy Persian sprawling on Fidel's head like a wig.

I only wished I could risk sending a link to Tania. She
might have gotten a laugh out of it.

"The site won't make a big difference," I said, "but it might
make a small one."

"I'm in," Ana said. "Once I edit the film that I shot, it's
gonna tell a story—not just about dance, but about Havana.

Nothing controversial, really—but not a pretty story either. We can publish it on the site." She hesitated. "If you like, of course."

"You kidding? That's perfect."

"I can help with the soundtrack," Lettuce said. "For when no one's dancing."

"Great," Ana said.

"You can credit us as Fidel's BlueNuts," Lettuce said.

We grinned at each other.

"Here's your ride," Lettuce said a minute later, with a grand sweep of his arm.

We were on the fifth floor of the parking garage. There was only one car here this time of night. A beat-up white minivan with tinted windows, parked in a dark corner under a dead light. A colorful illustration adorned the side of the van—two large misshapen peanuts side by side, tinged blue at the bottom. Tastefully ragged letters spelled out *The BlueNuts World Tour* underneath.

"This baby took us all the way to Poughkeepsie and back this summer," Lettuce said.

"As far as that?" Ana asked.

Lettuce nodded. He rapped on the side of the van, three short knocks. A moment later, the sliding door in the van's side edged open a foot. Inside it was dark—too dark to make out anything except the boom box sitting in the open door.

There was a click.

Ana and I started.

Horns sang out. Claves clicked together. The congas came alive in Yuri Buenaventura's "Salsa," an energetic, relentlessly cheerful track.

We exchanged a startled look.

The door slammed open all the way. People poured out. The guys of Lettuce's band, laughing, grinning. Flavia Martinez, her hair dyed blue, cheering wildly. And then Dad.

He stepped out last. In his blue Metro North dress shirt and dark slacks, he looked out of place among the kids. The smile he gave me was hesitant, like he wasn't sure he belonged here. "Rick."

I hugged him. Clutched him tight, as a matter of fact. A wave of relief washed over me as we stood there, Dad's solid form in my arms. I hadn't realized how much I'd missed him.

"You've put on some muscle," Dad said as I let go.

Someone tugged at my hand. Flavia. She nodded her head to the cowbell beat of the salsa. "*Vamos, salserito.*"

I wavered, cast a hesitant glance at Dad. But he moved toward Ana, offered her his hand. "May I?"

I stared dumbstruck.

"What?" Dad asked. "I learned a few steps."

So we danced. Flavia and I, and Dad and Ana, while Lettuce and the guys clapped and hooted.

I started out stiff, nervous, waiting for Flavia to laugh at me. But within a few bars of the basic step—back and forth, back and forth—I realized something. Flavia moved well, but she didn't really know much salsa. I did a few simple turns, guided her from side to side, and it was all she could do to keep up.

So I didn't push her. We danced the song simply, back and forth, side to side, a few basic turns. Out of the corner of my eye I watched Dad and Ana. He plodded through his steps, of course, but he had the rhythm down and seemed to be enjoying himself, smiling for all he was worth—to Ana's encouragement.

At the very end I released Flavia, did some improv—a shoulder shimmy, a torso circle, some fancy footwork. She clapped and yelled, "*Wepa!*" and laughed.

There was no mockery in that laughter.

I thought—this is all right. I could take on anything, feeling like this. Rob Kenna, come at me.

Then the song switched. Havana D'Primera's "Pasaporte," a chill, bittersweet piece.

"A demonstration, Rick!" Lettuce called. "You and Ana."

Ana looked into my eyes. I looked back.

"*Dale, dale!*" Flavia encouraged us.

I offered Ana my hand. She took it.

We may have been smiling. I'm not sure.

"Let's see what you've learned," Lettuce said, but the words seemed muffled, as if coming from far away.

Ana and I danced.

Valdes was thirteen hundred miles away. Pablo's judging eye was gone. And that thing between us, that tangle of awkwardness and hope and rejection . . . Ana and I had left it somewhere over the Gulf of Mexico.

Dad watched us, as did Flavia and Lettuce with his friends, but it didn't matter. We heard their oohs and yeahs and *wepas* and yet it felt like just the two of us there, on the fifth floor of a JFK parking garage.

That's all I will tell you about our dance. Maybe I'm selfish, but not everything should be shared. Not even if you're the Cat King of Havana.

Author's Note

Two passions inspired *The Cat King of Havana.*

The first was my passion for Cuba in all its complexity. An island that seems a utopia one day, a dystopia the next, and somewhere in the middle on your average Tuesday.

Between various trips I've spent close to a year in Havana, riding packed buses, standing in long lines for mundane errands, and enjoying leisurely strolls along the Malecón. Even so, I feel like I've only scratched the surface. Where this book succeeds it is thanks to the many Cuban friends and colleagues who advised me. Where it falls short, it is due to my limited outsider's perspective.

And yet, limited or not, I hope my vision of Cuba awakens in my readers a desire to go see for themselves—with respect and appreciation.

The second passion that inspired this book was dance.

I'm allergic to the words "you haven't got what it takes." Utter them in my direction and you might send me into an obsession lasting days, months, or even years—until I've proved you wrong.

This is how I learned English well enough to write fiction in it (my classmates, fellow Latvians, laughed at the idea). This is how I became a physics major in college (physics was the one black mark on my high school transcript). This is also how I learned to dance.

I didn't always have this allergy, though.

Back in elementary school, when I was on the verge of failing gym class, my family told me, "That's okay. You've got other talents. You're not made for sports."

I believed them. Years of clumsiness, bullying, and gym periods from hell followed. In high school, I finally decided enough was enough and joined a martial arts school. For three months of aikido classes, I couldn't do a simple back roll—something even the clumsiest of my classmates did with ease. But I kept at it, hour after hour, day after day, month after month.

Six arduous years later, I earned my black belt. By that time, I'd realized I didn't need talent to become competent at something. Sheer stubbornness would do the trick.

This insight came in handy when, on a chance trip to Cuba, I took my first salsa class. I loved it—and I was atrocious. A block of wood on two left feet, with a tendency to collide with any furniture foolishly left nearby. My Cuban teacher was too polite to say such a thing, but I could tell my dance potential wasn't exactly overwhelming.

It didn't matter. I was in love. I wouldn't let a lack of talent stop me.

Salsa took over my life. For the next few years, I danced twenty to thirty hours a week, took classes from all the best teachers I could find, and returned to Cuba to learn more.

Now, four years later, I teach salsa myself—even as I continue my own studies. I'm not the best dancer in the world, or even close, but I'm doing what I love and having a blast.

With *The Cat King of Havana*, I wanted to share my love of dance—but also to share my allergy, if such a thing is possible.

If you love something enough, it doesn't matter whether people think you've got what it takes. You may never become the best in the world. With endless hours of work, though, you can get pretty good at just about anything.

—Tom Crosshill

Acknowledgments

Writing has never been a solitary process for me, and this project was no exception. If you summed up all the hours friends, colleagues, and strangers put into helping me with *The Cat King of Havana*, there'd be time enough to write another novel.

I'd like to thank Ammi-Joan Paquette for her boundless enthusiasm for this project. Thanks also to the rest of the crew of Erin Murphy Literary Agency.

I'd like to thank Ben Rosenthal for sage advice and editorial guidance. This would be a different—and lesser—book without his input and that of the talented team at Katherine Tegen Books.

I'd like to thank the International Writing Program at the University of Iowa for providing an inspiring space to write this book. Thanks also to my fellow residents, whose friendship and encouragement kept me going. If I wasn't the most social of creatures, this book is the reason why.

I'd like to thank all my Cuban friends, teachers, and acquaintances who welcomed me to their island and have shared so much with me over the past few years. I couldn't have written this book if not for Leonardo Gala Echemendía, Mariela Cuellar Alarcón, Alina Peña Arevalo, Yoss, Ligia Casabella, and so many others.

Special thanks to Ivan Salazar Camue, who taught me to dance and changed my life in more than one way.

Thanks to Gerardo Contino, "El Abogado de la Salsa," for his advice on the title of this book and other matters (if you like salsa, check out his music!).

Thanks to Carlos Hernandez for his insightful Cuban-American perspective on my story.

Thanks to Jack Shepherd of Buzzfeed for sharing his cat video expertise.

Thanks to my many tireless beta-readers—Keon Parandvash, Spigana Spektore, Daiga Mezale, Sarah Brand, Karin Norgard, Nick Tchan, Stefanie Jellouschek, and Eric Olive. Particular thanks to E. C. Myers and Alaya Dawn Johnson, as well as the rest of Altered Fluid—the best writing group on the planet.

Thanks to Ruta Sepetys, Mary Robinette Kowal, Corinne Duyvis, and Mindy McGinnis for advice on launching a debut novel.

Thanks to David Farland, Steven Savile, and Kevin J. Anderson for their support and mentorship over the years.

My thanks and apologies to everyone I forgot to include above.

And finally, thanks to all my loved ones for putting up with me. I admire your patience!